ABOUT THE AUTHOR

Marjorie Sinclair, born in South Dakota, has spent most of her life in Hawaii and is the author of two important novels, *Kona* (1947) and *The Wild Wind* (1950), reflecting the life in the islands during the years just before and after Pearl Harbor. She has also written a biography of King Kamehameha's "sacred daughter" Nahi'ena'ena, edited an anthology of Polynesian poetry, translated two volumes of poetry (one from the Chinese with Lily Chong and one from the Japanese with Yukuo Uyehara), and has published short stories and verse; some of her poetry is collected in *The Place Your Body Is* (1984). In 1981 she received the Hawaii Literary Award for her total writings and long dedication to the written word in the islands. She is currently president of the Hawaii Literary Arts Council.

A graduate of Mills College, Marjorie Sinclair did graduate work there and at the University of Hawaii, and has long been known for her teaching of Pacific literature. (Of her biography of Nahi'ena'ena the *Times Literary Supplement* in London said that she had successfully written a life that read like a novel. Pearl Buck, who recommended the novels for publication, had high praise for the vivid pictures in *Kona* of life both on Oahu and on the Big Island.

Kona describes a family of mingled Hawaiian and Caucasian heritage at a time when Kona on Hawaii was untouched by the developers. The heroine's father, a Scot, and her part-Hawaiian mother rear her in the ways of her ancestry. However, she marries Winston Wendell, member of a highly respected New England family, and finds herself leading a divided life. "It's hard having two bloods," Martha Luahine Bell says. She has to learn to mold herself into a wife who reconciles the streams of life existing in Honolulu—but not without struggle and a small mutiny. Sinclair then depicts the problems of the next generation, Martha's daughter.

The later novel, *The Wild Wind*, tells the story of Lucia Gray, who comes to live in a village on the shore of Maui and marries a college-bred Hawaiian cowboy.

Marjorie Sinclair married Gregg Sinclair, who was president of the University of Hawaii in the forties and fifties. After his death in 1976 she married Leon Edel, the author and educator. She retired from her teaching at the University of Hawaii in 1980.

KONA

KONA

A NOVEL BY

MARJORIE
SINCLAIR

MUTUAL PUBLISHING
COMPANY · *Honolulu*

TALES OF THE PACIFIC

Printed in Australia by
The Book Printer, Victoria

Cover design by Bill Fong, The Art Directors.

Cover painting by Diana Hansen Young.

ISBN 0-935180-20-6

THIS BOOK CONTAINS THE COMPLETE TEXT
OF THE ORIGINAL HARDBOUND EDITION

FOREWORD BY THE AUTHOR

I wrote this novel in and about a Hawaii that no longer exists. With great nostalgia I remember those days in the 1930's when Honolulu was a sprawling small city. It reached up into valleys and moved out toward Kuapa Pond, now filled in and called Hawaii Kai. Its streets were hidden in the rich foliage of coconut palms, monkeypod trees, shower trees, mangos, poincianas. I remember spending summers in Kailua, Kona, on the Big Island. Those beautiful volcanic slopes of Hualalai and Mauna Loa were dotted with just a few villages then—some along the mountain road for coffee growers and other farmers, and other Hawaiian places along the shore that had been there at least from the historic past. There were only two or three hotels in Kona then, notably the Managa Hotel on the *mauka* road and Kona Inn in Kailua. There were few—very few— tourists in all Hawaii. There was little traffic in the streets of Honolulu or on the Kona roads. The days moved quietly. The islands still had remnants of the feelings and attitudes of the nineteen century. Jet planes had not yet interrupted the serene skies. Statehood was yet to come.

I remember the people of those days fifty years ago. Their lives were closer to the natural round of day and night, to tidal ebb and flow, to the growth, blooming, and fruiting of trees and plants, and to the constant awareness of human progress through the generations of families. There were, of course, the discords and struggles which occur when people of many different races come together in a small archipelago. But these had not, as yet, been complicated, intensified, dramatized by the rapid growth of big business and tourism and an exploding population.

My novel deals with some of those old harmonies and depths, some of the clashes within traditional Hawaiian ways. They are not to be confused with the older life before the coming of the first voyagers and certainly not with the ways of life that now exist. In the 1930's and 1940's I had many Hawaiian friends.

From their lips I heard the feelings and the yearnings expressed by some of the characters in this novel. Especially poignant was the desire to return to an earlier time, lived within comfortable and affectionate human relationships. And it was possible then to go to Punaluu on the Big Island, or Keauhou, Kailua, or Napoopoo, and enjoy the quiet, slow-moving days.

My story seems much longer ago than it was because of the remarkable and nearly overwhelming changes that have come about in Hawaii. It is almost a dream world, perhaps an edenic or golden age. But it was real. I was fortunate enough to live in it and to have found in it the substance of this book.

MARJORIE SINCLAIR

CONTENTS

PROEM

Most of the islands in the Hawaiian group have a region called Kona, which means south or southwest. But if you say Kona to an islander and refer to a place, he will think immediately and happily of a particular region situated on the slopes of Hualalai and Mauna Loa, Island of Hawaii. The district has a past rich in memory and romance; here Captain Cook died upon the black lava at Kealakekua Bay; along this shore the first missionaries worked and left as landmarks of their faith sturdy coral churches; in Kailua the royal kings of Hawaii built their sea-wind cooled summer palace, Hulihee; on these ginger-sweet slopes Mauna Loa and Hualalai have poured for centuries their flows of aa and pahoehoe lava, sometimes burying villages and always creating devastation; here also dwells Pele, the goddess of the volcano, who bestows good or evil upon her people. Islanders say that the air in Kona is sweeter and more tender, the sea more fragrant and delicate in hue, the rain gentler and more life-giving. They regard the countryside with a kindling warmth and sigh as they say, "Kona! That's old Hawaii." They mean by those words that life is a tranquil enchantment, that the halcyon influence of the Hawaiian people is strongest there. They mean that the atmosphere has an ineffable quality about it which makes one disposed to live quietly, simply. They know that once you have given your heart to Kona, nothing can extricate it.

BOOK I

LUAHINE, 1925–32

I

Martha Luahine Bell was sitting on the *lanai* of her father's home in Kona, trying to imagine what it would be like to live in green-dark Nuuanu Valley of Honolulu. She wondered how it would feel to become a mere visitor on this sunny hillside, to stay away for months at a time, perhaps years, from this polished air and from the view of the jagged Kona shore line sheltering in its coves the Hawaiian villages of Kailua, Napoopoo, Hoonaunau, Hookena, Milolii, whose names strung together are like an old song. She suffered an alien coldness and trembling in her heart, an anguish which she hoped that Winslow would never discover in her. He would only be puzzled by her "sentimentality," as he would call it. Winslow walked briskly through his life, disregarding the intervals of unpleasantness and of tangling emotion, keeping his eye on the goal of handsome and proper living. Martha envied him his ready poise.

"Luahine!" She recognized her mother's voice and rose from her comfortable position on the *hikie* to go to the *lanai* railing. She watched her mother, carrying an armload of ginger blossoms, climb the steps to the *lanai*. Mummy was a handsome woman, Martha thought. Her black hair shone like wet lava sand in the sun, and her brown skin had a warm red sheen over it. She moved with that flowing grace which most part-Hawaiian women possess.

"Luahine," she said, "I want you to go in half an hour to Aunty Kakae's to get the crown-flower leis for the center table."

"I'll go," Martha replied. When her mother reached the

top of the stairs, she chided her gently. "Mummy, please call me Martha—so you'll get used to it. You know Winslow likes my haole name better."

"Pfui on Winslow! For nineteen years I've called you Luahine, and your handsome fiancé is not going to stop me." Mrs. Bell emphasized the remark by letting her armload of ginger fall into a chair.

Martha looked thoughtfully at her mother and murmured, "He's queer in some ways. I really think he worries a lot about having everything just right. Isn't it silly?"

"That's just New England. What can you expect of a boy named Winslow Abiel Wendell the Third?"

Mrs. Bell went to the door of the house and called, "Pua, please come and get the ginger." Then she turned back to Martha and began massaging her fingers. "That ginger was heavy!"

"Mother!" Martha felt a quick twinge of guilt. "I'm afraid you're working too hard—grating coconut all morning and picking flowers all afternoon."

"*Keiki,* darling! The whole Kona coast and a goodly portion of Kau are coming to your *luau* tomorrow! Daddy had to get two pigs, and I don't know how many gallons of poi. Mrs. Ahuna is making pails of lomi-lomi salmon, and Aunty Kakae is doing bread pans full of *haupia*. Even the twins are working—squeezing coconut cream."

"The twins working! I can't imagine it," Martha said and relaxed again on the *hikie*.

"Yes, the rascals! They are as excited as you are. You'd think *they* were getting married." Mrs. Bell walked over and sat down next to Martha. "I saw Mr. Pukui at the post office, and he said that Kau people are planning to come in the morning and spend the day; it's going to be like one of your grandmother's *luaus* in Punaluu."

"So big? That sort of scares me."

"*Keiki,* dear, you mustn't be scared. They're all your old friends."

"I know. It's just having to say good-by to them that's so hard." She hid her head in the curve of her mother's throat. "Mummy, I hate to leave here." The sweet, dreaming quality of Kona land and water suddenly overwhelmed her, and a feeling of tears welled hotly into her eyes.

"My little *keiki*! You're all grown up now and almost a married woman."

Martha enjoyed her mother's encircling comforting arms for a moment and then gently pushed them away so that she could rise. She went over to pick a ginger blossom, and sniffed at its fragrance. Finally she said, "Mummy, I'm worried about something else, too."

"Luahine, darling! You have too many fears for a bride. Tell me, dear."

"I don't exactly understand Mrs. Wendell." Martha hesitated uncertainly and then continued. "I feel that she thinks I'm not good enough for Winslow."

"Every mother who has a son thinks that there's no girl good enough for him! Wait till you have a son of your own." Martha was startled by her mother's light laugh which interrupted her remarks. "Besides, of all people to be afraid of, Loralee Wendell! You should really feel sorry for her. When she first came to Hawaii as a bride, she was a pretty girl who had all the silly, charming ways of southern women. But through the years, Winslow Second has frowned so many times that she has become timid and restrained."

"But, Mother, she seems so stern."

"Not at all. She simply keeps people at a distance until she is certain of them."

"I'd never think that."

"You probably wouldn't, darling. She may be very kind to you and think of you as her own daughter who died."

"Oh, do you think so? . . . How long ago did that happen?"

"About ten years before Winslow was born. Little Laurie passed away of diphtheria when she was only eight."

"Poor Mrs. Wendell!"

"Yes, it is sad. The one creature who might have been a real companion for her died."

"It's a tragedy."

"Luahine, you must try hard to love Mr. and Mrs. Wendell. They are different from us, but they're fine people. Winslow Second is proud of his family; it's been here a long time, and in their way, they belong to Hawaii. He has a strong sense of the proper thing to do, something you'll have to try to fit in with as best you can."

"The proper thing," Martha said musingly. "That explains something, then. He once said that the house which Winslow and I bought was the right kind of house for Wendells. When I said I thought it was dark, he didn't answer but looked at me as though I were a two-year-old."

"Yes, Winslow would do just that. But he will care for you, simply because you are his son's wife. Later on, I think he'll love you for yourself."

Martha sighed and said, "I hope so. I've often wondered what Mr. Wendell, and Winslow too, think about—my blood."

"Be proud of the Hawaiian in you, Luahine."

"Oh, Mummy, I really am!"

"Grandpa Slator and Mr. Wendell's father were great friends. That makes a sort of family connection which Winslow Second respects." Mrs. Bell rose from the *hikie* and went to Martha.

"Don't worry too much about these things, *keiki,* darling. Just be your sweet self, and they can't help loving you. And remember that the important thing is the life which you and Winslow make for yourselves; nothing must interfere with that, and you'll be happy."

Martha was glad her mother had said the last sentence, because that was what she dreamed of doing, building a life with Winslow, creating days in which such simple things as a swim in the sea or tasting the first mango of the season were the components of their joint happiness. If only they could have a life half so warm and endearing as that of her parents! Of course it would necessarily be different in many ways. The Wendells had certain social and economic responsibilities in Honolulu, and as Winslow's wife, she would be expected to share in them. That was the part she feared. But in spite of these unknown duties, she had determined to be everything that Winslow wanted her to be, just as Mummy in her naturalness and with her warm heart had been all that Daddy had desired.

Martha rose early the next morning. She wrapped a kimono around her, went to the window, and breathed deeply of the air; it had the fragrant, silken quality typical of Kona. If she could work very hard today, she thought, some of the poignancy of leave-taking might be absorbed in fatigue. It was a choking thing to remember that only one night remained before the trip to Honolulu—and only four days until the wedding.

At ten o'clock when she was busy sweeping the lanai floor, she noticed several carloads of guests drive onto the lawn. Mr. Pukui's prediction had been right. These early arrivals were ranch hands and fishermen from Kau and residents of Punaluu, where Tutu Slator lived, and they came in rickety old Fords, bringing their children, ukuleles, guitars, and leis which she knew had been strung especially for Winslow and herself. They climbed out of their cars and lounged in the shade of the trees, talked and sang softly among themselves. She watched them for a few minutes. Sol Akau was clowning as usual; old Mrs. Kanakanui looked as handsome as ever in a black silk *holoku;* Lei and Joey were already holding hands down under the Tahitian breadfruit tree. Martha thought what wonderful, lovable people they were. But they were sensitive to snubs, real or imagined, and she would have to be very cautious of her behavior after she became Mrs. Wendell. She could almost hear them say, "Oh, Martha Bell! She too much high tone. She get marry that Wendell guy. Plenty rich, now." They had been hurt enough when she stopped attending the local school and had gone off to Punahou in Honolulu.

At lunchtime, Martha helped her mother put large bowls of potato salad, plates heaped with sandwiches, and buckets of iced soda bottles on the bare *luau* tables in the garden. Mummy called gaily to the guests, "I hope that'll be enough till the pig comes out of the imu." They grinned, thanked her, and mumbled, *"Maikai!* Plenty *kaukau!"*

Sol Akau teased Martha about her coming marriage and said, "Now you no can be rascal. You have one beeg boss."

"You're wrong, Sol," she replied with a smile. "I'm going to be number one boss!"

"O.K. We watch!" He grinned when he said those words.

"Just for that, you can give me this!" Martha said and snatched a sandwich out of his hand. She took a bite from it and ran back to the house.

When she was inside, she heard her father calling and went to his study. He was leaning back in the desk chair, running his stubby fingers through his thick reddish hair. The desk was the usual tangle of papers, books, and colored pencils. She paused on the threshold a moment; the odor of the study, a mingling of the aromas of mosquito punk, musty books, tobacco, and tea, a cup of which he always had near him, aroused nostalgia in her. She walked slowly into the room.

He said, "Hello, lass," and she noticed a familiar, teasing glint in his blue eyes.

"Daddy, what is it?" she asked.

"Guess!"

"Please, not today. Don't tease me."

"I just had a telephone call."

"He's on the way!" she exclaimed and felt her heart throb.

"Who's on his way?"

"Macpherson Bell!" she scolded. "You mustn't tease your daughter on a day like this. Are Tutu and Winslow really on their way?"

Mr. Bell pulled Martha down in his lap. "Aye, wee lassie," he said, using his strongest Scotch accent. "Winslow was fetched safely from Hilo this morning, and he and Tutu left an hour ago from Punaluu."

"Oh, Daddy, then I've got to get dressed. Let me go!"

He grinned at her and held her wrists. She tried to pull away. "Please let me go!" He released her, and she rumpled his hair when she rose from his lap.

In her own room, she dressed quickly in her new yellow silk *holoku,* which had been made for wearing at the *luau,* and fitted a lei of sweet-smelling *pakalana* about her black hair. Then she went to the twins' room, because it had the best view of the road down which Tutu and Winslow would come.

The twins, Jane and Janet, were dressing when she went in. They greeted her, and Janet, who had just finished combing her hair, sat close to Martha on the bed. She put her hand over her older sister's and squeezed it. "Oh, it's all so wonderful! Do you suppose everything will be so beautiful when I get married?"

Martha teased her, "Janny, I think you're going to be an old maid."

"I am not! I've already had two boys say they loved me. They even said I was beautiful."

Jane turned from the mirror where she was fixing a *pikake* wreath in her hair. "Janny Bell! You, beautiful! Look at your streaky hair, blonde and brown and every other color."

"I look like you 'cept for my hair. You're jealous because I'm blonde, and you just have black hair like everybody else."

"Jan, you terrible liar!"

Martha laughed at them. "Oh, twins! You both are beautiful, especially in your new green *holokus*. You'll probably steal the show."

"No, Martie, we won't steal it," said Janet. "Mummy will. She always does. I wouldn't be surprised to discover before the day is over that she and Winslow had eloped leaving you and Daddy in the lurch. Have you seen her beautiful red holoku?"

Jane spoke up. "And if Mummy doesn't steal the show, Tutu will. She's the cutest old flirt I know. Why she's lived stuck away in Punaluu all these years I can't understand."

"Punaluu's a wonderful place," said Martha. "I love it there, so peaceful with the sea crashing on the lava in front of you and behind you the Kau desert sweeping up to the green hills. I even like the barren old church."

"Martha, you always were kind of *pupule* about some things. I think you're sentimental." Jane went to the open window and put her head out to look up the road. She suddenly stood on tiptoe. "There's the car! I'm sure it is." She whirled around. "Martha, how do you look? Oh, your nose needs powdering."

Martha hurriedly patted the puff on her nose and smoothed her hair while the twins straightened the skirt of her holoku. She had planned this meeting with Winslow for days. He would come up on the steps of the lanai to find her sitting quietly in a wicker chair and reading a magazine. She would look up and hold out her hand to him, and he would lean over and kiss her. It would be a dignified greeting, just as a Wendell would do it.

She called good-by to the twins and ran down to the lanai to wait; her father was there, standing in the doorway watching the early guests. "Daddy," she said breathlessly, "I think they're coming now!"

Mr. Bell took her hand and held it gently. "You look very handsome today, Martie."

"Thank you, Daddy. I'm really happy!"

"I want you always to be happy—like your mother. That's all I ever need to say to you, dear. Be like your mother."

"She is wonderful!" The noise of a car sounded in the driveway. "Oh, they're here!" Martha forgot her carefully planned scene, rushed down the stairs and around the house to the car. As she crossed the grass, she waved to the guests gathered on the front lawn and told them that Tutu had arrived. "Winslow! Tutu!" she cried when she reached the car. She opened the door, offered her grandmother a hand, and helped her out. Then almost before she knew what had happened, she was in Winslow's arms. "Oh, Winslow," she whispered after his kiss, "it seems such a long time."

"It was a long time," he replied and held her away from him to look at her. "Yes, you are as beautiful as I remembered." He smiled at her and said, "Now let me greet your father." He turned to Mr. Bell. "How do you do, sir."

"Baby dear!" interrupted Tutu, using her pet name for Martha. "Can't you spare a kiss for me?"

"Of course!" Martha embraced her grandmother with warmth. Then she asked, "What do you think of your grandson-to-be?" She looked proudly at Winslow, admiring his tall, well-proportioned figure and his shining brown hair. His eyes, she noticed, had a calmness about them for all their gay sparkle. That was like Winslow, she thought; he never lost a certain cool poise in any mood.

"Winslow," said Mrs. Slator, "you are my first grandson, and I'm proud of you. My husband would have been pleased with this marriage; he would have found it very fitting." Martha wondered at the sudden sharpness in her voice when she said the word fitting.

Winslow smiled and said, "Come, Grandmother, and let your 'fitting' grandson help you up the stairs." He took her arm and escorted her to the lanai. On the way, many of Tutu's old friends cried out *aloha* to her, and she responded to them.

Martha, following behind with her father, whispered, "Isn't he wonderful, Daddy?"

"Yes, dear."

"He always knows just the right thing to do."

When they reached the top of the stairs, Tutu and Mr. Bell went on into the house, but Winslow took Martha's hand and led her to a screened corner of the lanai.. "I've been waiting, darling, to give you this." He took a string of pearls from a black velvet box and held them up against her yellow holoku. "A lei for you, my Kona sweetheart," he said, using his private name for her.

She felt her body go warm with love for him and leaned her head against his shoulder. "Thank you, dear Winslow," she said.

He clasped the pearls around her neck and then held her tightly to him. "Martha, my beloved!" he whispered in her ear.

By five o'clock most of the guests had arrived, and Martha took Winslow among them to introduce him. She wanted him to know the Kona people, to see beyond their simple manners and clothes to the genuine friendliness and happiness by which they lived. She realized that in Honolulu his circle of friends was restricted considerably, and she hoped that he would understand that in the country a person could know everyone. The guests were of all racial backgrounds—haoles, Caucasians from their large old homes, Chinese shopkeepers, Hawaiians from little shacks on their *kuleanas* near the beach, a smattering of Japanese coffee farmers from their green-stained cottages. When she introduced Winslow to Sol Akau, the Hawaiian said, "Luahine tell me she be the beeg boss. You betta watch out!" and he laughed at his old joke.

After leaving Sol, they sauntered toward the *luau* tables, which now had a striped canvas marquee over them. The tables had been decorated with ti leaves and hibiscus blossoms, and the servants, headed by Pua, were setting at each place bowls of poi and chicken cooked in coconut milk, dishes of salmon, *opihi,* bits of dried fish, pink Hawaiian salt, cold boiled sweet potatoes, and *haupia.* "Mmm!" Winslow exclaimed. "*Ono kaukau,* good food!" Martha smiled at him and was pleased that he was in the spirit of the day.

When they heard that the pig was being taken out of the imu, they hurried over to watch the men roll the hot rocks away and lift the brown, roasted pork from the primitive oven. The musicians began to play and sing, and Mr. Bell lighted the torches. Mummy called, "Come, children," and led them to the places of honor at the family table. "We must get things started now," she said.

Martha and Winslow sat down, and the guests crowded about to give them leis and gifts. Martha invited each one to visit her in Honolulu, and added, "I'll miss you—and Kona, too."

When she received an orchid lei from Toshi Yamaguchi, she turned to Winslow and said, "Toshi will be a famous painter one of these days; you just watch!" The shy smile of Toshi kindled her, and she wished suddenly that she could do something friendly, something generous for all of these people. She thanked Wai Chee Fong for a jade pendant and complimented her on the birth of her twins. "Wai Chee and I were schoolmates," she explained to Winslow. Isabel Wheeler brought ten strands of *pikake,* and Martha said, "How wonderful! Thanks, Izz. When are you going to join me in Honolulu?"

"Not too long from now," Isabel answered. "Jerry and I are going to be married in October. But, oh, Martie, how I hate to leave Kona!"

"Yes, that's the worst part, Izz," Martha agreed.

Martha sensed a moment of stir and confusion among the guests, and she looked up to see that old Samuel Kekela was moving toward the family table. The time has come, she thought, and her heart began to beat heavily. All of Kona had wondered about the bridal song which Samuel was preparing for her, and his chanting of it would be the high point of the luau. Many believed that Samuel's forecasts always came true. Martha watched him as he made his way among the chairs and tables. His back was now permanently bent, and she saw only his shining white hair, his stooped shoulders, and occasional glimpses of long brown fingers. Samuel had always been a special kind of friend to her. Whenever the house had seemed noisy, too full of the twins and their giddy friends, she would slip down to his cottage, where he lived alone at the beach. She loved the hours spent there, listening to the surf, watching his lean, nimble hands as he mended the nets, hearing the stories he would tell when the spirit moved him. Frequently he spoke of his dreams in which a red fish appeared and forecast for him the future.

When Samuel reached the family table, he turned to face Martha and Winslow; the guests settled into a deep quiet. He cleared his throat and motioned for the woman who held the gourd to start her accompaniment. Then in a deep, throaty voice he began; he chanted of years of happiness and peace in the Honolulu home and of the long lives destined for Martha and Winslow; he predicted a mainland trip which would bring Martha to a crossroads and that after that, her life would become "a polished pebble"; he described the two children, a boy and a girl, to be born to the bridal couple, and said that the girl would marry a man from Kona. Martha was thankful that Winslow did not understand much Hawaiian when Samuel described her with a poetic flattery which she felt certain would embarrass Winslow's New England reticence.

The bride is beautiful as the foam
Which sways upon the sea,
Her skin like the pale flush
Of the ieie *blossom,*

Her hair heavy and fragrant
As the night sea. . . .

When Samuel had finished, he hung a *maile* wreath around Martha's neck and whispered huskily in her ear, "Keep your heart open for Pele." She looked questioningly at him, but he only smiled and went back to his place.

Later when the guests could eat no more and the food remained untasted on the tables, the twins begged Martha to dance with them. She stood up with her sisters and saw the laughter and antics of the crowd; their merriment infected her, and she danced with ardor. At the end of the first song, the twins sat down and left Martha dancing alone. She saw the guests clapping and shouting in her praise and responded to them. She loved the movement of the hula and thought of herself as a tree swaying in the wind and of her hands as painting little pictures. In her happiness, she gazed at Winslow; but when she caught his eye, a tremor of hesitation passed over her. There seemed to be a fleeting look of disapproval on his face. Maybe, she thought, this was something a Wendell wouldn't do.

When she sat down, the guests urged her mother to dance, and Martha whispered, "Don't, Mummy! Please."

"Just one, darling. It'll be all right," Mrs. Bell answered and patted Martha's hand. She leaned over toward Winslow. "In the country, we are gayer and simpler, Winslow. And even some of us aged people are still inclined to dance. Forgive me if I yield to our guests."

Martha watched the slow, graceful movement of her mother. Her dance told of the pearly sea of Kona; her fluttering fingers showed how the sweet rain fell, and her arched palms portrayed the swelling slope of Mauna Loa. The beauty of her mother's hula reassured Martha.

It was long after midnight when the last guest departed, and the Bell family, Tutu, and Winslow went wearily to bed.

Martha did not sleep. She lay in a pleasant stupor, and her mind cruised in a dreamy rehearsal of the evening and the music, of the people, of Winslow, of Samuel's prediction. She wondered what Samuel meant when he said her life would be like a polished pebble. A polished pebble—it was a nice thing to think of, something smooth, gray-green, and shining, perhaps like a drop of water on a kukui leaf.

At dawn she rose and went downstairs. The dewy grass of the garden wetted her bare feet and legs, and she thought with a little catch in her throat that it was Kona dew. The departure from this beloved spot was going to be even more difficult than she had expected, and it would come now in less than two hours. She wished there were some small thing she could take with her which would be an embodiment of Kona. But there was nothing; for the enchantment, the sweet breath of this land was impalpable, was something composed of the aromatic balm of the atmosphere, of the fragrant flowers and trees and sea, of the hearts of the residents. She looked at the sea, drowsy in the cool light of dawn. A breeze from the mountain, which rose gently behind her toward its crater summit, tousled her hair. She walked down to the entrance of the lava tube, which was just large enough for a child to crawl into, and remembered how she had hidden there as a little girl and how one evening she had seen a strange old woman walking there. Pua in the kitchen had told her that it was Pele, the goddess of the volcano, coming to scold her for playing in the tube. Martha didn't really believe that explanation, but she had never gone in again. She thought of Samuel's admonition, "Keep your heart open for Pele." If he meant by that to remember Kona and all it stood for, he need never fear. Kona was so much a part of her that she wished she could rear her children on its slopes and let them bathe in its waters. She wondered about her children. Would they be a boy and a girl as Samuel had said? She would prefer to have more—three, at least. Would they look very Hawaiian? The blood was pretty well washed out by now;

Tutu was pure Hawaiian, but she had married a white man, and Mummy had married Daddy, who was Scotch, and now she was marrying Winslow. She hoped that one of her children would have black hair and eyes, but the rest of them could look like Winslow. Dear Winslow! She touched the pearls lightly and felt how warm they were from resting against her throat.

II

It had been a long day, and they were both tired. Picking up after a honeymoon, Martha thought, was a melancholy occupation. The clothes were soiled and did not fit neatly into the suitcases. The little cottage itself seemed dirty, in spite of the fact that the old Japanese lady had come in every day to clean and cook. When she had closed and locked the last suitcase, Martha went out to take a final look at the giant green cliff behind the cottage. The cliff had become a friendly thing for her; she had watched it in all lights—when the morning sun tinged its jutting rocks with gold, when the hot, bright glare of noon revealed its every cave and shrub, when the green-blue light of evening filled its crevices with mystery, and finally when the milky glow of the moon enchanted it and one could almost imagine a troupe of ghostly priests marching down from the *heiau* at the top. She knew of nothing like this cliff in Kona, but here on the island of Oahu, there were dozens of such *palis*. There were some in Nuuanu Valley, where her new home was situated, and she wanted to learn to love them rather than to feel shut in by their green steeps.

Winslow was busy packing the car and closing the shutters at the cottage windows. When he was finished, he came to her, put his arm around her shoulders, and said, "Now, darling, at last! We are going home." The word home resounded in her ears, and for one fleeting moment she thought of Kona. But she forced this tender memory from her mind.

As they drove toward Honolulu, she felt a curious mixture of uneasiness and joy in anticipating the days to come. There was so much she didn't know about the new house—the ordering of groceries, hiring servants. . . . And during the honeymoon, Winslow had talked about things and people in a way which frightened her. He planned his daily procedure with care and deliberation and studied the reactions of people to what he did and said. This was a new course for her. In the past she had simply been with people and liked them; her relationship with them grew as naturally as a hibiscus shoot.

After a while the soothing motion of riding lulled her uneasy thought; she became drowsy and leaned back against the seat to relax. When the images of the landscape again focused in her eyes, she realized that they had already reached Nuuanu Valley. Winslow turned down the avenue which led to the senior Wendells' home, and she asked, "Aren't we going to our house?"

"Yes, of course, dear, but I have to get the key. Mother's been putting everything in order."

"How nice of her!"

"You'd better come in with me and say hello." He turned into his father's driveway, parked the car under the porte-cochere, and opened the door for Martha to get out.

Mrs. Wendell greeted them in the drawing room. Martha had a feeling that she had been waiting there for some time with nervous impatience like a child waiting for Christmas morning. She was dressed in a long gown of pale green, which set off the well-brushed beauty of her graying blonde hair. She rose and moved toward them. "How are you sweet ones?" she asked. "I don't need to inquire if you had a marvelous time. I can see by your faces." Martha thought that her high voice with just a trace of southern accent sounded overly polished.

Mr. Wendell came through the door and shook hands with Winslow. "Welcome home, son." He kissed Martha on the forehead. "Our daughter! We have a daughter again, Loralee. Isn't it fine!" He took Martha's arm and patted it, and although she was used to a demonstrative family, she felt embarrassed by his gesture. He said, "Your home is waiting for you, Martha, and I hope that you will have every happiness in it."

"Thank you, Father Wendell. I'm sure Winslow and I will always love it."

"Winslow," said his father, "there are a few belated wedding gifts in the kitchen. Have Taro help you load them in your car. Meanwhile Mother and I will go on over to your house and see that everything is ready."

Martha was chagrined. Weren't the Wendells going to leave them alone the first night in their own home?

The late wedding presents, which were mostly crystal and chinaware, were packed in the back seat of the car, and Winslow drove with caution so as not to jostle them. Martha watched the rays of late afternoon sun fall in green-yellow splotches, like a blight, on the tree foliage, the gardens, and the pavement. This light seemed garish and sorrowful to her; it took away all aspect of comfort and friendliness from the houses of Nuuanu Valley and left them stark. She tried to throw off her melancholy mood and remembered that the fading time of day always made her faintly unhappy, even in Kona.

"Here it is, darling!" Winslow laid his hand on her knee when he turned into the driveway of their home. The lawn looked emerald green—almost too green, she thought, and the house was newly painted white.

They walked together up the curving path from the garage, and Martha paused a moment on the little bridge over the *awai,* the irrigation ditch. Wind rippled the papyrus growing in the water. She looked up at the steep mountains, which were dark against the evening sky. They seemed to rise ominously, like austere guardians, and she longed for a vision of the sun-warmed, gentle slopes of Kona.

"What's the matter, dear?" asked Winslow. "You look so unhappy."

"It's nothing." She laughed a little self-consciously. "It's just different, and I'm not quite used to it."

He put his arm around her. "Of course, darling. Remember I'm always here loving you and wanting to help you."

"I know, Winslow," she said.

She saw Mr. and Mrs. Wendell standing in the deep recesses of the lanai, waiting to welcome them. "Winslow, there are your mother and father. We'd better hurry."

When they reached the lanai, Mr. Wendell said, "You must carry Martha over the threshold, Winslow. I did it for your mother long ago."

Winslow lifted Martha and carried her with elaborate care into the house. He set her down and turned to his father. "I never knew, sir, that you are really a romantic at heart."

"I still have unplumbed depths, son," Mr. Wendell said seriously.

Mrs. Wendell spoke to Martha. "As soon as you young people are dressed, we shall have dinner."

"Dinner?" Martha asked wonderingly. "Is it ready?"

"Yes, Father and I have found a good cook for you. Her name is Yukie."

"Come on, Martie, I'm starving," said Winslow, and he took her hand and led her up the stairs to their bedroom. Martha looked eagerly around; the furniture was old and made of polished koa wood. The bed, of Hawaiian design, was twice the size of the average double bed. The draperies, of a heavy white material with large red polka dots, hung to the floor, and the bedspread, a Hawaiian quilt of the *popolehua* design, was also red and white. A large bouguet of Ixora was arranged in a calabash on the bookshelves under the window. Martha liked the room; a warm friendliness pervaded it, created by the presence of familiar island things. She had been fearful that Mrs. Wendell would furnish the room in a feminine and frilly fashion. In the month before the wedding Martha had felt rebellious at the manner in which the Wendells took over the furnishing and appointing of her house, but it had been easier to let them have their way, and she had relapsed into indifference. The happiness she felt to find the bedroom fitted perfectly according to her own taste brought tears to her eyes.

"Look, darling," said Winslow, "our clothes are all hung here in the closet. What are you going to wear?"

She walked to the closet door and fingered through her dresses, finally selecting a white linen sport frock. "I guess I'll wear this tonight."

"Don't you think, dear, it would be nice to put on a long one? Mother is dressed."

"Yes, of course." She felt the warmth creep up her neck and flow across her face. Dinner at home—the twins in dungarees, Mummy in a holoku, Daddy in a sport shirt, and probably all of them barefooted. She must remember that she was no longer at home.

The bath was warm and friendly, and when she stepped out she felt happier. "Winslow, darling," she called, "I love you. It's wonderful to be your wife!" She slipped on her robe and went into the bedroom.

He put his arms around her and kissed her. "Umm, darling, you smell sweet. That must have been nice soap."

"It's carnation. I feel good now, not so tired."

"That's fine! You've seemed sad at our home-coming."

"Not really, Winslow."

When they had finished dressing, they went downstairs. Martha thought that Father Wendell looked very handsome in his white coat and dark blue trousers. Perhaps Winslow would look that way when he reached his father's age.

Mr. Wendell took Martha's arm, and Winslow took his mother's, and they went into the dining room. Martha saw that the table was adorned with the silver candelabra which had belonged to Grandfather Slator's mother and with a simple flower arrangement of lotus buds. The set of spode china which Tutu had given her glistened in the candlelight. When they were seated, she picked up her soupspoon to examine her new initial, W. Then she heard the soft, high voice of her mother-in-law, "The grace, please, Father," and she hastily put down the spoon and bowed her head.

Mr. Wendell's voice had in Martha's ears the intonation of a person used to reading religious texts and praying aloud. "Our Father, we thank Thee for the blessings of this table and pray that Thou wilt guide us to an ever more useful life. We also pray that Thou wilt bless this young couple and make their lives worthy in Thine eyes. Amen."

She sensed that it was a very solemn moment and prayed she would grow to be all that the Wendells expected of her. Things flowed so smoothly, with such grace, when they took charge; everything was already accomplished in her household in an almost magical way. Would she be able to carry on in their fashion? She wondered about the maid dressed in kimono, who waited on the table.

Mrs. Wendell, as though in answer to her thought, said, "Martha, dear, this is Kimi, who will help you. Kimi, this is young Mrs. Wendell."

The servant bowed and smiled and went on with her work.

"I think I have things started for you in the house, Martha. If you have any difficulties, just call me. I know what it is not to have a mother near by."

"Thank you. You are very thoughtful."

"When you are settled, I'd like to introduce you to some of our friends. Of course I know you have some school friends here, but there will be business acquaintances of Winslow's you'll have to know and old family friends of ours." She turned with a gesture of helplessness toward her husband. "What was it the other day, Father? Oh, yes! The Mission Family Society called; they want to include you. It would be nice. It's good for a young bride to have these connections, isn't it, Father?" She fingered nervously the string of jade at her throat.

Martha said, "Whatever you think best."

"Your days are going to seem long at first—with Winslow gone for eight hours. Of course after you have children, it won't be so lonely."

"Mother," broke in Winslow, "you're frightening her. She won't be lonely, and you make her duties sound so grim." He looked at Martha. "Darling, your only duty is to me."

"I don't mean to frighten you," said Mrs. Wendell, "but I remember so well when I was a bride. There are some things men don't understand."

"Now, Loralee," said Mr. Wendell, "don't befuddle these young people with a lot of your feminine nonsense." He turned to Martha. "You have lived in Hawaii, daughter, and know the good New England virtues which are followed here. You understand that a home and children and community service make a happy life for any woman."

Martha searched for something adequate to say. "Yes," she murmured. After a pause she continued, "My Grandmother Slator is loved because she has done so much for the Hawaiian people. She has given me an example of community service."

"That's right, your Grandmother Slator is a fine woman. Your Grandfather Slator was also a fine person. My father spoke very highly of him. I could never understand why after such a full life with him Mrs. Slator isolated herself at Punaluu upon her husband's death."

Martha answered eagerly, thankful for something she too could talk about. "We none of us understand. But she has done more work among the Hawaiian people since then, and she's happy living very simply—much as she did when she was a girl."

"I guess she's just gone Haw—" He flushed and went on hastily, "Winslow, after dinner, we'll have a little business talk; there's a difficulty in the shipping department, and I think you can straighten it out."

Martha finished in her mind Mr. Wendell's incomplete sentence, "She's just gone Hawaiian, as they always do," and thought bitterly, it's what the haoles, the white people, invariably said when Hawaiians didn't live according to the prescribed Caucasian fashion but went back to some of the old Polynesian ways. She felt little tears of anger and hurt start into her eyes, but she brushed them away. She must overlook his mistake, because he was embarrassed and because they would expect her to be graceful about it.

When the dessert course, a mango compote, had been eaten, they rose and went into the drawing room to wait for Kimi to serve the coffee.

"Winslow and I will take our coffee in the library so that we won't bore you ladies with our business conversation," Mr. Wendell said, and, in passing, he patted Martha clumsily on the shoulder. She knew that it was his unspoken apology.

When the men had gone, Mrs. Wendell said plaintively to Martha, "I'm so glad to have a daughter at last. Little Laurie left such a gap in my heart, and now you have come, Martha, to take her place."

"I hope I shall not disappoint you, Mother Wendell."

"Oh, you won't, dear. And I hope that you will overlook Father's little—uh—difficulties. He's really very gentle and very devoted to you. I don't know quite what to say, but our men are used to certain ways and standards, and. . ."

Martha watched her as she spoke fumblingly, and pitied her that she had to smooth over her husband's hasty words. The shadows under her eyes were a deep violet, and they gave a tragic aura to her pale skin. The veins stood out, blue and large on the backs of her small hands, and made the sapphire and diamond rings she wore seem all too heavy for such frailness. Mummy was right about Mrs. Wendell; she was a sad person.

"I'm sure they love us, Mother, and want us to be happy," Martha answered consolingly and noticed that tears came into Mrs. Wendell's eyes. She put her hand gently over the older woman's in a movement of sympathy.

The next morning Winslow kissed Martha before he left for work. "It's starting, dear," he said. "Real life! Don't be lonely. I'll hurry home to walk with you this afternoon."

She watched him go down the path over the *awai* bridge to the garage. The words "real life" echoed in her ears. She waved to him when he drove the car out into the street, and then stood in the doorway for several moments after he had gone. There must be something to do now; maybe the meals should be planned. What would they have for dinner? She hurried to the kitchen where she found Yukie cleaning up after breakfast.

"Good morning, Yukie. I came to see the kitchen."

"Yes, Meesus Wendell. Everyting new—very nice."

"It looks nice. Now about the meals. I—er. . . ."

"Oh, yes. All planned for whole week. I show you. You no like, we change."

"You planned them?"

"Mrs. Wendell—that is, old Mrs. Wendell help me. She said this week hard for you."

"Oh, I see. Where's Kimi now?"

"She make the beds, sweep up."

"Yukie, I think I'll do the flowers for the house."

"Kimi already fix. She plenty good in flowahs." Yukie, after these words, offered Martha a paper with the menu for the week listed on it.

Martha glanced at it. "The menu looks all right. I'll help you next week."

"Tank you, Meesus Wendell."

Martha left the kitchen and wandered into the library. It was filled with books, sets of Emerson, Hawthorne, Thackeray, Jane Austen, Dickens, all soberly bound in leather or fine linen. The authors were much the same as in Daddy's library, but his books were shabby. She pulled down a volume of *Emma* and glancing at the first few pages, read, ". . . and with all her advantages, natural and domestic, she was now in great danger of suffering from intellectual solitude." She closed the book and put it back on the shelf. Then she walked over to the desk and opened the drawers. Inside were neat piles of stationery of varying sizes for the different uses and all marked with her initials in pale blue. Here at last was something to do; she could write the family. She sat at the desk and started her letter.

"Dear Mummy, Daddy, and Twins. Our honeymoon was marvelous. Somehow I wish it could have gone on forever, although that, of course, would be impractical. . . ."

III

Martha soon gave up the idea of directing her household. Yukie was such an excellent manager that it was easier not to interfere with her planning; Kimi kept the house so spotless that even Winslow with his meticulous nature could find nothing about which to complain. Furthermore, Martha admitted to herself, she was a little afraid of these servants. They knew just the proper way to perform each household duty, and she was never certain. How different they were from careless, easygoing Pua, who was almost a member of the family. Consequently, Martha turned to the garden. She liked Mitsuo, the gardener, for his artlessness, his devotion to the earth and its plants, the stray bits of prediction and information he offered her each day such as that the weather would be rainy, that there were fine first-break waves at Waikiki, that there was fresh asparagus at Wong Hop's grocery. Each morning after breakfast she went out to help him cut the flowers for the house, and invariably she had to search for him. Sometimes he was picking papayas in the back garden or raking up fallen mangoes. Sometimes he was down by the stream cleaning out the inlet of the *awai,* and frequently he was out behind the garage fussing with his orchid plants. She liked to watch his quick, expert motions as he worked with these delicate flowers.

One morning she found Mitsuo building onto the crude little shelter in which he kept his orchids. He was so absorbed that he did not notice her. She watched him a moment and then said, "Hello, Mitsuo."

He got up from his work and bowed in his Japanese way. "Hallo, Meesus."

"You have all these nice orchids, but no lath house. Too bad."

"Yeah. Too bad. I tink we need lath house."

"Where you think we build one?"

"Right here behind garage all right."

She spoke enthusiastically. "I think we grow orchids—plenty, yeh? And anthuriums, too." She saw his dark eyes sparkle, and a grin, which made his teeth look white against the earth brown of his skin, came across his face.

He said, "Yeah! I know plenty 'bout orchids."

"You teach me, yeh? I like garden kind work more better house kind."

"Yeah, I tink so."

She told Winslow of the need for a lath house, and he answered, "Anything, my dear, which will enhance the beauty of our house and garden is yours for the asking."

He hired carpenters and sent them to the house; she and Mitsuo watched over their work with eager care. When the lath house was finished, Mitsuo moved the plants in. He began immediately to teach Martha the mysteries of orchid growing, the delicate method of preparing for the germination of orchid seeds, how to renew the fern bark for the plants, how to pick off the scale with tiny tweezers, and all the routine of daily care. She liked this work, not only for itself but because she liked Mitsuo. He responded sympathetically and readily to her thoughts. Yukie and Kimi had absorbed a bit of snobbery from their former mistresses, but Mitsuo remained close to the earth.

Except for her work in the lath house, she passed most of the first few months of her marriage in a dreamy idleness; she thought only of the moment when Winslow would return, put his arms around her, and kiss her. When he brought her a dachshund puppy and said it was to keep her from being lonely, she merely smiled and thanked him. How could she be lonely when her heart and mind were so filled with him! She named the little dog Boki and took him on the afternoon walks which Winslow had instituted as part of the daily schedule.

She spent her afternoons in resting and reading or at occasional luncheon parties. She didn't care much for luncheons, because the conversation was about persons and situations of which she knew little. The most distasteful part was that she had to dress when she was feeling her laziest and sleepiest. However, Winslow insisted that she must assume as quickly as possible her rightful place in the society of Honolulu—that it would help his business and that it was expected of her.

So Martha went, but she would have preferred to lie, as she often did, on their big koa bed after lunch and remember Kona days, the feel of sea water against her skin and of hot sand on the bottoms of her feet, the scent of guavas ripe and rotting, the fragrance of ginger blossoms, the consciousness of living on the flank of a live volcano. She enjoyed recalling the strange things which happened in Kona and which no one could explain. One story had been told her by a friend who believed it implicitly, and Martha almost believed it herself. An aged Hawaiian lady who coveted the chief's kahili in the old summer palace planned one day to loosen it from the stand and steal it. Before she could even touch the kahili, it fell over on her and cut a gash across her forehead. She confessed her intended crime, because she said that the *alii* in his grave knew her wicked heart and that he had punished her.

Martha also liked to think, on her lazy afternoons, of the days of her marriage, how they passed in halcyon succession—smooth, even, beautiful days which one had only to feel. She turned over in her mind the varying sensations, the roughness of fern bark against her fingers, the smoothness of linen sheets, the gentleness of Winslow's hands upon her body, the coolness of rain on her hair and forehead. She smiled every time she thought of the daily walk; Winslow was so particular about it. It was the first thing he wanted to do at three-thirty when he got home, and regardless of rain or shine they took the walk. Their route was always the same, down their own street until they reached Nuuanu Avenue, up Nuuanu to Country Club Road, and along that street to the golf course and back again. On the way they had handsome glimpses of the mountains and the sea, of the luxuriant gardens of the valley. Winslow always took her arm and walked her at a fairly brisk speed; he never allowed a sense of strolling or dallying, a delicious feeling of leisure, and she wondered why the walk meant so much to him.

One afternoon when she was tired, she tried to beg off from the walk. "Not today, Winslow, please. I worked awfully hard all morning, transplanting ginger roots. I'm really tired, and my legs and arms ache."

"It'll do you good, darling—keep your muscles from getting set."

"No. You take Boki with you today. He loves to go walking."

"Darling, it's become so much a part of our custom, and I'm afraid the neighbors will talk."

"What if they do? Besides, they probably don't even notice us."

"That's not true. Mother said that Mrs. Rinton had told her she thought it was such a fine thing to see us walk every afternoon—that modern young couples seldom had such a nice, old-fashioned spirit of companionship."

"Oh, Winslow, you're so . . ." She tilted her head and looked at him with a partly mischievous, partly exasperated glance.

"What do you mean?"

"Nothing. Well, come on, let's go and get it over with." She ran upstairs to put on her raincoat. She felt very tired, but perhaps the coolness of the shower would refresh her. When she went down to the back door, he was not there yet so she took off her shoes and amused herself by dipping her toes in the puddles on the brick walk.

He came up behind her. "Where are your shoes?" he asked anxiously.

"I thought I'd be comfortable," she teased.

"Dearest, you're a married woman now, not a girl."

He was pompous like his father, and this irritated her. She wished he would not call her endearing terms when they were in this mood. It sounded so ludicrous, and yet he always called her dearest or darling during these moments and never seemed to recognize by word or tone that they were close to quarreling. She yearned, at times, for a good honest fight, because she thought it would clear the atmosphere. But he never let it happen.

She snatched her shoes off the back steps, slipped her wet feet into them, and hurried ahead of him down the path.

"Martha," he called, "wait for me!"

She went on without pausing.

By evening she was ashamed of her behavior. He had acted distressed throughout dinner and had asked her a dozen times if she still loved him. When they were having their coffee, he said, "I hope I haven't offended you, Martha. Sometimes I find it so difficult to understand your moods." She answered him gaily that he wasn't the first man who had had difficulty in understanding a woman, and thought to herself that men were certainly queer and childish at times.

The next morning while she was working with the orchids, she thought of the incident. Winslow was in many ways a strange person, not like anyone in her own family. His life was carefully planned, and he never wanted to deviate; she couldn't imagine what would happen if someone called up late one afternoon and asked them to go on a spur-of-the-moment beach picnic. She felt quite certain that he would be unable to rearrange his thought and program to cope with it. Maybe other people knew this quality well, because curiously enough in all their five months of marriage such an invitation had never come.

When she had finished spraying the plants with water, she sat down on the stool at the potting bench and looked at the orchids growing out of pieces of fern bark which hung along the central beam of the lath house. Winslow, she thought, was just like these plants; they both prospered better on schedule. She smiled a little. How Winslow would hate to be compared to an orchid plant! But he even had some of the more elegant and tender qualities of the blossoms. There were his charming gestures, such as the way he kissed her softly on the forehead each evening after he had seated her for dinner, or when on the weekly anniversary of their marriage he sent her a lei. But he had troublesome customs too—the walk, for instance, and the way he let nothing interfere with it. There was his insistence that he help her plan everything, whether it be a trip to the dentist or hairdresser, whether it be a luncheon for her own friends or a large dinner party at which they were both hosts. She must always consult him on every little thing she did. She remembered the first hairdresser episode, just two weeks after they had returned from their honeymoon. She had called Julie Beach, one of her new friends, to ask for help in choosing a salon. Julie suggested her own hairdresser, and Martha telephoned and made an appointment. When Winslow came home, he noticed that her hair had been washed.

"You went to a hairdresser today?" he asked.

She answered that she had, and commented on how observant he was. With a gentle protest in his voice, he said, "But you didn't tell me!"

She was amazed and asked why she should. He replied, "I like to know what you are doing through the day. I like to have a picture of you in my mind, living a beautiful, proper life. I hope you selected a good hairdresser and one who has comfortable equipment." There was nothing in what he actually said, but she understood from the tone of his voice that henceforth she was to tell him when she was planning to have her hair washed and waved. His manner made her feel as though she had committed the gravest of errors in not having informed him on this occasion.

Martha rose from her stool and walked down the aisle of the lath house, scrutinizing the leaves and stems of the plants, hunting for scale. She was so accustomed to this that her eyes saw the little green scale and her hand automatically grasped the tweezers to pull it off without her being completely conscious of the act. Her mind continued to dwell on Winslow. His interest in her daily life seemed beyond the natural desire of a husband to know about his wife. A week ago she had been brave enough to protest mildly; he had been surprised and puzzled and had answered that married couples were supposed to rely on and confide in one another. . . . That was the difficulty, she thought; he had a definite conception about how a husband and wife should behave toward one another, and he observed it as though it were a ritual, a sacred ritual which could not be altered or disturbed. She sighed and decided that the best way was to overlook the queerness and stiffness of his actions.

In the afternoon when he came home, she put on a gay mood and met him in the doorway. She sang a silly little tune, which had been one of Daddy's.

Come, my love, and take a walk.
Come, my love, my cherie.
I'll hold your hand along the way
Fol da rol down derry.

She stopped singing when she saw his face. He said, "Martha, why is it you don't like our walks? I've always thought they were very pleasant."

"I do like them, silly. But I don't want to be so rigid about them. I really think that if I were dying of pneumonia, you would drag me out at three-thirty into the Nuuanu rain."

"Martha, don't exaggerate so. Come on. Put on your coat."

She sighed and said, "All right."

Two mornings later she awoke with a headache. When she opened her eyes, they were dry and burning, and sharp little pains darted through her head. She closed her eyes quickly and pulled at the sheet until it covered her face; she couldn't get up today, not for all of Winslow's sense of routine. Anyhow, she thought irritably, his habits seemed to be closing about her, and she would have to free herself.

Winslow rose and bathed at the usual hour. When he had completed dressing, he went over to the bed and said, "It's time to get up, dear. Breakfast in ten minutes."

"Winslow, I have a terrific headache," she mumbled from behind the sheet. "I don't think I can get up so early today."

"A little coffee will clear it up, dear. Come on, now."

"I'm sorry. I just can't."

"But, Martha, darling, it wouldn't seem right not to start the day without breakfast with you."

"Just for today, Winslow."

She pulled the sheet away from her face and looked at him; he seemed to be puzzled and unhappy. "Try getting up, dear," he urged. "You can go back to bed when I leave. I'm sure coffee will do the trick, anyhow."

"No, I'm dizzy, Winslow."

He leaned over to kiss her and went downstairs without another word.

After Winslow had left the house, Martha had her breakfast in bed. He had been right about one thing; the coffee cleared her headache away. While she was eating, Kimi entered the room to say that Mrs. Wendell was below.

"Ask her to come up. I can see her." In a few moments Martha heard the light, tripping steps of her mother-in-law as she mounted the stairs, and the steadier but nevertheless light footfalls as she walked down the corridor.

"Good morning, Mother," she greeted her. Although Mrs. Wendell was stiff and nervous in a gathering, she was pleasant in a tête-a-tête.

"Are you ill, dear?" Mrs. Wendell asked with concern.

"Oh, no. I'm just getting over a bad headache. Why don't you sit right here on the bed?"

Mrs. Wendell seated herself daintily, took off her *lauhala* hat, and brushed the hair back from her forehead. Martha thought she looked much prettier when she was slightly disheveled.

"Have you had some aspirin, Martha?"

"No. I don't need it. The coffee seemed to cure me. Poor Winslow was very hurt that I didn't eat breakfast with him. But I couldn't possibly have gone down today."

"I'm glad you didn't try. He shouldn't insist. Men can be so thoughtless when things don't go their way."

Martha was annoyed by the tone of Mrs. Wendell's voice, which seemed to imply that husbands were something evil to be guarded against, and she said crisply, "Mother, Winslow loves me and I love him very dearly, but we just can't agree all the time."

Mrs. Wendell looked flustered, and Martha was sorry that she had been sharp. The older woman spoke hesitantly, "I know he loves you, and very much. . . . You look pretty in your white negligee. It makes your skin so golden and your hair so black. You ought to wear white more often."

"I guess I should. But you know me. I like color."

"Martha, dear, I came this morning for a special reason. The members of my reading club have been urging me for a long while to bring you. I delayed it, but I think the time has come when you might enjoy it. We meet once every other week at the beach. We go about ten-thirty, read an hour and a half, have luncheon and a chat, and then go home."

"It sounds very nice," Martha said courteously, anxious to make up for her sharpness. "I'm sure I'd love it. What an early hour for a club to meet!"

"It is early. But our reading club started twenty-five years ago when a trip to the beach was an all-day excursion. Mrs. Platton always does the reading, and she has a lovely voice."

"Is there anyone my age in the club?"

"Oh, yes. Juliette Beach. You know Sam and Juliette; they were married just two months before you were. And Sam's sister, Felicity—the unmarried one. Also there's Joan Hereford and Alexandra Walton. We've always tried to have women of various ages in the club. I think that's what has kept it alive so long—the young people coming into it."

"If they really want me, I think it would be fun."

"I'm glad, dear. It's not only a tradition in the Wendell family but in yours too. One of your Grandfather Slator's sisters belonged twenty years ago, until she and her husband went back to Boston."

"That must have been Grandaunt Alice. Tutu didn't like her very much."

When Mrs. Wendell spoke, her voice was so soft that Martha could scarcely hear her. "That was a strange match, Ululani and Richard Slator. She was not the sort of woman I should have imagined he would marry."

"What do you mean? He's such a mystery to me. Tutu never mentions him, and even Mummy doesn't speak of him. And he died before I was born."

"He was a good man, Martha. Don't doubt that."

"Everyone says that same thing about him—that he was good. And I can't get beyond that."

Mrs. Wendell rose from the bed and went to the long mirror to put on her hat. Martha knew that she was avoiding further answer. "I'm sorry, Martha, dear, that I haven't time to talk longer now. I promised Dora Stephens to help with the flowers for her daughter's wedding this afternoon. We're having a meeting of the reading club tomorrow. Could you come?"

"Yes, I'm free."

"I'll call for you then, at ten-fifteen. I hope you won't mind, but I've asked Mitsuo to cut some of your white spider lilies for the wedding."

"Take anything you want."

"Thank you." She paused on the threshold and gazed at Martha with moist eyes. "You are such a comfort to me, dear."

When Martha told Winslow that she was going to the reading club, he seemed pleased. "I like to have you go into the things Wendells have always had a part in. Besides, you've stayed home pretty much since we've been married."

"I'd much rather wait and go out with you."

"And so would I prefer it, my darling. But I think it's nice for you to be with women and have social gatherings with them from time to time."

"I suppose so. But when I have to be back by three-thirty, it limits my activities."

"Darling, that sounds suspiciously as though it were meant for me."

"It was."

"Well, you're a rascal, and you still have to be home at three-thirty for our walk." He laughed and put his arms around her.

The reading club gathered at the Waikiki home of the Plattons, where it had met for twenty-five years. The house was a low, rambly one with a large lanai fronting on the sea. It had been painted pink and the windows trimmed in blue green, but these colors had grayed in the sun and salt air until they were soft and blended into the hue of the water and the grass. The house smelled of sea dampness and well-polished wood, and it created a mood of dreamy peace in anyone who cared to sit in the cushioned wicker chairs on the lanai and listen to the waves break on the reef. Within five minutes, Martha fell into the spell of the house, and she knew why the club had lasted all these years. It wasn't the young women but rather the graciousness and peace of the Platton home which drew people back.

She discovered that the club was very systematic in its selection of books. It alternated a classic with a newly published best seller, and of course when any new book on Hawaii appeared, the club read that. At the moment, Jane Austen's *Emma* was the choice. Martha thought of the first day in her own home and how she had read that one sentence from *Emma*.

Mrs. Wendell introduced her to the club members whom she did not already know. Martha found a chair next to Juliette Beach and sat down to wait for Mrs. Platton to read. Julie whispered, "How do you like your initiation?" Martha grinned and was going to answer when she saw that Mrs. Platton had taken her place and was beginning. Her voice was low and at times blended so with the sound of the water that, except for the words, it was hard to distinguish between the quality of the two. Martha found it difficult to concentrate on what she heard, and to occupy herself she studied the members of the club. Mrs. Blake's hair was blue-gray and carefully waved. She was a remarkable person, always cool and crisp and apparently able to cope with any situation. But Martha knew from the gossip that Mrs. Blake was deeply concerned over the fact that Margie, her daughter, was still unmarried at thirty-one. Felicity Beach's hair with its natural curl looked very nice the way she did it in a casual wind-blown bob. She was a quiet girl, intent upon the resource within herself, but there was something in her unassuming manner which made one feel at ease with her. Juliette Beach was, Martha thought, the most beautiful person there. Her curly hair was golden red and her eyes were gray-green. Strange, she was the only girl in the group who was not island born, and somehow you knew she wasn't. Her voice was not right; it didn't have the rhythmic intonation of island people, and her clothes had a trifle too much style. Yet, except for Felicity, Martha liked her more than any of them, and she had been disgusted with the talk that Julie had snatched Sam Beach right out from under Margie Blake's nose. Poor Margie was a sweet girl, but unhappily it looked as though she might join the rank of island spinsters who sat their lives out in their fathers' houses.

Many of the women in the group were sewing and darning in the thrifty way of their New England forebears. Martha wondered if they were listening to the reading any more closely than she was. It was a tranquil, dignified gathering, one which made a person feel as though she belonged to a fine, gracious world. Yet in the midst of it, Martha wished she were down at the old church in Kailua sewing and chatting with the Hawaiian women there. She might learn how Mrs. Mahi's baby was who had tuberculosis or whether Lei was really going to marry Joey Kealoha. That was the trouble with her life now; it was so circumscribed within a correct little group, and she liked friends of all kinds, just as she had had in Kona. She wished the day would come when her thoughts did not continually scurry back to that beloved spot.

At luncheon she sat with Julie Beach. "Well, Martie, how do you like us?" Julie inquired.

"It's pleasant."

"I suppose so. There seem to be so many things in Hawaii you're expected to do because your husband's mother and great-great-grandmother did. I guess it's tradition, and I'm not accustomed to it. Besides, everything is so terribly leisurely."

"You'll get used to our island ways after a while. The weather will slow you down and make you accept things easily."

"Well, I am slowing down. I don't even have enough energy to play bridge. But I do have a new interest. Lissie has started to confide in me."

"Poor Felicity!"

"That's what you islanders always say, 'poor Felicity Beach,' 'poor Margie Blake,' poor this gal and that gal and any girl who can't snag a husband. I like Felicity, except when she gets on the subject of why she hasn't a husband. I can just hear her mother, 'And Felicity, she's such a worry! That's a problem we have with our island daughters. The boys go off to college and bring back mainland wives and that leaves no one eligible for our girls.' I've heard her say that fifty times; the first time was when she called on me the day after we returned from our honeymoon. And of course it has finally gotten to me that I snatched Sam right out from under Margie Blake's nose. And I never laid eyes on Margie or Honolulu until my wedding day!"

"Oh, don't take that seriously, Julie. The trouble with island girls is that they want to live in the islands, and they can't if they marry a mainlander, unless papa gives him a job."

"Why, you poor little dears! Wanting to live right at home!" She smiled when she said it and took the sharpness out.

"Some of us, Julie, are a bit sentimental. I hated to leave Kona just to come to Honolulu. It's not explainable, but there's something about these islands. . . ."

Martha felt the tenderness of Julie's glance when she said, "But you're different. You belong, in a way no one else here does."

IV

Martha and Winslow left the doctor's office. After the morning chill in the cement building, Martha was vibrant under the touch of warm island wind. The smell of the sea was strong, and she had a sudden desire to go swimming.

"Winslow, let's go to the beach."

"Do you think it's wise?"

"Don't be so silly. Having a baby doesn't interfere with everything."

"All right, dear. But perhaps we'd better go to Aunty Florry's—not to the Outrigger."

"Winslow, you're so funny! I don't even show it yet, and you want to hide me."

"It isn't that. It's just that I want to be very careful of you now. Think, darling, this is what we've been waiting for."

"Yes." She looked musingly at the flamboyant blossoms of a poinciana tree. "Winslow, let's get Lehua Kakae from Kona to be the nurse."

"Is she reliable?"

"Wherever a baby is concerned, she's fine. Besides she's a calabash cousin of mine."

"Oh, I see." He watched her face closely when he asked,

"Do you think it's wise to have a relative as a servant in our house?"

"A baby's nurse is a member of the family. Old Annie was part of ours."

"In Honolulu things are different, though."

"Oh, Winslow, let's not worry about it now. You are a wonderful husband, and I love you dearly, but you do have a faculty of making the simplest things complicated problems. Let's go swimming and forget it."

Martha was delighted to discover that she was not ill in her pregnancy. The only trouble was the annoying care with which Winslow and Mrs. Wendell watched over her. Their ministrations stifled her, especially when they insisted upon hours of rest and walking, when they urged her to drink milk at any moment of the day. But there were gaps in their hours of vigilance during which she enjoyed herself in a completely sensuous manner. When she felt like sleeping, she slept. When she was thirsty, she sucked the cool, sweet fruit of the mango. She went barefoot in the dewy grass of early morning and sometimes lay on the lawn and looked at the clouds and the leaf patterns of the trees; from the corner of her eye, she could see the *palis* of the Koolau range, jutting like chunks of jade into the sky. She squatted by the bonfire of leaves and twigs which Mitsuo made once a week and let the fragrant, woodsy smoke curl about her. Sometimes, in a childish mood, she toasted a marshmallow over the coals. Never had life been so desirable for her, and she cherished each moment of it.

She had not seen Julie for three weeks, and although she had wondered about her, she was too taken up with the magic newness in herself to telephone. So she was happy when she answered the door one afternoon, to find Julie there. Her friend looked weary and ill. "Julie, it's good to see you! How are you?"

"Well," she answered, "it seems that I'm going to present

the Beaches with a son and heir. That is, they hope it will be a son and heir and not another Felicity."

"How wonderful!"

"It's not wonderful. It's just nature. I couldn't have escaped it."

"Julie, what things you do say! . . . I'll be running you a race."

"What do you mean? Not you too?"

"Yes."

"Martie, you lamb! We can go through this ghastly, I beg your pardon, blessed experience together."

Martha smiled; sweet Julie, she was not as brave as she pretended to be. She asked, "When is yours expected?"

"In September."

"Mine too. Maybe we'll have twins!" Martha said and laughed.

Mrs. Wendell had insisted that Martha and Winslow dine at the senior Wendell home once a week after she had learned of the baby's coming. She said that it would relieve Martha of the responsibility of one meal and that she remembered how she had hated to think of food during her own pregnancies. On an evening of one of these dinners, the family had gathered in the drawing room for coffee. Mr. Wendell helped Martha settle comfortably with a pillow at the small of her back, and Mrs. Wendell sat down next to her and took her hand. Martha this time was grateful for their attention, for she was tired in the evenings from carrying her burden all day.

Winslow drank his demitasse and then said, "Father, Martha and I think now is the time to get a house in the country. We ought to have a place to take the baby for week ends and summers." Martha looked at him in astonishment; he had not once mentioned this idea to her.

"What about Hale Nani at Punaluu?" Mr. Wendell asked.

"But, Father, that's yours. We can't take that."

"We have six acres. That's enough space for two houses. There's a nice site near the beach."

Martha disliked Punaluu on Oahu, partly because it bore the same name as Tutu's village on the island of Hawaii and partly because she didn't want to be dependent on the senior Wendells when she and Winslow bought a country home. In the city she couldn't escape being dominated by the Wendells, but in the country she wanted to be free. In her heart she harbored the idea that perhaps she could recapture some of the old Kona life at a country place. She said to her father-in-law, "We don't want you to break up your property. There's so much of that being done now."

"My dear," said Mr. Wendell, "we aren't breaking it up. It was our thought when we got it to have a place for Winslow and his wife and children."

Winslow interrupted, "Father, that's very nice of you. Of course, we're most grateful."

On the way home, Martha said, "Winslow, why did you spring this on me? You've never mentioned a country house, and I didn't dream it was in your mind."

"Darling!" He acted surprised. "I thought I did talk it over with you."

"You certainly never did."

"Martha, dearest, you are so close to me that I guess I just take it for granted that you know my every inmost thought. I honestly thought I had discussed it with you."

His tenderness mollified her, and she asked, "Winslow, couldn't we look for a place of our own?"

"Don't you like Punaluu?"

"Of course I do. But we've imposed so much already on your parents. I feel guilty."

"They'd really be very hurt if we didn't build on their land."

"Hurt! They're always going to be hurt about something. You care more about preserving their feelings than mine."

Tears came into her eyes, and although she tried to stop them, rolled down her cheeks.

"Martie, darling, what's the matter? You don't feel well, do you?"

"Yes, I feel all right, but I just want to look for something that will be our very own. We don't seem to have anything that is our very own."

"Sweetheart!" he said. "Don't cry. Of course we'll hunt for something our very own. I'll ask Mr. Jamieson to come and take you to the country tomorrow. If there is a place to your taste on this island, he will know of it."

Mr. Jamieson arrived at nine the next morning, and Martha greeted him at the door. He looked affectionately at her and smiled. "Well, well, little Martha Bell. I came on the same boat with your father from Scotland."

"You did? Why, of course, Mr. Jamieson! I've heard him talk about you. He called you Jaimee. It's nice to hear your Scotch accent."

"Thank you. Now, what sort of place do you have in mind?"

"I don't know. I think always of something as like Kona as possible, some place back from the sea a little, up on a hill. A spot with a house where people have lived a long time and the trees are old and mossy-backed, and there's lots of yellow ginger around."

"Well, young 'un, you have your mind all made up."

"Yes." She laughed nervously. "I guess it's only a dream place."

"I think I know just the spot—near Waikane."

He drove her over the Pali, through Kaneohe and Kahaluu, past the taro fields and lotus ponds of Heeia. She watched the little cottages and was envious of the women and children who sat on the lanais, talking and dozing or roughhousing. She saw the taro patches and thought how seldom she ate poi now. That would be changed after the baby was born, because poi was considered a fine baby food. Near Waikane, Mr. Jamieson turned up a little road which led to a hilltop shaded by a grove of mangoes and coconuts. An old house with a rusted tin roof and lanais around three sides stood in the midst of a green lawn. A hoary breadfruit tree shaded the grass, and behind the house was a bank of ginger.

Mr. Jamieson stopped and spoke hesitantly. "Of course the house is old and would need some fixing. It was built twenty-five years ago. But it's in good condition. The Parken family had it, and they watched the termites, dry rot, and all that."

Martha opened the car door and got out. She looked at the sea view and at the mountain view and breathed deeply of the sweet air. She walked around the lawn, smelling the ginger, admiring the old trees, letting the spirit of the place soak into her. How could it be, she wondered, that her dream of a country home was actually real! When she went back to Mr. Jamieson, she said, "It even smells right!"

"I'm glad I could find just what you wanted."

"Of course I'll have to speak to Winslow."

That afternoon while they took their walk, she told Winslow. "And it's a reasonable price, dear. I think it's just the place for us and for our children."

He took her hand and looked tenderly down at her. "Poor Martie, you still dream of Kona, don't you? There's something about Kona which seems to gnaw into people's hearts." He squeezed her hand gently. "But, darling, you didn't really think we could refuse the offer of my parents? Besides, people would think it queer if we didn't build on the family's land."

She could scarcely believe his words. "But why . . ." She pulled her hand away from his. He had only been humoring her; she remembered the doctor's words, "Winslow, you'd better humor her while she's in this condition. Women sometimes have strange moods."

"No," she said bitterly. "I should have known that even in this there was the proper thing to do."

"Martie, what do you mean?"

"You wouldn't understand my way of thinking. Not a Wendell!" She saw the pinched, hurt look cross his face, and did not regret a word of what she had said.

When they reached home, she hurried out to the lath house, away from him. She sat on the high stool at her work table and rested her head in the palms of her hands. He had really deceived her, although he hadn't meant it so. He simply wanted to do the accepted thing for both of them. And to do that accepted thing, he had gone ahead without sharing his thought and plan with her. That was the most difficult aspect of her married life—remembering to do the proper thing regardless of its emotional satisfaction. She had wanted a bit of Kona for herself and Winslow and for the baby. But apparently that was wrong. And now this conflict was growing within her, the clash of two purposes. She yearned for something of Kona in their lives, and at the same time she wanted to be the wife Winslow expected her to be. Why were the two incompatible? Maybe she would never be happy until she had torn Kona out of her mind as a reality and made of it nothing but a phantom, a thing of the mists to which she knew she could never return. Perhaps she should recognize as an unalterable fact that the old, easygoing life, the life of feeling, was gone forever. It had been wonderful when she had only to accept the delightful sensations of everyday living, refreshing when she did not have to suppress the warm enthusiasms of her mother's ways. Now she must study her actions, ponder them, to make certain that she was fitting into the proper pattern. And when the baby came, there would be even more thinking and planning. She asked herself if every person had two lives, the one which must be lived and the one which was only a wraith in the heart.

She climbed down from the stool and went to the doorway of the lath house where she leaned against the frame and gazed at the laden mango tree. She sighed and thought that the primary wish, after all, was to keep her faith with Winslow, and if giving up the thought of Kona was necessary, that she must do.

V

Martha noticed during the months of her pregnancy a subtle shift in the relationship between herself and the Wendells. In the past she had been only a daughter-in-law, but now that she was to bear Winslow's child, she was becoming in truth a Wendell. It wasn't what they said to her but a delicate change in the degree of intimacy with which they approached her. Mr. Wendell occasionally put his arm around her and kissed her clumsily on the forehead; he discussed family finance in front of her and gave her an old garnet bracelet which had been his mother's. Mrs. Wendell talked of all her little nervous ailments in some detail with Martha, and spoke confidingly of her first years in Hawaii and of Laurie's birth and death. They began to assume that she knew of certain family matters which were not openly discussed, such as Mr. Wendell's invalid brother who had recently died in an institution on the mainland. Her reactions to this new intimacy were twofold. Sometimes it pleased her because she knew that now she was completely accepted in spite of blood or anything else; at other times she was afraid because the Wendells seemed to absorb her so completely.

Even Julie and Felicity apparently were changing the emphasis of their attitude. Martha felt the full force of this on a hot afternoon when they sat on her lanai and sipped glasses of iced guava juice. They spoke very little in the heat and simply enjoyed being together. Martha studied Felicity during this silence and admired her dark hair and eyes. She wondered why such a handsome girl had never married.

Lissie broke the stillness, speaking in a thoughtful tone. "You know, once Queen Liliuokalani spent a week end in this house. Maybe she sat on this very lanai and sipped guava juice on a hot afternoon like us."

"Lissie, you're such a historian at heart." Julie's voice was drowsy.

"Not really a historian. I just like to know these things. It makes life more exciting."

Martha said, "I understand. We always know about such things in Kona."

"Kona," Lissie murmured, drawing the word out into a sigh. "I want to go there and stay for years, sometime."

"You people! At it again!" There was disgust in Julie's voice. "Now if I were to tell you about Chicago and Al Capone . . ."

Martha and Felicity interrupted her with laughter and then Felicity spoke. "When, Julie, darling, are you going to relax and become an islander and a Beach?"

"Well, when is Martie going to become a Wendell? She still broods about Slators and Kona and what not."

Felicity looked at both girls with mock pity in her eyes. "You poor darlings, when your babies are born, you will become irrevocably part of your husband's families. And your children will take their rightful places as Wendells and Beaches in society."

Julie rose from her chair and walked heavily up and down. "Good God! Haven't you people in these backward islands heard of the rights of women? We're no longer chattels of our husbands."

"We know all of that, Julie," said Felicity calmly. "We're just being practical."

Julie sat down again and gulped the last of her guava juice. "I suppose so. And now, I'll give you a true confession. But kindly do not repeat it to anyone else. I already feel more a Beach than a Morrison. I don't know when or how it happened, but one morning I woke up and thought of myself as Julie Beach and didn't even remember that I had been Julie Morrison. Such is the insidious influence of marriage on the ruggedest individualist. Come, Martha, my sweet, relax along with me."

When the girls had gone, Martha thought over this conversation. Julie and Lissie didn't really understand her situation; there was a blood difference. The Hawaiian part of her called for all that life in Kona had meant, and it was insistent in its demands. Every day something happened—a sudden awareness of the salt fragrance of the sea, the taste of raw fish with lime juice, an island song strummed on a ukulele by a passing boy—these made her tremble with the desire to cast aside the artificialities of her present life. There was also the problem of people; Winslow and his family could not seem to understand why she was interested in all kinds of people, how she could wish to be friendly with them. The Wendells were certainly kind to their servants and patronizingly warm in their attitude toward persons of all races and of economic backgrounds less fortunate than their own. But to welcome them as friends on equal terms in their home—that was a different matter. Martha desperately missed the rich variety of her friendships in Kona, and while she realized that she must give up most of such things for herself, she did not want her baby to miss this experience. She was thankful for one thing; Winslow had agreed to having Lehua Kakae as nurse.

She felt an urgent need to send her parents a hint of this mood which had settled on her, and she went to the library and sat down at her desk. She took out pen and paper and wrote:

Dear Mummy and Daddy,

I've been feeling very well. As a matter of fact I can't believe it when Juliette Beach tells me how sick she gets at times. Her baby and mine may have the same birthday—isn't that exciting? I really show it quite a bit now, and I've taken to wearing muumuus *around the house because they are so comfortable. Winslow teases me and says I look like photographs of 1890. Mrs. Wendell has been very nice and understanding; I do feel sorry for her.*

I hope that you will try awfully hard to get to town in time for the baby's birth. It would mean so much to me to have you here. You don't know how much. I want the baby to see all his grandparents and know them equally well. I want him to know that he's a Bell and a Slator as well as a Wendell, and I want him to know that he belongs to Hawaii. I want him to realize that Kona is as much his as Honolulu; I really wish he could be born in Kona. It's rather hard to express what I want to say. I hope my baby will understand that nothing is forbidden to him simply because one doesn't do it, but rather it is forbidden because it's ignoble and would harm people.

I didn't really mean to go on this way. You must think I'm getting awfully philosophical. But I just want my baby to grow up in the wonderful way you let me grow. Please tell Lehua to hurry and come. We are ready for her.

With love,

Luahine

The early morning air was cool and moist when Winslow and Martha drove to the dock to meet Lehua. The people in the gay crowd, gathered to greet the interisland steamer, *Waialeale,* jostled one another, bought and gave away leis, laughed and cried, exchanged family news in swift volubility.

Martha watched the gangplank intently. "Oh, look, Winslow, there she is! The fat one with all the leis."

"The one in the red dress with an *akulikuli* lei on her hat?"

"Yes, she loves red. Doesn't she have a wonderful smile! Oh, it's so good to see her!" She waved the leis she had bought for her cousin and cried, "Lehua! Here we are!"

Lehua Kakae ran to Martha, hung a bright orange hala lei around her neck, and embraced her boisterously. Then she pushed Martha back and looked at her. "Tsk tsk, Luahine, you're almost as big as I am!" She laughed merrily at her own wit. Martha laughed, too, but with restraint, for she was worried about Winslow's reaction to this kind of humor.

"Lehua, in Honolulu they call me Martha. You'd better do it too. You remember Winslow from the day of the luau."

"How do you do, Miss Kakae," said Winslow stiffly. "We are glad you have come."

"Hello, Mr. Wendell," replied Lehua just as stiffly.

Martha was disappointed that Winslow had not accepted the hint that they call each other by first names. On the way home she questioned Lehua eagerly about the family. "How are Mummy and Daddy and the twins?"

"They're fine. You'd never recognize the twins. My, my! They're such young ladies with such airs."

"I'd love to see them all—and to see Kona."

"Kona's the same, always the same. We must take the baby over when he's old enough to travel. He ought to know it."

When they reached the house, Winslow called Kimi, Yukie, and Mitsuo to the lanai and presented Lehua. "This is Miss Kakae, who will be the baby's nurse. I want you to do all you can to make her comfortable. Miss Kakae, this is Yukie."

Yukie bowed Japanese fashion. "So please, Miss Kakae."

"This is Kimi." Kimi bowed.

"And this is Mitsuo." The gardener handed Lehua an orchid.

"Thank you, Mitsuo. Orchid number one kind, yeh!" The gardener beamed at the compliment.

Winslow spoke. "Now, Miss Kakae, Mrs. Wendell will show you to your room and the nursery. I must go back to the office." He shook hands with Lehua and smiled at her. "We have a serious responsibility, you and I."

Martha sighed. Just when she was ready to be angry at Winslow for his stilted, unfriendly behavior, he said something like that, and her anger fled.

When he had gone, they went up to Lehua's room. The Hawaiian woman scarcely looked at it, but grasped Martha's hand. "Is he good to you, Luahine?"

Martha smiled and answered, "I'm afraid that Winslow will seem a little strange to you. He's really too good to me—sometimes he stifles me with goodness. Don't worry, Lehua. Just try to understand him. He's not like us. Now look at your room. I've spent weeks getting it ready."

"It's beautiful, Lua—I mean Martha. Really too elegant for me!"

"You'd better say that, Lehua Kakae! Now sit down and tell me the latest from Kona."

"There's so much." She paused a moment. "We had a fine party before I left."

"Tell me all about it."

"Three days ago the twins called up and said how about going to Kailua and taking out a canoe. Well, we drove down in your father's car, and Sam Aukai was there with a bunch of haole tourists. He suggested that we get some food and paddle down to Keauhou. So we did, and what fun! The haoles had a car meet them there, and they drove back to Miss Payne's Hotel, but we decided to stay the night. Sam's old aunt, Mrs. Kahananui, lives there, and she put us up. The twins called your folks to let them know, and we just took over that household. That night we had an old-fashioned poi supper, and afterwards we sang and danced to Sam's ukulele. You remember how he plays that ukulele! And all the time the twins kept saying, 'If only Martie were here. This is just the kind of party she likes.' "

"Wonderful, wonderful!" Martha whispered. "It's been so long. . . ."

"What do you and Winslow do for fun?" Lehua asked abruptly.

"Oh, we're quieter. I belong to a couple of clubs, and we go to dinners. Once in a while we go to the country. We have a house near the Wendells at Punaluu."

"At Punaluu, yeh?"

"Yes, but it's not like Punaluu on Hawaii. It's greener and rainier, and many of the fashionable people have homes there. I never think of it as Punaluu because that gets me all mixed up with Tutu's place. I always call it by the name of our house there, Nani Wai."

"It must be nice, though, yeh? Have plenty picnics and good swimming."

"Yes, it's nice. But we don't often have picnics. Mostly eat inside. There's a nice dining room which opens out on a rock garden and pool."

"I guess you're too swank now, yeh, for such stuff?"

"No, Lehua. It's just in Honolulu things are different. Sometimes we broil steaks on the beach and have luaus in the garden."

"Martha, I forgot to tell you!" Lehua's eyes sparkled. "Comet's married! My baby sister—and she's living right here in Honolulu. I want to see her this afternoon."

"Little Comet! Why didn't anyone tell me?"

"Come on with me. She'd want to see you."

Martha felt a clutch of happiness inside of her. At last after almost a year, she could go into a home like Comet's and meet the kind of people who would be there. "I'll go! I'll go!" she cried. Nothing else seemed important at the moment but going to Comet's; it was a necessity.

After luncheon Martha said she would not take her nap, that they could start immediately for Comet's. "Where does she live, Lehua?"

"Somewhere in Kapahulu. I have the address on an old letter here."

Martha drove with Lehua to Kapahulu District. After ten minutes of looking they found the rocky, twisting little street and Comet's home. A Model-T Ford was parked in front of the house, and it had fishing poles tied to the side. Martha saw that there were nets, glass-bottom boxes, goggles, spears, and other fishing gear in the car.

Lehua ran up the steps of the lanai and opened the door, shouting, "Comet! Comet! It's me, Lehua!"

Martha followed her more slowly. She saw Comet come out of the house and embrace Lehua. Comet too was going to have a baby, but somehow she seemed as beautiful and lithe as ever. "Luahine Bell!" she cried when she caught sight of Martha. "Come in! You're in time for some poi and *laulau*. We're just eating, and then we're going fishing. Come and go with us."

Martha walked up the steps and embraced Comet. "It's good to see you," she said. "I didn't even know you were married."

"Please, go in," Comet said and held open the door. Martha entered the little house and looked around her engrossed, yearning to find the atmosphere from which she had been away so long. And here it was, here was what she had been wanting to see. The room had plain wooden chairs and tables, a scuffed *lauhala* mat on the floor, garish pictures of Hawaii tacked on the walls, nets and spears and glass floats stacked and draped across the corners, shriveled leis hanging over the lamps and chairs, and a huge *punee* filling one whole end of the room. She had been in many such houses in Kona.

"Luahine, this is my husband, Gabriel," said Comet, and pointed to a handsome Hawaiian youth. "These are his brothers, David, Solomon, and Samuel. And my mother-in-law, Mrs. Hartwell."

Martha greeted each in turn and shook hands with Mrs. Hartwell, a large, brown woman who was in a comfortable, loose dress. Mrs. Hartwell looked at Martha and said, "Oooh, *maikai* yeh! You get keiki too. Dat one t'ing I wait for—Comet's keiki. Dat my first gran'child."

Martha sat down at the table and helped herself to poi and

a *laulau,* completely forgetting the luncheon she had already eaten. She asked, "Where you get *laulau?*"

"Aala Market," answered Mrs. Hartwell. "Roselani Paki have one stand there. Plenty good Hawaiian *kaukau.*"

"Long time since I eat *laulau.* Number one kind!" Martha said and suddenly realized that she had slipped into pidgin. "Where you go fishing?" she asked.

Gabriel answered. "We go Blow Hole. One friend say plenty *uku* run today."

When everyone had finished eating, they left the table as it was, heaped with dirty dishes and scraps of food. Comet ran to get her *lauhala* hat and found others for Martha and Mrs. Hartwell. Lehua said she didn't want a hat, that such a mop of hair as she had was enough protection. Martha offered to drive her car and take the women.

The men put on their swimming suits and dark goggles and climbed into Gabriel's car. They waved good-by and started on their way. Comet put a couple of straw mats into Martha's car, and some bottles of soda pop and her ukulele, and the women started. As they drove toward the Blow Hole, Comet strummed on her ukulele and Lehua sang the songs. When they arrived, the men greeted them and helped them carry their equipment down the rocks to a small sandy beach. Solomon Hartwell took Martha's arm and guided her carefully to a comfortable place in the sand. She thanked him, and he smiled warmly at her. When the women were settled, the men went off with their poles and nets to the rocks at the edge of the sea.

Martha took off her shoes and dug her toes in the sand. She luxuriated in the warmth of it and the softness. "This is heaven," she sighed. "Perfect heaven!"

Comet glanced at her shyly. "Maybe you don't do this so much any more."

"Not in just this way—so relaxed."

"When you want, you come our house."

Martha was embarrassed that Comet appeared to guess so much. "Thank you," she mumbled.

"Don't you worry, Luahine Bell," said Lehua. "Now that I've come you're gonna relax more often. Your baby's more important than all this tea-party stuff."

Mrs. Hartwell interrupted, "Dere's only one important ting. Keikis. All my life, all I want is one keiki in my arms. Dey so tiny, so cute."

The surf roared and echoed loudly against the rocky cliffs which surrounded the small beach. The noise made it difficult to talk, and the women soon stopped trying. Mrs. Hartwell lay down with her hat over her eyes and dozed. Comet took up her ukulele and sang to herself, and Lehua went off with a cloth bag to gather seaweed from the rocks. Martha leaned back in the sand and enjoyed the complete repose brought on by companionship with these familiar people and by the sun warm on her skin and the rhythm of the sea assuaging her spirit. She too dozed.

Gabriel startled her when he came back with two fine *uku*, which he buried in the wet sand to keep them fresh. She looked at her watch; it was three-thirty-five. Her heart throbbed heavily; Winslow would be home, and she not there!

She rose awkwardly from the sand and walked to the rocks. She called, "Lehua! Lehua! I've got to go now. I had an engagement at three-thirty. You stay and come home with the others."

Lehua glanced over her shoulder and said, "O.K. You go ahead."

On the way home, Martha reproached herself. She had determined to push her childhood dream away, for Winslow's sake. She wanted to accept the responsibility of being his wife, to fit into his pattern and his way of living. Already she had broken her secret faith with him.

When she reached the house, she hurried to him and said, "I'm sorry, Winslow. I'm terribly sorry."

He looked at her with an expression she could not interpret. "Martha, there are some things about you I can't . . ." He shook his head. "Sam Beach saw you when he was coming back from the ranch. He said you were at the Blow Hole with some —er—people."

"I was with Lehua, her sister Comet, her husband, and his family."

"You didn't remember that you had promised to go with Mother to the Mission Family Society?"

"Oh, Winslow!" In a voice of shame she said, "How could I forget!"

VI

One morning in the week the baby was expected, Martha called Lehua, after Winslow had left, to sit with her over a second cup of coffee.

"Do you feel all right?" Lehua asked as she poured cream into her cup.

"Uh-huh. Fine."

"You've seemed so listless since my first day here. That is, since we went fishing with Comet."

"I made a mistake that day, but it's all right now."

"You shouldn't have to worry about anything with the baby coming."

"Maybe not. But I've learned one thing. There are some times when you have to stand absolutely alone. Parents, nor husband, nor friends can help."

"I think the climate in this valley is affecting you."

"No. It's not that."

"When the baby arrives, we must go to the country for a

while and get you out of this rainy place. After living in Kona, it's depressing."

"But it's a beautiful spot. The mountains are always green and the foliage fresh. I can see how people love Nuuanu dearly."

Lehua twisted her coffee cup about on the saucer and seemed to be hunting for words. "I think there are too many—too much feeling of *akuas* here."

"Don't say that. You know it's superstitious."

"I suppose so. Your mother and father always say that in Kona too. But even they can't explain some things that happen."

Martha rose heavily from her chair and walked to the window. She stood gazing at the green pali cliffs a few moments before she spoke. "Sometimes at dusk I see an owl fly three times around the mango tree. I wonder why he does it just three times."

"Oh, *pueo!* A good sign. Don't harm him."

"I showed it to Winslow one night and he said the owl was hunting for rats that climb to get the mangoes. I asked him why three times around, and he said I couldn't count straight. He was disgusted with me."

"You ought to know, Martha, that there are some things you mustn't talk about with people like—uh—Winslow. Besides, it's better for you not to think of such things in your condition. Let's go and look at the orchids."

Martha bent forward slightly and clutched at a chair. She looked at Lehua, and her face was pale. "I wonder if it's come."

"You had a pain?"

"Yes. A sharp one. Lehua, I think I'm frightened."

The Hawaiian woman put her arms about Martha. "Poof, poof! Before long you'll have a handsome baby in your arms, and you'll be tired but happy. Now you just come and help me a little. We have a lot to do before you go to the hospital."

"First, let's call Mummy and Daddy so they can get tomorrow's boat."

In the late afternoon when the pains came frequently, Winslow drove Martha to the hospital. "Dearest," he said, "you are more precious to me than any child. Remember that."

She felt tears spurt into her eyes at his words. With great seriousness she said, "Winslow, this baby will be the beginning of a new life for us. It will make us a real family and will help me to know the right thing to do."

"Darling, I don't want you to become too grave about life. Part of your charm is your fresh, naive enthusiasm, your tendency to daydream."

She looked at his face and set her mouth firmly. "Don't say that to me or you'll spoil everything I've accomplished."

He put his hand on her knee. "Martie, dear, just be my little Kona sweetheart as you've always been."

The baby, a girl, was born near midnight of the following day. Martha slept on for several hours before she saw her daughter. At noon the Wendells and the Bells gathered in her room to congratulate her. Mrs. Bell kissed her and exclaimed, "It's a beautiful child! And, darling, she looks exactly as you did the first moment I set eyes on you."

"Really, Mummy? Did I have so much black hair?"

"Every bit as much."

Mr. Wendell went up to Mr. Bell and shook his hand. "Well, Mac, we are now *puluna*."

"*Puluna*, what's that, Winslow?"

"You've been in Hawaii these thirty years, and you don't know *puluna*? It means grandparents of the same child."

"Well, well!" Mr. Bell turned to his daughter. "Martha, what are you going to call this child who makes me a *puluna*?"

"I don't know. If it had been a boy, it would have been so easy—Winslow the Fourth. But a girl! We didn't think of girls' names."

Mrs. Wendell spoke softly. "Martha, dear, call her Laurie."

"Laurie," Martha whispered. "It's a pretty name. I could call her Laurie and then Ululani for Mummy and Tutu. What do you think, Winslow, of Laurie Ululani Wendell?"

"It's a fine name, sweetheart," he replied.

Martha learned, while she was in the hospital, that Julie's son was born just ten hours before Laurie. He was given Julie's maiden name, Morrison. When the babies were five weeks old, they were introduced to one another. Julie wheeled Morrison to the Wendell home and made a ceremony of the occasion. She lifted her son from his silk-lined buggy and held him so that he could look down into Laurie's basket; she said with mock solemnity, "Miss Laurie, may I present Master Morrison. Morrison, this is Laurie." And she dipped her son in a little bowing gesture.

Martha smiled and said, "I'm sure they'll remember this introduction as long as they live."

Julie put her baby back into the buggy, and then she sprawled out on the hikie. She threw her arms up in the air and said, "What can you do with a name like Beach? Anything you give the poor child is reminiscent of hot dogs and cheap concessions. I wanted to call him Sandy, but Sam would have none of it."

"Of course I shouldn't tell you this, but I know a Morrison Beach in California. When I was at school, some friends took me on a picnic there."

"Then there are two Morrison Beaches in the world. Hooray!" She paused to light a cigarette and then went on. "I suppose you know about Felicity."

"Well, I know she's in the country."

"Yes, to stay. At the Parken place at Waikane. Old Grandaunt Lucillia willed it to her—she died three weeks ago."

Martha felt her heart pounding. "At the Parken place? I thought it was for sale."

"It has been on and off for years. But Aunty Lucillia kept changing her mind. About two months ago she altered her will and left it to Lissie."

"How nice for Lissie!"

"Yes, how nice!" exclaimed Julie ironically. "She's fought with the whole family over it. It apparently gave her ideas. She's going to write a book."

"A book! What about?"

"The Parken place. She's doing all kinds of research about family life way back when, using old letters, and about the Hawaiian servants who were connected with it. I guess the hero is the house—another bit of Hawaiiana, you know. Papa Beach has already plunked several thousand in the bank for its publication."

"I always heard Lissie was a talented writer in school."

"She's talented enough. It'll probably be a good book, too. She's now living out there all alone with the servants. And what a quarrel she had with Mama to do it! I can still hear Mama's voice, 'But, Lissie, you can't expect to get anywhere when you bury yourself.' And Lissie's shrill answer, 'Mother, for seven years you've been trying to marry me off. Now I'm going to do what I want to do.' And so Lissie moved to the country with her pile of paper and her typewriter. She seems to be very happy."

"Let's take the children out someday," Martha said and thought how wonderful it was to know the person who owned that house.

"A good idea! Lissie has been trying to get me to come. But she stipulates afternoon; she says she writes all morning and she allows nothing to interfere with that. I really think she gets a little lonely in the evenings."

"Oh, afternoons. Then I suppose I can't go unless we get back by three-thirty." Martha knew that the disappointment was apparent in her face.

"Martha, as I've told you before, you're *pupule,* crazy."

Julie smashed her cigarette out with vehemence and flicked it out into the garden. "Something for your gardener to do."

In later years Martha thought that the first eleven months of Laurie's life were among the happiest of her marriage. She lived in a private little world with Lehua and the baby and was excused from many of the social obligations and other wearying activities which might otherwise have absorbed her.

It was different after Winslow Fourth was born; he was a boy and his father's own special property. But Laurie was a girl, and there was no mistaking her Hawaiian blood. During these eleven months Martha loved Winslow again with the fresh, bright passion she had known on her honeymoon. It was a love grown from herself as an individual, not a love carefully restrained and fashioned by polite convention. And Winslow seemed especially tender and considerate.

But when at eleven months Laurie started to walk, the little girl entered into Winslow's world, and slowly he began to fit his pattern over her brief waking hours. Martha remembered the very day he started. It was a hot, muggy August evening, and when dinner was finished, he said, "Martha, let's have our coffee in the library. I want to talk to you about something very private."

She was surprised and irritated by his manner; he had that pompousness of his father. But she answered, "All right, dear." To Kimi she said, "Please serve the coffee in the library tonight."

He courteously held her chair when she rose from the table and took her arm to lead her to the library. There he seated her comfortably on the sofa covered with gold and green obi cloth and kissed her lightly on the top of her head. She thought to herself that he had successfully created for his taste another picture of the perfect husband and wife relationship, and she wondered how he could love her and still be so artificial about it. The thought troubled her with little glimmerings of premonition.

He leaned against a bookshelf and took the cup from the tray proffered by Kimi. "Thank you, Kimi. You may go now."

When she had closed the door, Martha spoke. "Winslow, you are frightening me with your formality. It must be something serious."

"It's pleasant, my darling, because it's about Laurie."

"Oh?" She was puzzled.

"Darling, now that Laurie can walk, I think it is time to train her a little. When she was a small helpless baby, she was really all yours. But now that she's walking and beginning to talk, her world opens out, and I want more of a share in it. I think we ought to work out a little routine for her so that she will grow up knowing how to discipline herself."

"Winslow, she's still a baby!"

"Of course she is. But I want her to be a well-behaved baby. I have always been thankful that my father started his guidance of me when I was only a year old."

Martha wished that she had the flip, crisp mind of Julie. Then she could think of something to say which would show Winslow how ridiculous he was being. But she could only say with a partial groan, "Oh, Winslow . . ."

"Life in Honolulu is a little different, you know, from that in Kona."

That beloved word he used gave her courage, and she said sharply, "You can plan my life for me all you want, but Laurie is going to be free to grow as I grew in Kona!"

"Martha, dear, you are only starting a quarrel by such statements. We must discuss our child in a dispassionate way and decide above and beyond our personal feelings what is best for her."

Martha felt anger make her body rigid. "How can I discuss my child dispassionately? I love her, and I want her to be happy. If she grows up with an exaggerated sense of her position in society and a feeling that she must do things simply because others do them, she'll never be happy."

"How absurd, dearest. A woman always belongs in her class, and if she knows the rules of it and abides by those rules, she will be happy."

"You and I don't agree there. I've always known people of all classes and have been friends with them."

"Martha, please remember that Laurie is a Wendell."

She took a sip of coffee and held it a moment in her mouth before swallowing. Its hot bitterness was exactly what she wanted to taste. "Yes, she is a Wendell. But she also has my blood, and we don't know yet which will predominate."

He disregarded her words. "And something else. Mother is very troubled over Lehua's care of Laurie. She said that the other day she was in to help with the baby's bath and that Lehua threw the little girl high in the air and caught her again. Laurie laughed and seemed to like it, but Mother was frightened. What if Lehua hadn't caught her?"

"Lehua knows what she's doing. She's handled twenty babies."

"Mother adores that child. Sometimes I think she looks on her as the little Laurie who died."

"I know, poor dear. She almost smothers the baby with her love, and Laurie doesn't like it."

"That's what I was coming to. Can't you do something about that? When Mother even goes near Laurie, the baby screams bloody murder."

"I've told Laurie a hundred times that she must love her grandmother, and I've scolded her when she behaved so disgracefully. But she's just a baby, and your mother can't seem to approach her in the right way."

"A little discipline would help that. She must learn early to fit into her place in society."

"Discipline will not make her love your mother."

"Nevertheless, Martha, I've thought it over and decided

that we must begin to guide Laurie with a strong hand. Now that she's walking, she's no longer utterly helpless; she's become a little citizen and must share in the routine of the household. I want her to join us in our daily walk. Of course I realize that she can go but a short distance, but even that is sufficient. And I want a regular time with her each day—say for a half an hour after she is bathed and ready for her supper. She could begin to have her breakfast with us in the morning, and we could train her table manners. . . ."

He continued with his plan, but Martha no longer listened. She recalled instead the first night at her dinner table in this house and how she had prayed so ardently while Mr. Wendell was saying grace that she would become all that the Wendells expected of her.

When he had finished, she said softly, "We'll try it. If you'll excuse me, I'll go up and see if she's tucked in." Her mind was numbed by the droning multiplicity of his words. It was easier to shut out the meaning of them, not to think of it at all. Laurie would some day decide for herself, anyway. Already she showed a strong will of her own.

Martha climbed the stairs and went into the nursery. Laurie was asleep, her black hair curled upon the pillow, and her skin sunny golden against the blue blanket. Martha was engulfed in a tender adoration for this baby, her child. She realized suddenly that she wanted her daughter to reach a fulfillment of life which she herself would never know. She whispered, "Remember, darling Laurie, there is no pattern that cannot be broken."

VII

Winslow came home one afternoon in May when Laurie was twenty months old and with restrained eagerness told Martha that he had bought steamer tickets to the mainland. "Things at the office are now settled enough so that we can actually go to my fifth class reunion! I've talked a great deal about going and written old friends about it, but it always seemed unfeasible. Now Father urges me. He says these contacts are good to keep up, and that while we're at Cambridge, we can visit some of the relatives in Boston."

"What about Laurie?" Martha interrupted the flow of his speech. "Shall we take her?"

"I think not. She's pretty young, and you'd have a much better time without the responsibility of a baby. We can leave her with Mother."

"Probably we'd better make arrangements for her to have some time with Mummy too."

"Of course! She can divide her time between her grandparents," he agreed.

Martha loved the trip from the moment they set out. She and Winslow walked around the deck each morning, enjoying the sun's warmth which seemed to her like a cashmere veil lying over their heads and down their arms. They spoke of Laurie and how they missed her, and in missing her together found a strengthened bond. Sometimes Martha went off alone to watch the green and white wake; its motion filled her body with a sense of ceremonial dancing, her eyes with a hypnotic fixity. In the midst of these watchings, she would feel a sudden loneliness, as though the sea and its vastness had taken possession of her, and tearing herself away from this enchantment, she sought out Winslow. With her arm locked in his and conscious of his eyes smiling tenderly at her, she felt a thankfulness in belonging to him and a refreshed love for him.

They stopped in San Francisco for a week while she bought clothes and while they enjoyed together the French and Italian restaurants. Martha had not been in California since her year and a half at college, and she wanted dresses with the proper mainland flavor to wear in Cambridge and New York. She bought clothes of darker colors and fitted herself with hats and gloves, two articles she never wore in Honolulu. One day when she was trying on hats, she paused to look at her reflection in the mirror. In this dress and hat, she thought, she showed no trace of Hawaiian blood, and not even the clerk could guess that she had any. The clerk called her madame and treated her with the polite and flattering servility she used for any rich and fashionable client. But what if she knew? She might think it was romantic, as many girls in college had. And then again she might not. Martha enjoyed the little masquerade until she went down into the street and passed a flower stand which had gardenias on display. Their fragrance assailed her; her body was poignantly filled with memory of Hawaii, and she was ashamed of her pleasure in the masquerade.

When she crossed the bay to visit her college campus, she found herself a stranger. The students appeared awkwardly youthful and unfledged. Only the professors and buildings were familiar, but even they had suffered a change, a turn toward shabbiness, in the four years since she had been there. Her three semesters in college were not long, and she had already forgotten much of what happened. She had had no favorite professor, no special friend, and although the girls had been interested in her because she came from Hawaii, they also succeeded in making her feel apart from them. She wondered what it was that made Winslow so devoted to Harvard.

When they reached Cambridge, she was shy before Winslow's classmates. They did not know of her Hawaiian blood, and she anticipated the moment of their discovery of it with some misgiving, not for her own but for Winslow's sake. Contrarily, she was chagrined that Winslow never told them and wondered if he were really ashamed of her blood. His classmates' wives were slender girls, fashionably dressed, possessed of cool, clipped voices and of graceful yet aloof manners. She found herself imitating them in an effort not to appear different, to fit in for Winslow's sake. Although they welcomed her as an exotic, she knew she was not really one of them. Winslow, however, was satisfied with their approval, and that was the only necessary thing.

In Boston they stayed at the home of Father Wendell's cousin, Ephraim Hale. Martha trembled when they reached the Hale threshold, but she was met with courtesy and friendship. The Hale family was one from which all young people had gone; the only child, Margaret, had married a New York man against her fond parents' desire. After her departure the household had settled down and become, as Mrs. Hale expressed it, "a quiet pool away from the stream of life." Sarah, Mr. Hale's spinster sister, lived with the family.

When Martha stepped into the drawing room, she felt that the furniture had not been rearranged in years; the brocaded sofa seemed to have grown like a dark mushroom into its corner; the rosewood table with the blue glass lamp and silver cigarette box had stood before the Chinese hanging long enough for a line to be noticeable where the tapestry had faded above the table and kept its dark, rich colors beneath. The red mahogany fernery must always have stood in the bay window. Within a few minutes Martha herself felt as settled as the furniture; it was partly because of the quiet, old-fashioned dignity of the room and partly because of the friendliness, properly restrained yet warm, with which the Hales welcomed her. Mrs. Hale suggested a quick tea in the library where, she said, "the furniture is more comfortable." She continued, "Martha, you might tidy yourself in the little dressing room under the stairs. Later you may go up for your bath. But I think you need a bit of tea and relaxation after your long journey."

Martha went into the dressing room and removed her hat and gloves. She washed her face in cold water and ran the comb briskly through her hair. The door had not been latched securely, and it opened a crack, just enough for her to hear Sarah Hale say to someone, ". . . but you'd never guess it! She's a pretty girl—looks like the dark side of the Hale family. You say her grandfather was a Slator? I think there's Hale blood in that family."

Martha gazed at her image in the mirror and ran her fingers tentatively over the lines of her face. Cousin Sarah was right. One might never guess it, especially with her skin as pale as it was now and when she was dressed in these clothes so alien to Hawaii.

Martha discovered to her astonishment that in Boston she was content to fit into the pattern of being acquainted with the right people and doing the proper thing. Although actually she was bored with the continual round of calls on which Mrs. Hale and Cousin Sarah took her, she found a curious pleasure in knowing that she was well dressed and well mannered and that she, Mrs. Winslow Abiel Wendell III, was sitting in a correct Boston parlor and sipping tea from an eggshell cup which was a family heirloom. It was like acting in a play, and her success in creating an impression of polished, gracious, and fashionable womanhood was reward in itself. She had no temptation to break away from the carefully fenced limits of this society, and she was startled to find that going barefoot even in the privacy of her bathroom had become distasteful to her. Apparently the sense of correctness had penetrated into her very core so that even in her private moments she was impelled to do the accepted thing—she who took every opportunity in Hawaii to kick off her shoes! The Hales taught her how proud she should be that Winslow had gone to Harvard and that his family had originally stemmed from Boston, and she felt safe in knowing that everything in her situation was sanctioned by the right people.

She was sorry when the visiting in Cambridge and Boston was over, and she and Winslow traveled on to New York. In Boston they had fitted into a society, but in New York they became tourists again. Martha no longer felt a compulsion to pitch her voice higher and clip her words, to assume the little air which delicately and unobtrusively proclaimed her, if not a superior being, at least a sensitively attuned one. There was a feeling of laxity in New York, because no one cared how she looked or what her manner was. The fun of play-acting was gone with the correct Boston audience, and something else was also gone. The feeling of being complete, of fitting into a world uncomplicated by divisions of blood and allegiance, was gone, and Martha, at times, had a sense of being distrait. She thought of Samuel Kekela's statement that her life would become a polished pebble. Was this what he meant, this growing taste for a gentle propriety in behavior, for quiet restraint in emotion? A polished pebble was something self-contained and shaped handsomely by its environment. A polished pebble —the very words brought to her mind a vision of a piece of jade, shining, luscious, desirable.

Martha forced herself to enjoy the three weeks they spent in New York. But she was thankful when they traveled across the continent to San Francisco and the boat which would carry them home.

She spent the days at sea thinking of her mainland adventure. Adventure! That was a romantic word for it. Actually it had been a quiet trip with no startling event or mishap. She had shopped, had gone to the theater and concerts, and had met people—Winslow's people. In knowing these people, his classmates and his family, a comprehension had come to her of the reasons for much of his behavior which she had never before understood. She felt that she had moved further into his orbit and was thankful that she had been able to see in Boston the source, the very beginnings and reasons of a young man like Winslow. The weeks in Boston enabled her to understand more clearly his approach to life, and she admitted that his concept had great appeal in its cool order, its civilized and thoughtful ways, its aloof graciousness.

As they neared Honolulu, she thought more often of Laurie and wondered how much the little girl might have changed in the three months. Laurie had spent her first six weeks with the Wendells and the second six weeks with the Bells. Mummy had written that Laurie now talked fluently and that she also could speak Hawaiian. "She is almost as much of a Kanaka as I am. You had better hurry home to rescue her; Winslow might not approve."

On the fourth day out of San Francisco, Martha stood at the rail of the ship. The ocean's blue had changed from the cold, crisp hue of northern waters to the soft, flowing blue of southern seas, the flying fish were skimming in the wake, and the air had taken on a sweet balm. She was tinglingly aware of these changes and felt that something was melting within her and moving as a tide. She clung to the rail, and her body trembled. The blue of the sea was flooding her eyes.

She turned suddenly and ran to the stateroom. She snatched a brush from the dressing table and pulled it furiously through her hair, destroying the careful waves set by the hairdresser. She flung the brush back to its place and went to the closet where she snatched her mainland dresses off the hangers, rolled them into a ball, and stuffed them into a trunk drawer. Then she unpacked the cottons and linens which she had not looked at since her arrival in San Francisco three months before. She put on a bright dress with a large red and yellow print of hibiscus flowers, kicked off her shoes, and danced round the stateroom in her bare feet.

That evening Winslow smiled at her when she pinned in her hair the faded gardenia, bought in San Francisco, and said, "It's good to have you my Kona sweetheart again."

The next day Martha rose at dawn and went out on deck to catch the first glimpse of Makapuu Point. A morning haze clung to the horizon, and she strained her eyes in an effort to peer through it. The boat crawled along, and she rose on tiptoe in impatience at its slowness. Finally she could make out in the faint, green-gray shadow on the horizon the familiar outline of Makapuu Point; her eyes filled with tears. She was glad Winslow was not there because he might have been embarrassed at her weakness. She noticed an old Hawaiian lady, who had tears rolling down her cheeks, and went and put her arms around her, and they wept together. The Hawaiian lady sobbed, "Hawaii *nei*, Hawaii *nei* at last!"

It was wonderful to be home again, to smell the dampness, the earth, the ginger, the guavas. She had never realized how much of the memory of Hawaii was bound up in its fragrances and in its color. Mainland color was drab beside the azure of Hawaiian seas, the emerald green and lemon yellow of Hawaiian foliage, the red of Hawaiian earth.

Laurie's little body was sweet and tender to the touch. She now talked in a quaint mixture of English and Hawaiian, which amused Winslow by its baby charm, but also displeased him. Mummy had been right; Winslow found Laurie too much of a Kanaka for his taste. Martha set about unobtrusively to correct the little girl's ways.

The first few weeks at home sped by while she taught Laurie and played with her, while she swung the household routine back to normal and worked over the orchids in the lath house. The experiences of the trip began to fade, and there were left in her mind only impressions of the quiet dignity of the Hale family, of the delicious pleasure she had had in play-acting in Boston, and of her own overwhelming joy upon returning to Hawaii *nei*.

VIII

Although Martha did not realize it at the time, an incident on a late Sunday afternoon in early November foreshadowed the course of that whole month. She was sitting on the hikie on the lanai, staring dreamily into the garden. Winslow came in from a game of tennis and saw Laurie's toys spread around the floor. He started to pick them up. In the midst of it he apparently decided that the little girl should learn to do it herself. He called her and when she came, asked her to help him clean up the mess she had made with her things. She looked at him with an impudent innocence and answered simply, "Waste time!"

"Laurie!" he exclaimed. "You must help Daddy and not say things like that."

She said calmly, "Waste time, *hapai* those toys."

He spanked her gently and filled her little arms with a load and sent her off to the house. Then he turned to Martha and said, "I can't understand your Mother letting this happen to her—this Kanaka talk."

Martha felt the fearful choking sensation which came to her whenever Winslow suggested in his words a censure of her blood. That sentence rankled in her mind for days, making her miserable.

A week after this incident Mrs. Wendell came to take Laurie to the beach, a custom she had adopted while Winslow and Martha were away. Martha and her mother-in-law went into the nursery where the little girl was just waking from her nap. Mrs. Wendell bent over the crib and said, "Laurie, honey, where's your bathing suit?"

"Mummy knows," Laurie answered sleepily.

"Yes, but don't you know?"

"I don't want to go to the beach with you."

"Why, Laurie, Grandma wants to take you to the beach. She loves you."

"I don't love you. I love Nanna Bell. I want to go to Kona."

"Laurie!" Martha gasped in a shocked tone.

"Laurie, darling, you don't know what you say," Mrs. Wendell whispered, and her eyes filled with tears. She picked the little girl up and held her close.

Laurie struggled to get away. "Let me go! You smell too sweet!"

Martha scolded, "Laurie! Behave yourself. You're a naughty girl."

Mrs. Wendell laughed with a suggestion of hysteria and said, "Laurie often says she doesn't love me—that I smell too sweet."

"Laurie Wendell," threatened Martha, "I'm going to punish you. You must never say you don't love your grandmother."

She took the child from Mrs. Wendell's arms and spanked her soundly. Laurie's great brown eyes filled with tears, and she whimpered quietly to herself. Martha put her on the floor and knelt down near her. "You have hurt your grandmother's feelings, and she's going to cry. I'm ashamed of you, and I want you to go right now and tell Grandma you're sorry."

Laurie walked slowly to her grandmother. "I'm sorry, Nanna."

"That's all right, darling. Your Nanna just wants you to love her."

Laurie suddenly smiled. "I love you, Nanna. My bathing suit is over there. I show you."

In the evening, Martha worked up courage to tell Winslow of the episode. It was important that the story come to him quickly and from her lips. But she dreaded the recounting, especially because Winslow had recently been so critical of Laurie's behavior.

When she had finished telling him, she said, "It's a great shame. I've worked hard with the child to overcome this. And your mother is so devoted to her. I think the real trouble is that she fusses with Laurie too much."

Winslow sighed and rubbed his hands together. "Poor Mother! I sometimes think that Laurie is not really disciplined. Are you sure that Miss Kakae is the best nurse for her? Laurie has become very strong-willed, and I don't think her stay in Kona was good for her; it seems to have destroyed most of her training."

Martha felt the anger rising in her like a hot wave. "Of course you realize you are criticizing my parents."

"Not at all! It's Miss Kakae I'm criticizing."

Martha looked boldly into his eyes. "You haven't liked Lehua from the first, and after more than two years you persist in calling her Miss Kakae in spite of the fact that she is my relative. I wonder why."

"Frankly, I have disapproved of her. She is sloppy about her clothing, her speech is not the best, and her friends are uncouth."

"Yes, she's sloppy, but she's clean. Her speech can be what she wants it to be, and you know it. Her friends are Hawaiians of all types, nice people but poor. Laurie adores them. And you know how she feels about our friends!"

"That's it! Our Laurie prefers Hawaiian riffraff to my mother! I sometimes wish, my dear, that you didn't have your Hawaiian connection."

She blenched and was unable to move for a moment. She stared at the flesh pulled tight and white across his cheekbones and unconsciously picked up a slim jade figure from the table, which she clutched as if it were an overhanging branch and she were drowning in a stream. When she felt that her voice would not quaver, she spoke. "I'm glad you said this, Winslow. It makes something clear between us, which has been suppressed. The first day we were in this house your father started to say that Tutu had gone Hawaiian. I should have realized then, but I was a bride, and you were so perfect that you and your family could do nothing wrong. Now I know better. You belong to those people who have lived here for generations and found it pleasant and convenient to befriend the Hawaiian—even on occasions to marry him. But underneath, you are contemptuous of us and regard yourselves as superior. Oh, you are kind enough to us! You pose as a friend, and what are you really?" She turned and walked from the room.

"Martha, Martha!" he called after her. "I'm sorry for what I said. Martha, please!" She heard his words echoing down the corridor, but went straight on to the nursery and the comfort of Laurie and Lehua.

The next day Martha packed her clothes and Laurie's and took the steamer to the Island of Hawaii. She told Lehua to follow her as soon as she could, that she was going to Tutu's in Punaluu. Winslow would not think first of Tutu's but of Kona. Her note to him was brief.

Dear Winslow,

Please do not follow me. I need time to think.

Martha

P.S. Laurie will have the best of care. Tell your mother not to worry.

When she reached Hilo, she did not go immediately to Mr. Gonsalves for a car; he would ply her with friendly questions which she could not answer. Instead, she strolled slowly about the streets with Laurie, trying to find repose for her mind.

A fine rain was falling. It would not be Hilo, she thought, without a shower. Even if she were blindfolded, she would know it was Hilo by the smell of the rain and the green foliage. She would know it by the fragrance of Japanese food, of shoya and sugar, of rice and daikon. She thought intently of Hilo because it was restful to remember the river and its vine-entangled banks, the coconut island, the cool swimming off black rocks.

"Mummy!" Laurie pulled at her hand. "Mummy, when do we get to Tutu's? I'm hungry."

"Poor baby, it's a long ride yet. We'll get you an ice-cream cone."

They went into a drugstore where Martha ordered a cone for Laurie and a coke for herself. She sat on the familiar chair with the curved wire back and remembered how when she was a small girl she had felt she was in a city whenever the family went to Hilo. And now Hilo was only a village compared to Honolulu.

When they had finished, they went to Mr. Gonsalves.

"Meesus Wendell!" he greeted her. "How nize to see you!"

"It's good to be here. Could you take us to Punaluu—to Tutu's?"

"Of course, of course. You got any bags?"

"They're down at the pier. Perhaps we can pick them up there."

"Of course, of course. And how iss your good husband and good mother and father?"

"They're fine, thank you."

"And thees leetle girl. Isn't she the pretty one?"

On the ride to Punaluu Martha tried to rehearse a little speech for Tutu, but her mind refused to be troubled. The beauty of the passing landscape lulled her into a dreamy stupor, and when Laurie fell asleep in her lap, she too dozed.

Martha felt the car stop and opened her eyes. They were at Tutu's. She got out of the car and paid Mr. Gonsalves. He said, "Any time you want me, you just call. I come quick."

He looked admiringly at Laurie. "Such a fine leetle one!"

When he had driven away, Martha looked toward the sea and breathed deeply of its salty air. Tutu's home was half a block from the gate cut through the white picket fence which surrounded the lawn. The building was old, weather-beaten, and shabby, and the garden was filled with mossy-backed mangoes and coconut palms. Martha had always thought of Punaluu as a strange little oasis at the edge of the sea, with a lava desert about it. The desert grew only hardy ferns and a few low shrubs. The Hawaiians had lived there in the past because of the springs of fresh water just off shore. The haoles had come to build on a hill overlooking the settlement a gaunt gray-brown church in the stern New England Congregational fashion. The church was large, but it had an attendance of only a handful when the minister made his monthly visit. There had been a time when its congregation was numbered in the hundreds. Martha was superstitious about the church; as a child she had thought the steeple had eyes and could see her if she were naughty.

She opened the gate and said to Laurie, "Go and tell Tutu we are here."

Laurie ran down the path and Martha followed her slowly. She saw her grandmother come out on the lanai and heard the startled, "Why, Laurie, what are you doing here?"

Mrs. Slator sat down on the top step of the lanai and pulled the child into her lap. When Martha came up, she said, "Hello, dear. I hope you and Laurie can stay a while."

"We shall, Tutu, dear," Martha said and kissed the old lady. "Laurie's pretty hungry."

"Oh, poor sweet baby! Darling, run to the kitchen and tell Lei you are hungry. She'll give you something good." Laurie went off to the kitchen.

Martha looked round the garden, noticing how the mango leaves shone in the sun and how green the grass was for November. She breathed deeply. "Everything looks the same. Even the old tree house in the mango."

"Yes, I tried to get Joe to take it down. But he said no, that it would do for Laurie."

"Lehua will arrive in a few days."

"You don't need her here."

"I know. But I couldn't leave her. She'll probably go to Kona first and see Mummy and Daddy."

"That's good. What about Winslow?"

"He's not coming. I don't think he knows I'm here."

"No?" Tutu moved along the step until she could lean against the banister. She spread the skirt of her *muumuu* carefully over her bare feet. Martha sat down close to her and took her hand. When she spoke, her voice trembled a little. "It's too soon for me to know what I'm going to do."

"If you don't know now, you'll stay with him."

"What do you mean?"

"It happened to me too."

"To you?"

"Yes, a long time ago. If you don't know now that you can leave him, you'll stay."

"I loved him so much once. Sometimes I do now, but he has such—such a way of killing it all the time. And he doesn't even know."

"Grandpa was like that. For all my education, I was just a simple Hawaiian girl, and it took me a long time to understand."

"He was—like Winslow?"

"In some ways. At times he made your mother's life miserable. But I stood up for her. He wanted everything to be 'fitting.' "

"That word again! You said it at the luau when you called Winslow 'fitting.' You were wiser than I."

"No. It just slipped out. I don't know why I said it. Sometimes, Luahine, when I think that if I had married a Hawaiian, I would have changed the destinies of so many people . . ." Tutu left her sentence unfinished and looked out to the sea which crashed in huge breakers over the lava. Then she went on in a low voice, "But my father was a minister, and he wanted me to be educated in a young ladies' seminary. That made me different from most young women in Kona in those days."

Martha sighed and said, "It's hard having two bloods. Everything gets so mixed up inside."

"Not really so hard, Baby dear. I know just about what it

is, because I married a haole and had your mother whose every dream and thought I knew. In one way people like us are lucky. We can choose, and haoles can't. I chose when Grandpa died, and I'm happy."

Martha rose from the steps and smoothed the wrinkles in her skirt. She kicked off her shoes and pulled off her stockings. "I just want to be quiet while I'm here and think. Tell Mummy and Daddy not to come. I love them too much, and they would only mix me up. In a few days maybe, I'll go see them."

"What of Winslow?"

"It's hard to know. I left a little note. I think he'll let me alone for a few days."

IX

Martha loafed at Punaluu. She swam in the pools formed of lava rock, whose water was constantly renewed by waves and springs of fresh water; she fished, lay in the sun, gossiped with the neighbors. She went over to Mrs. Hoomanawanui's to help her with the quilting of a large comforter in the lava fern design. Sometimes she mended the nets with Mr. Hoomanawanui or took walks with his son, Kimo. When Lehua came from Kona, she brought baskets of guavas, and Martha and Lei put them up; they made jelly and juice. They stewed the guavas in Tutu's special way, carefully peeling and cutting them in half, scooping out the seeds, and cooking the shells and the seeds separately. Later Tutu would serve this guava preserve with ice cream, and there was nothing more delectable. Martha could not do her thinking in these fine, busily idle days. The sun hot on her skin, the noise of wind and water constantly in her ear, Laurie's body soft and sweet against her own, the fragrance of cooking guavas in her nostrils—these were the stuff of a precious way of life, and there was no need to think.

The only interruption to these idyllic hours was the day she went to Kona; Daddy had tried to question her, and she knew she hadn't satisfied him. She couldn't make him understand that in Punaluu she couldn't analyze things. She had to let time and feeling tell her what to do. In Honolulu, maybe, one could plan, but not in Kona or Kau.

She spent many hours with Tutu; sometimes they fished off the rocks or gathered *opihis,* and when they did this, the waves were usually so loud that they couldn't talk. Other times they just sat in the shade of a mango and drowsed. At dusk Tutu liked to sit outside, and she became loquacious. She recalled incidents of her young womanhood, and sometimes repeated tales and legends of ancient Hawaii. She told Martha that in the old days, the *pueo,* the owl, had been the talisman and protector of her family and that to this day she never allowed any of her servants to harm an owl. Martha thought of the owl in the garden at home, which circled the mango tree three times, and she wondered. . . .

She watched the beautiful, mobile expressions which crossed Tutu's face. The old lady was of the type of Hawaiian who is narrow-faced and has a high-arched nose and large round eyes. Her appearance was aristocratic and melancholy, and people instinctively listened to her with respect and admiration.

When they sat together after supper, Martha frequently said, "Tutu, let's talk about the old days again."

Tutu's eyes glistened and she said, "Just think, once there was a hotel in Punaluu and a wharf. It was gay."

"I can hardly believe it! Why should there be a hotel? It's all desert round here."

"It was mostly for the plantation. But they also landed tourists for the volcano here." Tutu turned her face away and was silent for a few minutes. Then she spoke in a voice which suppressed an emotion Martha could not appraise. "Lanterns in the dark are so much prettier than electric lights—not so harsh. When a house was lit with lanterns, it looked friendly, inviting."

Martha asked gently, "What do you mean?"

"Richard and I were among the first in Kona to get electric lights. We were always among the first. He said it was for the Slators—not for ourselves. I never quite knew what he meant. Because he was the only Slator left, except Alice and some remote cousins in Boston."

"Was Grandpa—so—difficult?"

"No. He just had strange ways. When he looked at your mother for the first time, he said, 'I think this is all we want, just this little Ululani.' I was hurt. I wanted many children."

"I should think he would have wanted a son. How strange!"

"He never told me why. But I guessed the reason. Your mother's skin was dark—dark as mine."

"Oh!" Martha felt that horrible, empty place in her chest which she felt when Winslow's manner or words reminded her of her Hawaiian blood.

"He loved your mother passionately, but he was stern with her. She never cared for him. He forced her to be a constant little lady, and she wanted to be a tomboy. Winslow's grandfather once tried to get him to be more lenient—when Ululani ran away."

"Mummy ran away?"

"Yes, but not far. She walked down to a fisherman's family on the beach and asked if she could be their little girl. They were delighted."

"How terrible for you!"

"It was much worse for him. He only lived about five years after that. I felt, at times, as though I watched him die because his daughter didn't love him." Tutu sighed and looked at Martha with seriousness in her eyes. "No, Martha, people like you and me can't destroy the faith which our husbands have in us. We can't because it breaks men like them. They are strong, but they are highly refined."

"Tutu!" Martha said, and began to sob. "Tutu, am I always going to be caught in a—in a cage?" She hid her face in her grandmother's skirt."

"Baby dear!" Mrs. Slator whispered. "Baby dear, dry your eyes. Here's Kimo."

"Who?"

"Kimo Hoomanawanui. He's come for a walk, probably."

"Oh!" She sat up. "He mustn't see me crying. Talk to him a minute, and I'll go in and dry my eyes."

Martha rose from the grass and ran into the house and upstairs to her bedroom. She combed her hair hastily and patted the powder puff over her nose. Then she went into the nursery and kissed Laurie.

"Good night, my baby sweet."

"Night, Mummy. Where you going?"

"I'm going for a walk with Kimo."

"Oh, Kimo. He's a nice man. Mamma, why isn't Kimo my daddy?"

"Darling!" Martha said and smiled. "You go to sleep now."

"All right, Mummy. Night!"

Martha tiptoed out of Laurie's room and went down the stairs and into the kitchen. She took some Kona plums from the ice chest. At the front door, she paused for a moment and looked at Kimo and Tutu talking together on the lawn. Kimo was a handsome, sweet-tempered boy, and she liked him. She chuckled at herself for thinking of him as a boy, because he was the same age as she was. But in many ways he seemed immature after Winslow. Yet there was a charm about Kimo which Winslow could never have.

Martha walked down the lanai steps and across the lawn to greet him. "Hello, Kimo," she said.

"Hello, Martie. What about going up by the church tonight? We can see the moonlight on the mountain as well as on the sea." He turned to Mrs. Slator. "May I, Tutu?"

"Kimo, I don't know why it is you're always so polite to me when Martha is around," she teased.

"It's not Martha, Tutu. It's you—your beauty, your charm!"

Martha stuffed the plums into Kimo's pockets. "They're for later," she said. "Now, come on before you two dish out any more of that *hoomalimali.*"

They walked down to the edge of the sea and along the rocks; the moon was so bright that they felt no fear of unseen holes. Kimo took Martha's hand, and they went along in silence. The spray, whitened with moonlight, fell like sea birds' feathers on the dark rocks, and the roar of waves enchanted the air with gigantic rhythm. Martha watched and listened, and a spirit of exultation filled her. She pulled her hand from Kimo's grasp, flung her arms out, and stretched her body as though she were going to dive. She stood poised a moment in that position and then relaxed and let her arms fall to her sides. "Kimo," she said, "sometimes I have the silliest ideas. Like right now. I suddenly thought it would be a fine thing just to plunge into that great white breaker. There could be no more wonderful experience."

She thought that that was something she would never have dared to say to Winslow.

Kimo looked at her face. "Yes, I know. Sometimes I too. . . ."

They walked on in silence until they came to the road which led up the hill to the church. Kimo said, "We go up here," and they turned their backs to the sea and started the climb. At the top he pointed. "Look! You can see the whole mountain tonight. I don't think I've ever seen it before after dark. It's beautiful in the moonlight."

She saw rapture in his face, and thought, Kimo is free; he can love with passion and hate with passion. He can cry out when he wants to and show by every gesture of his body the emotion within his heart. He never has to pretend.

She said, "It is beautiful and mysterious. I can almost believe that a spirit like Pele's lives in that volcano."

"Pele," he whispered. "I have seen her." He tossed his head back and laughed. "But *you,* of course, will not believe me."

"But I do believe you!"

"No, you too much Honolulu. I know Honolulu; Tutu gave me money go school there, but I find waste time. More better fish and loaf."

She smiled because she knew he was not aware of the pidgin he had used to emphasize his conversation. "More better believe Pele," she mocked. "By and by lava come; no more Punaluu."

He grinned. "I no catch good kind speech Honolulu side. . . . Come on, Martha. Let's sit down a while." He pointed. "Here's a nice clump of grass."

They settled themselves on the turf and watched the path of moonlight across the sea. There was a great restfulness in this moment, Martha thought, almost a primitive peace. The two little figures, hers and Kimo's, in the landscape were unimportant. The moon, the sea, the night, and Mauna Loa were the essence, and like a fragrance pervading everything was the remembrance of generations of Hawaiian people who had lived and fished in this spot.

When some time had passed, Kimo spoke. His words were so soft that she barely heard them. "Martha, I love you." The sentiment was a surprise to her but a pleasing one, and she simply looked at him to study his face and the beauty of his eyes. He put one arm around her, and with the other hand he gently touched her breast. Her body tingled in response, and she let him kiss her; the kiss was light, like a sip of some sweet beverage, and she craved for more, for long, deep drafts of it. As though he felt her desire, he pulled her to him until they lay close upon the grass, and he clasped her in a strong and passionate embrace. "Martha," he whispered, "you do not belong to Honolulu. You belong to us here."

"Oh, Kimo, Kimo!" she murmured.

"Don't talk, my darling," he said and kissed her lips.

She could see over his shoulder the surf white against the black sea, the road climbing up toward the church, the church itself, and glistening in the moonlight like a shaft of white jade, the steeple. "The steeple!" she gasped and pushed Kimo away from her. "Let me go! Let me go!"

He looked at her with shock and hurt in his eyes. "Martha, what's the matter?"

"It's the steeple. No, it's more than that. It's Laurie and Tutu and Winslow! Kimo, I've been so wrong."

"But I'm sure you love me, Martha."

"It's the night I love, Kimo—you and the night together. But it's wrong."

He rose from her side, walked over to the steps of the church, and sat down. He put his head in his hands. She turned away from him to look at the mountain.

In a few minutes he called, "Everything's all right now, Martha. Come and have a plum."

She said nothing but walked over, sat beside him, and accepted a plum.

"Martha, let's go get some *opihis* tomorrow," he suggested.

"Wonderful idea!" She laid her hand, palm up, on his knee for another plum. He leaned down and kissed her hand before he put the fruit in it. "Forgive me," he said.

A few days later Martha was sitting on the lanai, shelling peas which had been grown in Tutu's garden. She looked up from her work and saw Winslow walking down the path toward the house. He had not written of his coming, but she was not surprised to see him. She had been gone a fortnight, and that was a long time for him to leave her alone. He looked slim and well built in the sunlight, and his dark hair gleamed as though it were newly washed. She was proud that he was her husband. But she felt a tinge of guilt when she remembered the evening with Kimo. Yet, perversely, she was glad it had happened, because now she knew about such moments and would never again think that an experience was missing from her life.

He kissed her and said, "It's good to see you. Where is Laurie?"

"She's in the house." They walked through the door together, and he put his arm around her shoulders.

Tutu greeted him and Laurie ran up to be kissed.

He asked, "Laurie, did you and Mother have a nice vacation?"

"Yes, Daddy. And I caught a fish, a great big fish."

"All by yourself?"

"Well, Kimo helped me a little."

"Who is Kimo?"

"He's a most wonderful person."

"Well, that's nice. I hope you were a good girl."

"Yes, I was."

He turned to Mrs. Slator. "Thank you for taking care of my two dear ones. It was a fine vacation."

Martha realized that he was still the same old Winslow. To him, she had merely been on a vacation. What a wonderful quality he had, to be able to refashion the world according to his own vision!

When they were alone, she said, "Perhaps your way is best, Winslow. Just to overlook these things. It's amazing how time makes them seem less important."

"You are learning. There are things which people like you and me should always overlook because they are beneath our notice."

"Perhaps you had better say no more or I shall be angry again."

X

When Martha returned with Winslow to the city, she fitted contentedly into the old pattern of her Honolulu life. It was now comfortable for her, like a worn kimono which has shaped itself to all the curves of the body. She went back to mornings with Mitsuo in the orchid house and enjoyed the acrid, ferny odors, the precise work with tweezers and flasks, the delicate and sometimes fragrant beauty of the final blossoms toward which all the work was bent. The dreamy hours at the reading club had a renewed comfort, and she looked at her old friends with a fresh glance. Julie was still the favorite, but Martha was disappointed that Felicity, since her move to the country, no longer attended; Felicity was the one person who, she was certain, never thought at times, "Why Martha Wendell, after all, has some Hawaiian blood!" There was a delicate rapport between them, almost as though Lissie shared the double blood. Martha planned a series of dinner parties and studied cookbooks for suggestions of preparing meats with herbs, of concocting creamy, cold deserts, of baking crispy, flaky rolls, and she showed Yukie how to prepare Tutu's guava preserve. She was happy in her round of domestic and social affairs.

Laurie was the only problem. Winslow complained that she was strong-willed, and Martha worried about the child's quick, tempestuous flares of emotion. Sometimes there was no apparent reason for her display of rage, and it almost seemed as though the child enjoyed the excitement of a tantrum. Fortunately these moods did not come often, and much of the time Laurie was irrepressibly gay, practicing little hulas to the radio music, trying to sing by herself, running out of doors and smelling the flowers, begging to be taken to the beach for a swim. Martha tried to quiet her ebullience by reading to her and interesting her in picture books. But Laurie pushed these occupations aside with impatience and ran out in the garden to dig in the sand pile or romp with Boki.

Occasionally the remembrance of Kimo troubled Martha. She felt a little tremor of fear when she recalled how close to madness she had been that night. If the steeple had not been glistening in the moonlight and she had not seen it with all of its childhood connotations, she wondered what would have happened. Sometimes she clasped her hands together and murmured, "Thank heaven, thank heaven for that steeple!" She was safe now within her and Winslow's pattern. Why, after all, a pattern was a refuge, and she had never realized it! Even Kona life had a pattern when you thought of it that way—but that sort of life would work only there or in some such country district. Honolulu was more complicated, and there the pattern must be more rigid and circumscribed; it could not be loose and tenuous.

Since their return from the mainland, Winslow had been advanced in his father's business, and his new work absorbed more of his time. Now he seldom reached home as early as three-thirty, and the afternoon walks, which had been an important ceremony in the first years of their marriage, slowly slipped out of existence. Martha was relieved because it gave her more time to spend with Laurie and Julie, and she could now make trips to the country to spend the afternoon with Felicity at the Parken place.

At the reading club and at dinner parties Martha heard strange accounts of Felicity and her activities in the country. A Hawaiian youth was seen frequently on her lanai or sitting under a mango tree at her gate. The two had been observed walking down the roads together in the moonlight, and they had all the aspect of lovers. But no one knew exactly what it meant, not even Julie.

One morning Martha, remembering the talk at a dinner party the night before, asked Lehua, "Do you know someone named Solomon Hartwell? He's part Hawaiian."

"Solomon Hartwell?" Lehua stopped folding Laurie's newly ironed clothes and looked questioningly at Martha. "Why you want to know?"

"Someone mentioned him last night."

"It's about Felicity Beach, isn't it?"

"How did you know?"

"Solomon is Comet's brother-in-law. You met him."

"Oh! Solomon! I remember! He helped me climb down the rocks."

Lehua gazed sternly at Martha. "I hope you people are not going to mess into that affair. Sol and Lissie are both happy for the first time in their lives. You know how Lissie's life has been muddled by Mrs. Beach. Well, Sol has his story, too. He was just about to get married once, and his girl died in an accident the day before the wedding. He tried to kill himself when he heard, but Gabriel saved him. He's gotten over it only since he's known Lissie."

"Do you think they'll get married?"

Lehua shrugged her shoulders. "Why should they get married and bring a storm about their ears from Lissie's family? They're happy now."

"But they can't go on forever this way."

"They just relax. Why worry about that?"

"What does he do?"

"Nothing much except fish and grow taro at the family's country place. Can't you imagine what would happen if Felicity Beach married a Hawaiian fisherman?"

Martha shook her head. "They're going to get into trouble. If they're in love, they can marry and criticism won't matter. Society demands something of them; they've got to think of the future."

Lehua gazed at her for a moment, which seemed an hour to Martha. "You've changed. You used to understand these things."

"What do you mean?" Martha inquired sharply.

"I mean that Winslow is having his way with you," Lehua said, and gathering up the baby's linen, she walked out of the room.

Lehua's words echoed through Martha's mind. "Winslow is having his way with you." The realization of all that sentence meant overwhelmed her, and suddenly the comfort she had had in slipping into the Honolulu pattern was gone. She felt imprisoned in a frosty, desolate life in which she always did the right thing just because people said it was right, a safe life but one which was devoid of freedom and fire. The walls of the room seemed to close in upon her, to press against her temples, and she hurried into the garden and lay down under the mango tree in the plushy, Japanese grass which Mitsuo had planted.

This was the old struggle again, she thought wearily; the two tides had swelled and clashed within her for so long now that she felt racked and spent. She looked up into the deep, dark green of the tree. Somewhere below the surface of conscious thought, her mind was simmering, and she waited patiently, watching the green winter mangoes sway on their delicate stems in the wind. An idea pressed itself into her mind as softly, as persistently as Boki pushed his nose into her hand when he wanted to be petted. She must recognize that there would always be two parts of her, two parts which must be satisfied and at least partially reconciled. She must not crush one for the benefit of the other. At the emergence of this thought a wave of relief splashed over her with a cooling, refreshing shower. This was the conclusion she had been waiting for all these years—that she was two things, that there was nothing wrong with being two things. She must explain it to Lehua. Then her cousin would understand and not feel unkindly. Also she could help her to remember. Martha stood up and called excitedly, "Lehua, Lehua!"

There was no answer, and she walked over to the house and tried again, "Lehua!"

"What you want?"

"Please come down. I want to tell you something."

"O.K. Just a minute."

While she waited, Martha thought of how she must phrase the idea so that Lehua could perceive it and be sympathetic.

The Hawaiian woman came around the corner of the house. She apologized, "I'm terribly sorry if I hurt your feelings."

"It's what I needed, so let's forget it. Sit down in the grass with me. I have some things to say, and I know you are the only one who can understand it."

"Baby dear!" murmured Lehua, using Tutu's pet name for her; her voice trembled in compassion.

When they were comfortable under the mango tree, Martha began speaking in a hesitant fashion. "I have two lives, Lehua. One my parents and my blood made for me, and one my love for Winslow and my sharing his destiny are making for me. I've always tried to live completely in one or the other, but I can't. . . . Now an old thought has come back to me, one I had when Laurie was a baby. Only I understand it better. I shall always have these two lives; the one with Winslow will be my active life and the other will be my dream life—or my Kona life. The Kona will come out only in very secret moments when I'm with you or Laurie. . . . And when you can't understand what I do, Lehua, remember what I'm saying now." She looked beseechingly at Lehua. "And please, you must help me to remember what I've said—to remind me."

"Baby dear, I'll do everything I can to help you," Lehua exclaimed and put her plump, brown arms around Martha's shoulders. Martha felt a flowing, peaceful strength move from Lehua's body into her own. That was Lehua's way of comforting, she thought—loving arms and tender caresses.

Martha let a moment pass and then said, "Maybe after a

while when this idea has become a part of me, I'll not need help."

"Poor Baby dear! I don't know why life turned out so complicated for you."

"It's not too bad really . . ." She brightened her voice from its contemplative mood and said, "I think I'll go see Lissie this afternoon. I have a sort of urge to do it."

In the afternoon Martha drove alone to the Parken place. She had an inexplicable desire to see Felicity, but she also wanted to try out her new plan at the Parken place. If she could love and enjoy the resemblance of the old house and its location to her home in Kona and still not be unsettled for life in Honolulu, her battle was partly won. She drove slowly to enjoy the landscape. Little intermittent showers hung veils within the mountains' steep-sided valleys and drifted across the banana and papaya groves to the sea. Flecks of blue sky reflected in the flooded taro patches and lotus fields. A curious idea crossed her mind that the Hawaiian countryside was mystically enmeshed by water—the rain, the wet fields, the sea—all stealing their gray or blue from the sky. It was this very wetness which made the fragrances of the flowers so poignant and which steeped houses in the damp and musty odors, which she loved, but for which she knew the newcomer to Hawaii invariably felt distaste. She liked to go to bed at night and smell the boggy "south wind" aroma of the pillows and the sheets, because it took her back to the days when she slept in Tutu's beach house in Kona under moisture-heavy mosquito nets which smelled that way.

She turned into the driveway of the Parken place, drove up behind the house, and parked the car. Waves of fragrance from the ginger bank impelled her, and she walked over to pick a blossom for her hair. "Lissie!" she called. "It's me. Martha."

Felicity's Japanese maid appeared on the back steps and said, "Miss Beach in front part house."

"I'll go around, Asano. Thank you." Martha walked to the

lanai steps at the front and climbed them. She paused on the top step and looked out at the sea. It was like Kona, the same blue, the same sweet balm in the air, the same whiteness of the surf. The round tops of the mango trees were cloaked in tawny new leaves, and hau trees twisted and hugged the beach in their tortuous way. She could hear the waves as they crashed on the reef, that same dulled, distant surf roar she heard in Kona.

"Martha Wendell! What charm is working that you should arrive when I wanted you so much?"

Martha turned to Felicity. "I don't know. I just felt an urge to see you."

"Come in! I've got something to tell you." Felicity grasped Martha's hand excitedly and led her into the study. Martha looked hastily around and saw two large pieces of furniture—a desk and a hikie. The desk was littered with papers and books and encumbered with two typewriters, both of which had sheets of paper in them partially used. There were two small bookshelves within easy reach of the desk and an open safe in which Martha could see yellowed papers covered with Victorian script. These must be some of the old family letters Lissie was using to write her historical account of the Parken place. The hikie was covered with Javanese batik material and had innumerable pillows on it. Martha stretched out on the hikie, and Lissie sat at her desk.

"I'm breaking one of my stern regulations by allowing you to enter this sanctuary. But this is really an important moment, and today marks a new life for me."

"What's all this mystery? What are you talking about?" demanded Martha.

"Martie, darling, you are in time for my wedding! And furthermore I beg you to be my attendant."

"Your wedding! Why, Lissie, how exciting!"

"I wanted to ask you all along, but I was afraid you'd spill the beans to Winslow. You see, my parents don't know. They wouldn't approve if they did. Oh, you must have heard the gossip in town. But I'm so excited, because I think my favorite kahuna really works and that the gods brought you here specially today."

"I'm glad they did!"

"I'm marrying Solomon Hartwell. I think he's connected with your family by marriage, through Comet and Lehua. We shall soon be calabash cousins."

"I met Solomon once. He's a handsome person."

"He's handsome and he's wonderful. Martie, I love him very dearly."

"Then you are making no mistake, Lissie."

"I knew you would think and say that."

Martha was startled to notice the tears gleaming in Lissie's eyes; she had always thought her friend to be cool and unemotional. Martha rose and walked over to put her hand on Lissie's shoulder. "If you really love him," she said, "in time you will find a way to reconcile everything else to that. But there must be a lot of courage and strength."

Lissie did not answer immediately, but when she did, her voice had great delicacy and gentleness. "I've had a feeling, Martha, that you've had to do a lot of uprooting and rearranging in your life with Winslow. That's why I thought you'd understand."

"Tell me about you, Lissie," she said.

"First, we must have a bottle of Aunt Lucillia's heirloom sherry to drink to the occasion. Aunty loved her sherry, and the basement is full of it, enough to last a lifetime."

She went to the door of her study and shouted, "Asano! Bring a bottle of sherry, two glasses, and some *cha siu*." She turned back to Martha. "I haven't been able to celebrate with anyone, and there's lots of celebrating to be let loose from my soul."

Asano brought in a tray with the wine bottle, small glasses, and a plate of red-edged slices of Chinese roast pork, each piece pierced with a toothpick. Felicity poured the sherry and handed a glass to Martha. Martha raised it and toasted, "To your deepest happiness." They both drank the tiny glasses empty, and Felicity refilled them. Then she sprawled on the hikie and placed her wine on the floor within reach.

Felicity traced the pattern of the batik with her finger a moment before starting her story. "Six months ago I met Sol. His family has a little taro patch down the way, and he was living alone in the shack on the land. Each evening he went to the Waikane store to drink soda pop and sing and play the ukulele with the other Hawaiians who gathered there. I went down sometimes myself, because the people were friendly, and I enjoyed being with them. Sol began walking home with me, and we liked talking together. He has an observing mind, and his comments on the Waikane neighbors were interesting and shrewd. I liked the way he was contented with his life. He is happy just being a fisherman and farmer. Such very simple things please him and give him real joy—a good meal, a song and a hula, a swim at night in the sea. I'd never known anyone like him, simple in taste, yet interesting to be with."

She paused to sip her smooth, golden sherry and to nibble a piece of *cha siu*. "After a while he began to hold my hand on those walks home. And then one night he made love to me, and I—I—liked it. But I was afraid. Was it because I never had known anyone like him, and only his novelty appealed to me? . . . Fortunately, none of this had come to the ears of my parents as yet, and I had freedom to search my own mind and heart. Writing became more difficult; it was like pulling teeth. I would scribble a few words and then gaze out the window for an hour. I had to make a rule that Sol absolutely must not come before noon. After that rule I began to watch the clock. So finally I had Asano hide all the clocks. As you can see, I was in a bad way. But still I wondered if it were a love that would last."

She got up and went to the desk for her cigarette case. She offered it to Martha, who waved her hand in refusal. "That's right. You don't smoke," Felicity said, and lighted one for herself. "Oh, Martie!" she exclaimed and combed her fingers through her hair. "When you're twenty, every love is a love that will last. But when you're twenty-nine, there's doubt."

She smoked vigorously for a few moments and then snuffed the cigarette out in a jade ash tray. She returned to the hikie and sat down, leaning back against the cushions.

"How did I discover that it was the love I wanted? I'm not certain. But one day we climbed to the top of the ridge and ate a little lunch we had carried. After eating, we lay back in the grass and let the sun beat on us. It was warm and fragrant, and I went to sleep. When I awoke, I found that Sol was watching me. He said, 'We are at peace, Hoku.' Hoku—that's his name for me. I guess you know it means star. I continued to lie there in utter relaxation and happiness, and I knew that the peace of which he spoke was in me. For an hour we lay there with only a few inches of grass and fern separating us. He didn't once touch me, nor did I touch him, and we were silent. At the end of that hour I knew, and I said to him, 'You're right, Sol. We must be married.' "

Felicity stopped and sighed. Then she glanced at her watch and jumped up. "Martie! It's two-fifteen, and we have to be dressed and down at the Waikane church at three. Come on upstairs. Hurry!" She pulled Martha off the hikie, and in the process spilled her wineglass. "Never mind. We've got to rush."

Upstairs in her bedroom, Felicity took a white silk holoku from the closet. "This is my wedding dress. Asano made it for me. You can wear my green holoku; we're about the same size, and Asano can tuck it up where it needs it."

Martha felt impelled by a dreamy momentum throughout all the details of dressing. She scrubbed Lissie's back, rubbed her shoulders and arms with cologne, and helped her while she slipped into the smoothly fitted holoku. Then she bathed herself quickly and put on the green holoku. It fitted her very well. All through their dressing little items of Lissie's story floated in her mind; the story was more like a poem than like life, a bit of enchantment more than reality, and Martha felt the same sort of detachment that she had when she left the theater after watching a fine play.

Asano brought a bouquet of white and green orchids from the lath house for Lissie and a spray of yellow ginger for Martha. Martha unclasped the strand of pale, water-green jade she had around her neck and put it on Lissie. "My wedding present for you," she said. "It's nice with your white dress and your dark hair."

Felicity kissed her cheek and said, "It's my first and most precious wedding gift." Then she shrugged her shoulders. "Maybe it's the only one I'll receive."

"Such nonsense!" Martha said. "Come on, it's two-fifty; we have ten minutes. Let's go in my car."

The Waikane church, small and cream-colored, was set far back on a lawn of green. A neat cemetery with a few blooming plumeria trees lay in the shadow of a steep green hill. On the other side two giant monkeypod trees spread their umbrella of shade upon the grass. Martha held Felicity's hand while they walked up the cement path, and Asano, in her finest kimono, followed carrying the two bouquets. The minister, a short, plump Hawaiian, greeted them in the foyer of the church and told them that Solomon and his brother David were already waiting near the altar.

"Are you ready?" he asked Felicity and looked at her with kindliness.

She whispered yes, and the minister inquired gently, "What is your full name, please?"

"Felicity Sophia Beach."

"Thank you. I think we can start now." He motioned to the Hawaiian woman who was sitting at the piano, and she began to play the wedding march. Asano handed the bouquets to Martha and Felicity and tiptoed to a seat in the back pew.

Martha kissed Lissie lightly on her cheek and then holding her spray of ginger carefully with both hands, she started slowly down the aisle. The church held a scattering of Hawaiian children and old men and women; they looked very solemn and watched with great, round eyes. Martha glanced ahead and saw Solomon and David and the minister waiting near the altar. The minister must have rushed to reach his position so quickly. Martha took her place and turned to observe Felicity, who walked proudly and happily down the aisle; her body radiated strength and peace. In the aquatic dimness of the church, Martha thought she was like a column of white light in a green dusk.

Solomon watched his bride with a tenderness which in its gentle persistence reminded Martha of the fingers of grass which continually crept over the feet of the stone figure in the Nuuanu garden. He was right for Felicity, she said to herself. He would understand why his wife preferred to sit on the turf and watch the sea rather than go to Mrs. So-and-So's reception. Not only would he understand, but he would be content to let her have her way.

The minister read the ceremony in Hawaiian, and the words, rich in vowels, resounded through the church. There was a lilt to his way of reading, reminiscent of the old Hawaiian chanting, and Martha felt her blood stir. For some reason she could not fathom, she recalled the *pueo* which flew around the mango tree.

When the ceremony was over, Martha kissed Felicity and wished her happiness. Solomon kissed Martha and said, "I'm thankful you came today. It seems more than mere coincidence."

Martha looked at the seriousness in his eyes. "Yes . . . there are such happenings."

Felicity interrupted. "You two look as though you are spinning magic. But I have an even greater magic for Martie to spin. Martie, will you tell Mother and the family when you go to town tonight—as gently, as tactfully as you can. Tell them I'll come to see them in a week, when the honeymoon is over. Tell them, Martie, darling, that it was in a church, that it was beautiful—that I'm utterly happy."

XI

Martha was amazed to find that the Beach family accepted Felicity's marriage with grace, once it was accomplished, and that they welcomed Solomon Hartwell with a quiet but friendly dignity. Felicity and Solomon stayed in the country, living much the same life they had before the wedding. Lissie said that her writing sailed along easily now and that she hoped to finish her book before long. Martha drove out once a week to spend an afternoon with them, and she often took Laurie. The four spent lazy hours together, sometimes walking back into the hills and twisting fern leis for their heads to keep off the beating sun, or hiking down to the beach for a swim. Sol took Laurie fishing and carried her out to the reef on his shoulders. He showed her the limu, which was good for eating, how to get opihis, and pointed out the bright-colored fish which lived in the pools of the reef. He taught her to surf and how to study the waves and to decide whether a wave should be caught or ducked. Occasionally the four of them sat on the bench in front of the Waikane store, sipped bottles of orange soda, and listened to the gossip of the community—how Mrs. Keala had taken another *hanai* child, a Filipino one this time, although she already had ten children, seven of her own and three adopted, of whom one was Chinese, one Japanese, and one part Hawaiian. They listened to the story of Roselani Kukui, who refused to marry Johnny Amoy in spite of the fact that he was the father of her baby daughter;

she said he was lazy and that it was "waste time" to marry him. For this one afternoon of the week Martha escaped from the careful pattern of Honolulu life. It was her day of refreshment and renascence, her day of succoring the Kona part of her, and she returned to the city to play her role of fashion and propriety.

She developed a pride in her ability to live impeccably the life required of her, and she studied the manners and the customs of the older women, how they greeted their guests, what dishes they served for dinner, luncheon, or tea, what their emotional and intellectual reactions were to all the happenings of their life. She copied these, not slavishly but with selection and taste and with consideration for her own generation and background. It became a game for her, in which she sipped the stimulating draft of success. When she discovered that Winslow was aware of her victory, she felt a warm, mantling pride within her.

"Darling," he said once, "you are the perfect wife. Everyone compliments me on you and tells me how gracious you are, how beautifully you entertain, what a pleasure it is to be with you." Every shred of this success, Martha knew, was possible because of the one afternoon a week she spent at Waikane.

Only Julie looked at her with skeptical eyes, and Martha wondered what she was thinking. She did not have long to wait. One afternoon they lay together on the sand at the Platton's. The reading club had met in the morning and the younger members had decided to spend the rest of the day in the sun and water. With breath-taking suddenness Julie said, "You're a big fake, nowadays, Martie, and you know it. You've let Winslow with all his stuffy ideas take you in. I liked you because you were relaxed and natural. You're not that now. You're a beautiful, artificial creature who belongs in a museum. And how all the old dowagers dote on you!"

Martha felt an inward flush, but she replied evenly, "I'm sorry, Julie, you feel that way. I confess that in some ways I have consciously remade myself. But not all of myself. I have obligations, you know, to Winslow and his family."

Julie persisted, "What I can't understand is why Lissie and Sol still swear by you. They aren't taken in by all this cultured nonsense."

Martha shrugged her shoulders. "Perhaps they see beneath the surface."

"Maybe that's it. But I suspect it lies in the blood—yours and Solomon's." Julie poked her first finger deep in the sand. "Sometimes I wish I had Hawaiian blood. I feel shut out. I'll always be shut out from the core of this island life. I know why, too. My instincts are to be the way you could be. My marriage to Sam makes it impossible, and I'm spending my whole life being someone else."

"Hawaiian blood wouldn't help you."

"Oh, yes, it would. No matter how much I displeased them, they could not deny that I belonged."

"Poor Julie! But your children will belong. That's some comfort."

"Yes, it is. But also it takes them away from me. Already I have the feeling about Morrison when he is with his father that they belong to an exclusive society to which I can never aspire."

"Julie, you're imagining things that aren't there."

Julie drew figures in the sand for a few moments and then said, "Martha Wendell, I suspect that somewhere you have refuge. You've never seemed so happy—so integrated—as you are now."

Before she realized what she was saying, Martha said, "And that's why you find the new me distasteful. When you were the calm one, it was all right."

Julie scooped the sand violently with the back of her hand and sent it spraying down the beach. "I didn't know you would say a thing like that."

Tears came into Martha's eyes, and she grasped Julie's hand. "Forgive me. I didn't mean that."

"Forget it, Martie. This has shown me one thing; the struggle is still there."

After this Martha, although she still felt tenderly toward Julie, avoided her as much as possible, and she knew that Julie was doing likewise. Julie really belonged to the masked side of her life, and it was better to leave her there. She was vaguely unhappy about the unfortunate turn of their friendship. But the only two things that really mattered were the preservation of her Kona self and the cultivation of her position as Winslow's wife. Thank heaven, Laurie shared in both.

Martha was going to have another baby, and although she was as well as when she had been carrying Laurie, she pretended to little illnesses. Somehow it seemed more delicate and was more acceptable to Winslow's friends.

Mrs. Wendell commiserated with her and said, "You were so fortunate with Laurie. It's too bad this had to happen now —most unusual too. We must be very careful, dear." Martha submitted graciously to being careful and accepted the constant ministrations of Winslow and Mrs. Wendell.

In the fifth month of her pregnancy she told Winslow that she was tired and that she wanted to go to Kona for a few weeks. Now was the time, she thought, to see how her remembrance of Kona life, encrusted with more than four years of tender imagining, had changed from the actuality. She suspected that the creation of her mind was more suited to her now than the actuality would be, and she felt that before this second baby was born, she must know it. If it were true, then there was nothing for her to long to go back to, because the love of her mother and father remained, in spite of changed circumstances, as warm and guardian as ever.

Winslow readily agreed to her going, but she was tartled by his comment. "I think it's time, my darling, for you to refresh not only your tired little body, but also your tired little spirit."

"My tired little spirit! Winslow, what do you mean?"

"When I married you, you had a charming, easygoing quality which I loved in you—and, I must confess it, which I envied. I'm afraid that in the years of our marriage, I've afflicted you with my disgusting sense of responsibility and worry about doing the right thing. I never wanted to do that."

"Winslow!" she whispered tensely.

"Don't misunderstand me, sweetheart. No one could have made me a more perfect wife than you have. And you have certainly won my mother and father; they think you are wonderful and compliment me on my choice. This isn't a criticism, dearest. It's just that—well, perhaps you are a little too controlled. I think you need the sun and the laziness. And you'll come back my little Kona sweetheart again."

"Yes," she replied, "I'll try to." She excused herself and hurried to the nursery. Laurie was asleep in her little bed, and Martha sat on a cushion on the floor. Now it was all so clear, she thought, why Winslow had married her and she had married him. They each yearned for something in the other and thought that marriage would help them to possess it. He desired the part of her she had tried so hard to suppress for his sake. And she had wanted some of his coolness, some of his perceptive, well-regulated approach to life. Yet—and at this idea she smiled—he was fundamentally ashamed, although he did not realize it, of those same qualities in her which he admired and coveted. Thank heaven, she had learned to think such things through, or his comment would have thrown her into a turmoil of unhappiness. She saw clearly that she must continue in the same way. To revert would only be to displease him.

She took Laurie and Lehua to Kona with her; only Mummy and Daddy were left in the big old house, and she was afraid it would seem lonely without the twins, who were at college in California.

She spent the first day at home in exploring the house and garden. Laurie, although she was only four, made a fine companion. She seemed instinctively to know what Martha wanted to tell her.

"Here's where I used to slide down the banister until the termites weakened the posts."

"Mummy, can I?"

"You're too little. Maybe in a couple of years. If you fell down, you'd break your head."

They went to the kitchen, and Laurie asked, "Mummy, why has Nanna got two stoves?"

"A long time ago, honey, we could use only wood for cooking, and this old stove is that kind. Now we use electricity. Do you understand?"

"Uh-huh. Mummy, are there any cookies?"

"I think we'll find some in a jar in this cupboard." Martha took out a covered crock and offered Laurie a large sugar cookie. "This is the stool, Laurie, I used to stand on when I watched Pua knead the bread or fix the poi."

"What's kneading bread?"

"It's taking the dough in your hands and going this way," Martha said and went through the gestures.

"I wanna go outdoors, Mummy."

Martha smiled and thought, "You're my little outdoor girl." They toured the garden, and Martha showed Laurie the best hiding places, the old lava tubes, her favorite trees and flowers. She pointed to the sea and named the little villages along the shore and asked Laurie to breathe the air and discover how sweet it was. It made no difference that much of what she said was beyond Laurie, for the child listened with a round-eyed assumption that she understood everything.

In the evenings when Laurie was in bed, Martha sat on the lanai with her mother and father and thought of the afternoon just before her marriage when she had looked at this same landscape, trying to imagine what it would be like to live away from it. That had really been the start of the division within herself. Now her Kona life had become even more precious because it lay so deeply within her, so unalterably a part of her. "It's fine to be home," she said and looked toward her mother and father with tenderness.

"We're glad to have you. You seemed to have slipped away from us, Luahine," commented Mrs. Bell.

"Not really, Mummy."

Mr. Bell interposed, "Laurie is so much like you when you were at that age. When I hold her in my arms, twenty years fall away."

"Yes, I feel she is like me. I don't know what this new baby is going to be like, but Laurie will always have a special nook of her own. It can't be helped when you see an image of yourself. But Laurie has something I haven't—a deep love of music. She dances and sings and listens enrapt to any kind of music."

"The little rascal!" exclaimed Mrs. Bell. She looked at her daughter and said, "Keiki, darling, you seem very tired."

"I'm just unwinding after so many years of city life. Oh, Mummy and Daddy, I don't want to have my shoes on the whole time I'm here! I want to lie in the grass and the sun, go swimming at the beach, go fishing, eat lots of pork and poi and opihis. I want to remember how it is to feel."

Mr. Bell rose and went over to kiss Martha lightly on the top of her head. "Be Luahine Bell for a while," he said.

A few days later, Lehua awoke Martha from an afternoon nap to announce, "I've just been talking with Felicity and Sol. They arrived this morning."

Martha rubbed her eyes sleepily. "Felicity and Sol! What are they doing in Kona?"

"They're looking for a place."

Martha sat up. "A place? What for?"

"They want to live in Kona part of the year. Sol was born here, and Lissie has always yearned to live here, she says."

"Yes, she did say once she wanted to spend a long time in Kona. But the Parken place. What of it?"

"They'll keep it. They want to spend three or four months in Kona each year and the rest of the time at Waikane."

"Four months in Kona. Oh, Lehua, what shall I do?" Martha cried and burst into sobs.

Lehua took her hand. "Luahine, what's the matter?"

Martha sobbed, "That one afternoon at Waikane has made my life possible. Now it's gone—gone! What shall I do?"

Lehua wrinkled her brows and scratched her head and said, "Baby dear, there are other ways to remember your Kona life. We'll make one together." She wrapped her arms firmly about Martha's shoulders.

Martha's sobbing ebbed, and she dried her eyes. "Lehua, you are so good to me. Whatever would I do without you?" She felt the warm comfort of the plump, brown arms and thought, "These indeed are my one haven, my one consolation —these tender arms of Lehua. Not even Winslow's arms can comfort me in this way."

After a few minutes Martha said, "I'm going down and ask Daddy to fetch Sol and Lissie for supper tonight. I'd better run a comb through my hair first, though. What a mess I am!"

When she had smoothed her hair and washed her face, she went down to her father's study, opened the door, and walked in. He was writing in a large book, and she went over and put her hands on his shoulders. "What are you doing, Daddy?"

"Writing in my journal?"

"Your journal? Oh, yes, I'd forgotten."

"I've kept it for thirty-five years."

"I didn't know! What did you have to say every day, for heaven's sake?"

"I've kept records of the growth of you children, of the tides each day, of the growth of certain plants and the coffee, the births and deaths in the neighborhood, what people say to me, what I think and dream. Sometimes I copy off from my readings poems and passages I like. It's a wonderful occupation."

"Daddy, how exciting! You have our whole life in Kona written down!" she exclaimed. The thought came to her that here was the substitute for Sol and Lissie's months in Kona, here was a matrix, a crucible out of which she could take the stuff necessary for her happiness.

"It's just the skeleton of our life," he said. "Also I've been studying Chinese and Japanese, and I record my progress in those languages."

"Daddy, you're really a scholar!" she said in amazement.

"Your Grandfather Bell was a true scholar. I'm just a dabbler. But he gave me certain literary and philosophic tastes. He was disgusted with me when I wanted to be an agriculturist—and then on top of that had to be lured by my countrymen to savage isles in the midst of the Pacific."

"But, Daddy, why didn't I know this about you?"

"You were always so much your mother's child."

"Oh, no! I belong to both of you."

"I loved you more for being your mother's child," he said in a voice which in its tenderness seemed to Martha to express all the years of happiness he had spent with Mummy.

"May I read your journals some day?"

"Of course. They are primarily written for you children."

"Could I start today?"

"Why don't you begin with the year you were born? It's over in the case by the window. With the green cover, the fifth from the end on the second shelf."

She went to the bookcase and pulled out the volume labeled, "Macpherson Bell, 1906." The book lay like a Pandora's box in her hands. She was fearful of opening it lest the contents do mischief to her. But only for a second this doubt assailed her, and after that, she opened it straightway. The pages were foxed, and the ink had faded to brown.

Mr. Bell interrupted her examination. "Please, sweetheart, don't read it with me here. Take it to your room."

She snapped the journal shut. "Of course, Daddy." With a light chuckle, she said, "But I almost forgot to tell you what I came about. Sol and Lissie are down at the Kakacs'. Could you go and bring them up for dinner?"

"Of course, keiki. Now you run off with the journal there. I have several more paragraphs to write."

"Thank you, Daddy," she said and rumpled his hair in affection before she left the room.

She hurried upstairs and curled herself on the bed, still disarranged from her nap. She opened the journal at the first page and began to read. Her father's style was brisk and matter-of-fact except in certain lyrical moments of emotion when he wrote with a poetic flourish. She learned how thrilled he was at the expectation of his first child, of the quivering tenderness which beset him whenever he thought of a tiny, helpless baby which was his very own. He hoped that it would show the Hawaiian blood and would have dark hair, large black eyes, golden skin, that it would have the temperament of his wife. She read of the day when Mrs. Wong Wah Yuk had brought a gift of pigs' feet, which she said were the best food for women in Mummy's condition, and how the very idea of pigs' feet had made Mummy sick. She read how Daddy returned from a business trip in north Kona to find Mummy smiling and happy as she lay in bed with the baby by her side. Mummy had said to him, "I thought of Luahine, my ancestress who was a chieftess right here in Kona, when the baby was born, and I've named her Luahine." He had answered, "That's a pretty name, my darling. Let's add Martha, my mother's name, to it." And Mummy had murmured the full name for the first time, "Martha Luahine Bell."

Martha was startled when she felt the cool, slim fingers which suddenly slipped over her eyes. "Lissie?" she gasped.

"This is a fine way to greet your guests! I don't even think you expected us," Lissie said as she removed her fingers and sat down on the bed.

"Yes, I wanted you. That's why I sent Daddy. But I've been reading his journal, the year I was born, and it absorbed me."

"I should think so!"

"Lissie, what's this I hear about your moving to Kona?"

"It'll be just a vacation place for three or four months. We'll not be going to the mainland every year or so the way the rest of you do. And we need some change."

"Whatever will I do without you?"

"What you really ought to say is, 'What will Sol do without Laurie?' He adores that child," Lissie answered. Martha felt the glance of her friend to be poignant with some unknown emotion.

"I know, and she loves him," Martha said. A curious thought crossed her mind—that Laurie should be Sol's and Lissie's child. They could offer her the life she would love, the life for which her little body and spirit had been created. She remembered what Tutu had said about Mummy running away to a fisherman's family, and fear assailed her. She must take care that Laurie never felt her home unfriendly to her warm spirit—as much, really, for Winslow's sake as for Laurie's.

Lissie sighed and spoke almost as though to herself. "It's a great shame. It's the big, big sorrow of my otherwise perfect life."

"What do you mean?" asked Martha.

"That I can have no children. Sol wants them so badly."

"Oh, Lissie, I didn't realize."

"No, neither did I till after we were married."

XII

At the end of her second week in Kona Martha became restless. She had no share in the simple routine of the Kona household except to enjoy its quiet comfort. Each day she was conscious of gazing at a garden no longer hers, one which did not beckon her with little tasks, weeds to be pulled from the nasturtium bed, ginger roots to be transplanted, a lime tree to be sprayed for scale. It was only a garden to look at and to walk in. The meals were plain and their choice was left to Pua, who preferred poi, steamed cabbage, roast pork, and rice. Martha missed the delight she had at home in planning dishes to please the members of the family and expected guests. Flowers were picked in large bunches and put in vases just as they happened to be arranged in the hand that gathered them. There was none of the delicate trifling with buds and branches severely clipped in formal lines, of using spiked frogs to hold a blossom or two in chaste simplicity. The Kona house ran as uncharted, as easily, as artlessly as a path through a guava thicket, and Martha was bored.

The days became amorphous, wearying, and she realized that her supposition was true, that the vision of Kona life was better suited to her now than the actuality. The play-acting had become necessary; it was like following an art, only instead of paint or stone the fragile stuff of everyday living, manner, emotion, planning was her medium. In Boston she had had her first pleasing taste of it, and since that time she had added many elements to its complicated ritual. In Kona she felt as a pianist must feel who has been too long away from his instrument, and she yearned to get back to Honolulu. The one new perplexity to be faced would be the months which Lissie and Sol would spend in Kona. Martha knew that she still needed the refreshing draft of her day at Waikane. There was another source now, however—her father's journal. He had promised to let her take a few volumes back with her; perhaps they would carry her over the gap.

On Friday of the third week she packed and returned to Honolulu with Laurie and Lehua. When she kissed her mother and father good-by, she blushed with guilt over her white lie to them. She had said that Winslow had written urging her to return. But he had actually urged her to stay as long as she wished.

When she walked over the little awai bridge, she paused to look at the green mountains of Nuuanu. They were a proper setting for her, she thought, because they were dramatic, like a stage prop. She loved them dearly for all their moods, and now she understood them.

Laurie tugged at her arm and said, "Mummy, when can we go back to Kona? I don't like these old dark mountains."

"Honey, these are beautiful mountains!"

"No. They have akuas in them."

Martha looked intently at her child and asked, "Laurie, where did you get that idea?"

"I just know."

"There are no such things as akuas."

"Maybe," the little girl said and ran on to the lanai of the house. Martha watched her and wondered from whom in Kona she had picked up the notion about spirits.

Martha first saw her son, Winslow Fourth, as he lay in the nurse's arms, and she knew he would be a proper child. His skin was not red as is that of most newborn babies but was fair and delicate. His brown hair fitted his head neatly, and his tightly clenched little fists lay quietly at his side. Even when he cried, there was a certain dignity about him. Somehow he didn't seem to open his mouth as wide as most babies and display his toothless gums, nor did his face redden much. His crying was purely a matter of exercise, not of temperament, and he seemed to want his mother to realize that fact.

When Win had passed his seven-month birthday and she began to have to say no when he clutched for things or crawled and climbed about, he obeyed readily. She was tempted to hold him up as a model to Laurie but never allowed herself to do that. Laurie's attitude toward Win was too unsettled.

The little girl was torn between her natural response to a baby and her chagrin over what she considered his lack of spirit. She was almost indifferent to him, except in moments when she thought she was alone. Then she caressed him and called him baby names. When she first saw him lying in Martha's arms, she said, "Oh, he's just like a girl—so pale!" Sometimes she tried to play with him, dangling ribbons or rattles before his face. He might reach sedately for a bright color, but he remained placid; this disgusted Laurie, and she said, "He's nothing to play with." One day Martha overheard her talking in the garden to a neighborhood child. "Oh," she said plaintively, "I wish I had a real boy for a brother like yours. It looks like mine's going to be sissy."

When Martha saw Winslow with the baby, she saw the satisfaction which flowed from him that he should have such a son. Here was a creature he could understand, a little one not subject to vagrant moods and flares of temper. Here was a person who was going to be like himself, cool, logical, dignified. This was a son to fulfill a man's dreams. Martha was certain that Mr. Wendell felt as Winslow did and that he looked into the future and saw that the temperament of Win was one which could be molded into that of a shrewd and successful businessman.

Mrs. Wendell's affections clung to Laurie. She duly admired Win and congratulated Martha upon having a son, but Laurie bore the name of her dead daughter and that made her especially precious. Mrs. Wendell frequently said to Martha, "Laurie is made of a stern stuff. She will not be imposed upon." And Martha thought of Mrs. Wendell's sad, pinioned wings and how she would love to see Laurie grow up a liberated feminine spirit.

With Daddy, too, it was still Laurie who was the favorite. Laurie was a carrying on of Mummy and of Martha herself, and any child who was that held Daddy's heart securely. But Mummy embraced both children in her capacious affection. There was equal room for Laurie and Win. She accepted the children as they were, loving them because they were of her own flesh and blood and because they were small and needed care and affection.

One day when Win was ten months old, Lissie came to call. Martha saw her standing on the awai bridge, gazing at the mountains, and she felt a moment of apprehension, because Lissie seldom called on her friends in Honolulu. She always expected them to come to her in the country.

Martha greeted her on the lanai. "Lissie, what a pleasant surprise!"

"Thanks, but when I get through, you may not think so."

"Sit down and relax and don't be so mystifying."

"Have you got any cigarettes in this pure household?"

"Of course. I have an impure husband." Martha reached for a lacquered box on the lanai table and opening it, offered Lissie a cigarette.

Lissie smoked silently for a few moments. Then she walked to Martha and took her hand. "Martie, Sol and I are leaving next Monday for our first sojourn in Kona."

"Oh!" exclaimed Martha in a breathy whisper. "It's come!"

"But we both want you to feel that whenever you wish, you may go to Waikane. Asano and her family will be there. The house will always be open, and you know many people in the village."

"Yes, that's right. I do. And I could take Win. He's old enough now."

"As a matter of fact, I hope you will take him. And this leads to what I want to ask you."

Although Martha was listening carefully, underneath in her mind there was a flow of amazement that she was not particularly disturbed that it had come at last—Lissie's leaving Waikane. Daddy's journal was always at her finger tips; she could see within her mind now the five volumes she had on the shelf near her bed, their green covers spotted with a yellow mold. Win was another consideration. He needed so much care that she didn't have many hours for the country now.

"Martie, darling, I took my manuscript up to Professor Reed at the University. He had kindly consented to criticize it, and he has made some fine suggestions. The biggest fault he finds is in my treatment of the children who necessarily come into the story. He says that my handling of child life is hopelessly sentimental and untruthful and suggests that I make a point of studying children, their reactions, what they say and do; he points out that they are fundamentally very practical little people. I thought if I could have Laurie in Kona for a couple of months, it would help me. She's nearly six now, and not so much of a baby. And she knows Sol and me so well." Lissie moved closer, and Martha noticed that her eyes had a glistening suggestion of tears. "Sol would love to have her. You know that."

Martha answered in a low voice, "Laurie would love it, too."

"Please let her. We both of us need her so much. Couldn't you spare her a couple of months?"

"I'd have to convince Winslow."

"Try hard. I'm sure he'd agree if you presented it just right. Win's his favorite anyhow."

"That's certainly true enough." Martha paused and twisted the pearls at her throat. In a moment she said, "Lissie, I'll do it for you, and I'm sure you know why."

"Martie, you're a brick. We'll never be able to repay you."

"You already have. Anyhow, it's really for Laurie's sake I'm doing it." Martha saw the puzzled look in Lissie's eyes and raised her hand in a little gesture which besought her not to ask.

When the time came for Laurie to go, Martha pushed Lehua out of the room and packed Laurie's dresses and play clothes herself; she felt that somehow this was the first significant thing to happen to her daughter in her five years and that she herself was giving up a certain aspect of Laurie's life which she might have claimed for her own. Letting the child go had not been difficult for Winslow; he had been playing with Win when Martha asked him and had replied rather indifferently, "It'll probably be good for her." Martha wanted her daughter to know that she had packed the suitcase with tender hands, and she stuffed little sweets and tiny presents in odd corners. The thought suddenly came to her that Laurie was the only actual part of her Kona life left. Win had never even entered that life and never would. But Laurie—yes! . . . Laurie could become the embodiment of it! At the unfolding of this idea Martha felt a warm flooding of excitement. It had blossomed so easily, so naturally in her mind that she wondered if it had lain there as a seed, quiet and dormant, waiting for the proper moment. She could create two lives, each distinct, each peculiarly her own, and each embodied in a human being. She herself would become irrevocably the finished fantasy of Winslow's wife. And Laurie would live in the warmth and sweetness of her Kona dream. Sol and Lissie didn't know it, but they were helping both Laurie and Martha herself to their destinies. The idea seemed so tremendous, so fearful to Martha that she sank to her knees and whispered, "Dear God, let me help my child, my daughter, to the right way for her."

Ten days after Laurie had gone with Sol and Lissie to Kona, Martha felt the old restlessness, the old yearning to be free of her bonds, and she bundled Win into the car and drove to Waikane. Asano greeted her at the Parken place and bade her be at home.

She admired Win. "One beeg boy, yeh? More like Daddy, I tink."

"Yes, Asano, he certainly is. He and Laurie are very different."

"Yeah. Laurie, she Hawaiian kind. Win, he haole kind. More better, I t'ink."

Martha smiled at Asano's conservatism. She could be expected to prefer the son over the daughter. And it was probably natural that she would assume that Martha would want her children to be haole through and through.

"I'll stay outdoors, Asano, out in front so baby can get some sun."

She carried Win to a hillock which had a fine view of the water and sat down with him under a breadfruit tree. A breadfruit had fallen and smashed near by, and flies and gnats swarmed about it. Win crawled toward it and daintily poked his finger into the fermenting mess. He withdrew it and started to lick his finger. Martha cried, "No! Win, don't put that finger in your mouth!"

He looked at her with a startled glance and holding his finger high in the air, hitched back to her in his peculiar crawling fashion. She wiped the finger and started him off in another direction. She thought that Laurie, in the same circumstances, would have returned immediately to the breadfruit, to examine it until she was satisfied that it no longer held any mystery for her. But Win was happy in taking his mother's suggestion.

Martha lay back in the grass to enjoy the warm wind and the laziness of the day. She stretched out and tried to relax, but the grass prickled her arms and legs, and busy ants crawled over her hands, leaving an unpleasant tickling sensation. It was curious that in all the times she had lain in this grass, she had never before noticed these little discomforts. She brushed the ants away, but more came. Some were little red ants that bit sharply. In disgust she rose from the grass and picked up Win. "Come on, son, let's go down to the store and hear the gossip."

She called good-by to Asano and drove to the Waikane store. Old Mrs. Mookini was sitting on the bench in front, watching two or three of her grandchildren and gossiping with Mrs. Hauoli and Piilani Jones.

"Hallo, Meesus Wendell," they greeted her.

At that moment there was a loud shriek from the children, and the women rushed over to the little bridge where the young ones were playing in a stream. "Whassa matta?" called Mrs. Mookini to a tall, slender little girl.

"Joey fall from da bridge in da watta. He O.K. now. Hannah ketch heem." Hannah brought the wet, naked, screaming three-year-old Joey to Mrs. Mookini, who slung him nonchalantly on her hip and sauntered with all the slow grace of her rotund person back to the store.

She settled down on the bench with the little boy in her lap and yelled, "Mr. Wong! Bring me one bottle orange soda, yeah?" When Joey held the soda bottle in his small hands, his crying ceased abruptly and he drank greedily.

"Well!" exclaimed Martha. "I arrived at quite an exciting moment."

"Yeah," said Mrs. Hauoli. "Only Joey, he fall in all da time. Someday he break his neck."

Mrs. Hauoli, who was the real mother of Joey but who had given him to Mrs. Mookini, said her words with a certain careless indifference, but Martha knew that if anything ever did happen to Joey she would be grief-stricken, inconsolable for weeks. The whole village would be concerned and would care for the little boy with tenderness.

"We miss you," said Mrs. Mookini. "We t'ink maybe now Hartwells gone, you no come."

Martha laughed a little self-consciously. "I just can't stay away."

"Waikane one nice place. But not like Honolulu," said Piilani. Her eyes shone with envy, and Martha said to herself that she must ask Piilani to come in town and spend the day with her sometime. The girl would be enchanted.

Mrs. Mookini admired Win. "You have number one boy there."

"I think so. His name is Win. Named after his father."

"More like fadda, I t'ink. Haole kind. Not like Laurie."

"No," said Martha, "not like Laurie."

She felt the silence which settled abruptly over the group. This had never happened when Sol, Lissie, and Laurie were here. She tried to think of something appropriate to say, hunting frantically through her barren mind like a woman searching through her cabinet for a misplaced jewel.

Finally Mrs. Mookini said, "You got pretty shoes. They no hurt your feet?"

With those words Martha realized the trouble. She was dressed for town, not in the slacks and gay shirt she usually wore in the country. This set her apart from them, raised the mysterious barrier which fine clothes could form. The clothes reminded them that she was an interloper, not one of them.

"No," Martha answered, "they don't hurt." She rose from the bench with Win in her arms. "Please excuse me now. I have to get back to town. I'll come out again when I can."

"*Alo-o-oha!*" the women called as she waved good-by from the auto.

When she reached home, she gave Win into Lehua's care and went up to her bedroom. She stretched out on the great koa bed and thought of her afternoon's experience. She was certain of one thing, that she would not return to Waikane until Sol and Lissie were there again. Alone, she was not strong enough to capture the mood, the atmosphere, which refreshed her. What upset her even more was that she had apparently lost her ability to make the villagers feel at ease with her. She wondered if the people in Kona had begun to say, "Martha Bell, she too much high tone." The thought hurt her, and she reached for a volume of her father's journal to find solace. She opened it at random and glancing down the page, read:

January 24, 1919. Weather: a sunny, windy morning. Light showers in the afternoon. Sea: heavy swells with white caps. Extremely low tide this evening.

Poor bairn, Martha! Late this afternoon she came into the study and stretched out on the hikie with a book. I knew she was only pretending to read and was watching me from the corners of her eyes. So I said, "What is it, wee thing?" She jumped from the hikie and ran over to stand by me. "Daddy," she said breathlessly, "I was down with Samuel Kekela today." I remarked that I hoped she'd had a good time. "Oh, I did," she said. "Wonderful!" She stopped abruptly, and I waited for her to continue. Suddenly she flung herself into my arms, and in a voice muffled against my shoulder, she poured out her wee heart. As nearly as I can remember, she said, "Oh, Daddy, I've been thinking so much about life and about what will happen to me. Oh, Daddy, you may think I'm crazy, but I want to be just like Samuel Kekela. He has the most beautiful, peaceful time, living down there by the sea, always hearing the waves, and catching fish, and mending nets, and always happy. And his mind is so full of wonderful things and stories, and he knows that the sea is his friend and Pele is his friend. And he knows everything about what the changes in the sea and the weather mean. And he's never lonely because he has imaginary companions to be with him when no one is around. Oh, Daddy!" and her voice trailed off into something which sounded suspiciously like a sob. I kissed her and told her that Samuel's life had much to commend it—the simplicity, the quietness, the wonderful resource he had within his own mind. And I told her that men who had this inner resource were apt to be happier than others who depended on external things. She listened to me, and her big dark eyes fairly seemed to pierce me through. What a wee lassie she is!

Martha put the journal back on the shelf. She rose from the bed, walked to the window, and looked out, trying to shape the idea stirred in her by what she had read. Dusk had come into the garden, and she saw the owl hovering round the mango tree. The bird made a sudden swoop into the foliage and startled her; in that moment she understood what was happening to her in the absence of Laurie and the Hartwells in Kona. To conjure her Kona life she no longer had *to do*—to go to Waikane and hike or loaf or swim. She had only to think intently, to glance at Daddy's journal, and Kona would blossom in her mind; the resource was within her. It was now, she thought, Laurie's turn to *do*.

INTERLUDE

THE LATH HOUSE

The lath house, as years of rain and light and wind beat upon it, weathered; its boards became streaked with a golden lichen and splotched with the velvety darkness of dry rot. Laths worked apart from their nails and slid out of place under the buffeting of the trade winds. Something came loose on the roof and beat in the wind a rat-a-tat against the tin eaves' gutter. Long blades of grass, which Mitsuo could not reach with the mower and forgot with the clippers, made a shaggy hedge around the base, and hidden in the grass, mango leaves rotted, giving off a sweetish, acrid odor. Bamboo shoots strayed from the awai banks and started a feathery clump close against the back.

Laurie chose a hiding place, a spot she kept a secret from Win's bright, curious eyes for several years. She entered it through a gap left by broken laths and hidden by the bamboo clump. Her place was under the table where indifferent cattleya experiments were shelved. She was shielded from view on the inside by the luxuriant growth of maidenhair fern which covered, except for the cement paths, the floor of the lath house. Her place was usually snug and dry, although Mitsuo on occasions watered a little too vigorously, and dampness seeped below. Laurie would lie for hours at a time, listening and interpreting the varied movements sounding about her—the passage of a lizard under a dried leaf, the creaking of tree branches in squally weather, the wind like a shower in the bamboo, and most interesting of all, the little scraping, gurgling, and cutting noises of her mother as she worked among the orchids. She peered out at Mummy and saw the way she pushed her tongue between her teeth and lips as she prepared the culture for the germination of seeds. Laurie flushed warm and trembling with the pleasure of being able, thus unnoticed, to observe her mother. She kept a doll in the hideaway, and when Mummy was not there, she pretended that she and the doll lived in ancient Hawaii; they fished off the reef and hunted for limu; they surfed and climbed the mountains for bananas. When she was tired of the doll, she brought her ukulele to the lath house and improvised songs with Hawaiian words, playing them over a few times and then forgetting them. The songs expressed her whims and poetic observations. Her mind was charged with the melodies, and safe in the hideaway, she did not need to answer Win's prying, nagging question, "What's that you're playing? I've never heard that."

When Laurie was old enough to be concerned about keeping her play clothes clean and after Win had discovered the secret, she abandoned her sheltered spot and moved to the outside. She found an old stool which she painted yellow-green and set against the clump of bamboo. There she sat and strummed her ukulele or read. One summer Win made a garden bench for Mummy's birthday, and because of its ungainly lines it was set out next to the stool. Laurie abandoned her little yellow-green seat to sprawl upon the bench. The family thought she was rather queer to like that particular spot where the garden was its most unkempt, and she had to explain to them that it was the smells and the weedy green which she liked. The family seemed more and more frequently to find things that were singular about her, and Laurie began to puzzle over her difference. At times she rejoiced in this difference; it was exciting because they took special notice of her. But at other times she was troubled by it. When a sense of the discord welled up inside her and she had to express it vigorously, passionately, she had seen her father look at her with irritation, her mother with anxiety, and Win with childish and cutting contempt. But although she tried to curb some of her tastes of which they disapproved, such as her preference for Lehua's friends, she stubbornly clung to her spot behind the lath house.

Martha, however, was pleased that Laurie liked being close to the lath house. While she was working among her orchids, she enjoyed the sense of her daughter's presence and the sound of her ukulele. It gave her a tender, peaceful sense of living. Martha had ferreted out the richness in herself since that afternoon she had read in her father's journal of her day with Samuel Kekela. She had taught herself to savor moments, incidents. She would whisper, "Let me remember that this moment is what life really is," and somehow it became a throbbing, living thing, not merely a passage between past and future but an experience intrinsically valuable in itself. When she pulled the blanket off in the morning and felt the coolness of early air against her sleep-warmed body, she thought, "This is something people have done for centuries and something they will do for centuries." And once while she wiped with a soft cloth the water stains from the washbasin, she had said aloud, "Why, I'm part of the parade of all women who for generations have been cleaning and caring for their families. This is my share in the eternal!" And she felt joy moving within her, as whirling and abandoned as smoke from a beach bonfire.

One morning she rose and looked out at the lath house and saw that it was shabby, rotting, in need of repair. In a flashing second the idea came—"We'll rebuild it, have a new one, twice as large and with a lava stone base." She told Winslow of her plan, and he sent the carpenters, and they built a new orchid house with a glass roof and a stone base and screened-in sides.

When she and Mitsuo moved the plants in, they exclaimed to each other in antiphonal chorus, "It's wonderful! Plenty room! No bugs can get in! Number one sprinkle system!"

But some of the joy over the new orchid house was dissipated when Martha discovered that Laurie would not go near it. "What's the matter, darling?" she asked.

"It's new!" Laurie declared contemptuously. "It smells of

cement and varnish and metal. You can't smell the plants or the grass. . . . It's like Honolulu."

"Like Honolulu!" Martha repeated in astonishment.

"Yes. New buildings! Waikiki is cluttered with them. Everywhere swarms of people and new buildings and rawness."

Martha laughed and put her arm around Laurie. "In a few months, darling, you'll be back to the orchid house. Time acts quickly."

And it was true. Mitsuo let the grass grow tall at the back, allowed the mango leaves to rot, and yellow ginger to spread helter-skelter. And Laurie was once again playing her ukulele there.

But Martha continued to think of Laurie's poignant words, "swarms of people, new buildings, rawness," and of the things that were happening in a growing Honolulu. The old quiet spreading and gentle shifting were gone. This change came in spurts and frantic efforts, and Martha watched it with mingled reluctance and pleasure, reluctance for the disappearance of old buildings and trees, of large sheltered gardens, of the last bits of swampland at Waikiki, and pleasure at the excitement and mystery of unfinished shops, new canals, luxury liners. She liked people whose roots were deep, deep within the Hawaiian earth. Now one met more often those who regarded Hawaii as a nice spot in which to winter or met service people who were doing a tour of duty here, either liking or hating it, and always eager to know the townspeople and not understanding why it was so difficult. New government agencies and new businesses brought in persons who had no feeling of permanence. Hawaii was on trial in their eyes, its virtue and glamour to depend on the money they were able to make. The most troubling quality about these *malahinis,* Martha thought, was their ability to live and work and play almost completely oblivious to the Oriental and Hawaiian peoples living and working all about them. They overlooked much of the significance of Hawaii, and it frightened her, this curious stratification they seemed to achieve.

More and more the old families were slipping purposely into the background, living their lives quietly and watching and wondering, holding tenaciously to what was theirs. But there was a young generation growing up which was discontented with the ingrained, tranquil ways. When they married they built lavish houses, unlike the simple homes of their forebears, and they welcomed the new, smart people from the mainland. And Honolulu, which had had only a night club or two found itself acquiring several.

Martha wondered if this discontent shown by the young people were not a variation of the restlessness that was festering into war in Asia and Europe. It was difficult to make the picture of death and hunger come alive in her mind when she sat on a lanai in Hawaii and looked at shining leaves and a turgid, azure sea. War! One round, hard syllable which meant that men were thrusting at the very meaning of existence. Winslow said that before too long the United States would be involved, and Hawaii as an island extension of the mainland would feel the war sharply. He began to lay in supplies and to make plans to gear his business to war conditions, to prepare for shortages of material and labor. He encouraged some of his young employees to join the Army or Navy and purposely did not replace them so that his business would learn to function with less help.

His father laughed at him and said, "The United States will never go to war. We're a peace-loving nation. Why should we entangle ourselves in these European and Oriental brawls?"

And Winslow replied courteously, "I want to be prepared for any event. And I'm afraid I disagree with you, Father. Just consider what we've seen and heard here in the Pacific in the past ten years—the stories of travelers and refugees, the scrap iron and weapons, the suspicion and fear. We can't stay out of it, even if we want to." Winslow had said to Martha privately, "The children must be prepared for war. I purposely talk about it so they'll get used to the inevitability. Win doesn't worry me. But Laurie—she's so emotional!"

It always came to that, Martha sighed—worry about Laurie. She was at the same time the most complicated and the simplest of girls. When she rubbed banana leaves between her palms to feel their silken-soapy smoothness, Winslow complained, "What in the name of heaven is the child doing?" But that was the simple part of her, Martha thought. It was the sudden stubbornness, the unexpected flow of tears; for all her careful study, Martha could never be certain when these gusty moods were coming. They usually burst upon an unprepared family, filling everyone with uneasiness, sometimes repugnance. Only Mummy and Daddy in Kona accepted Laurie for what she was and said, "You're lucky to have such a warm-hearted, talented child, Martie."

The war did come, unexpected yet half-expected, on a bright, wind-shaken December morning. Laurie sat out behind the lath house. "It's not safe!" Winslow stormed at her.

But she answered calmly, "Shrapnel can go through the walls of our house just about as easily as it can the air."

Martha begged, "Please, for all our sakes, come in."

But Laurie said, "I'd rather die, if it's to be, in the open, in the grass." And then with a warm, affectionate smile, "Don't worry, Mother, dear. I'm quite safe here, hidden from the sky by the green."

In the first week after the blitz Laurie offered herself to the Red Cross and soon was engulfed in work. She served at canteens, delivered books to out-of-the-way posts, rolled bandages, typed volumes of papers. When the war had been blazing for more than a year, a Red Cross official told Winslow, "Mr. Wendell, your daughter is a marvel. I don't know what we would have done without her—especially at the first. And what is she—only seventeen or eighteen? With her friendly ways, she has the toughest people eating out of her hand. She accomplished some things I could not have done without stirring up considerable ill feeling."

But helping the Red Cross was not enough to satisfy the growing Laurie felt within herself. "This work is all for the urgent, sorrowful present," she thought, and wondered with most of her friends what the peace, which, after all, would mark the important years of her life, would bring. She decided to take courses at the University of Hawaii; perhaps they would help her to understand some of the puzzles and bring her maturity. More than anything else she felt the need of maturity to cope with the emotions and ideas which flooded in upon her. But she failed her courses, and tried again, and failed again.

"Mummy, I can't concentrate! Why? Why?" she lamented. But she knew why; it was because of Jerry Wakinekona whom she had met at the University. She had first loved him, and then after her father's harsh, blundering interference, she had hated Jerry. Eventually time blurred these impressions, and Laurie remembered most poignantly the whispered, agonized words of her mother, "Child, child! Why is it you call out the worst in your father?"

During the troubled years Laurie often took refuge in the lath house. "Mummy!" she had once cried. "This is the only spot I can get away from the smothering feeling of being a Wendell. This is the only place I can know myself."

She watched with a deep content as the lath house settled unobtrusively into the garden, decking itself with streaks of golden lichen. The rocks of its base became green with a fine moss, and crevices opened to let in lizards with whispering feet and hard-shelled bugs that tumbled and rustled among the maindenhair ferns. Sometimes at dusk an owl would perch on the peak of the skylight and stare down as though he thought the tenderest of mice must dwell in that lush spot. And Laurie would sit motionless and stare up at him, murmuring to herself the Hawaiian words which came and went like shreds of mist in her mind, "The owl with the golden eyes, with the green fire in his golden eyes. The owl that stares at me with the eyes of all my ancestors."

BOOK II

LAURIE, 1946

I

Laurie Wendell sat behind the lath house on the unstable garden bench which had been Win's handiwork. She strummed on her ukulele, but she did not sing. She was thinking of what Tutu Slator had told her, Tutu whose eighty years had turned her thoughts toward dying. Laurie felt an uncomfortable stricture in her throat and a trembling of her pulse whenever Tutu repeated that sentence which had become a frequent prelude to her statements, "I want to get these things all straightened out before I die."

Last week she and Tutu had been sitting on the black sand at Punaluu, having one of their delicious hours of enjoying together the sound and color of the sea and smelling the tart wind which blew in from the surf. Tutu had taken her hand and said, "Laurie, I want to explain something to you so you won't think I've overlooked your mother or that I loved her the less. It has always been taken for granted that I would leave this Punaluu home to her, because she enjoyed it more than anyone else in the family. But in the past ten years things have changed. Your mother has changed too. She still loves the house, yes, but only as an object out of the past, a place filled with tender memory. She could never live here now—as you could. So, Laurie, darling, it's to be yours. Your mummy already knows it."

Tutu had stopped talking a moment and had released Laurie's hand; she scooped up some black sand which she let fall through her brown, bony fingers. When she continued, there had been a sparkle of merriment in her voice. "Maybe . . . who knows? Samuel Kekela at your mother's wedding luau foretold that you would marry a man of Kona. And if you do, you may want to live here."

Laurie remembered with perplexity the scantiness of her words of gratitude to her great-grandmother. "Thank you, Tutu. Thank you for such a—a wonderful present!" was all she had said.

But Tutu had understood. "You don't have to say anything, keiki. Just enjoy it when and if you live here."

Laurie had looked at the old home for the first time with the knowledge that someday it would be hers. She felt a gentle swelling of pride, for the possession of it somehow established her. Now she would have a place peculiarly her own, a home apart from her family, and she could live each day without wondering fearfully how Daddy would interpret her actions. She had muttered again, "Thank you, thank you, Tutu." In the silence which followed, they regarded the old house, admiring its crisp New England pattern and the comfort offered by the broad lanais, dreaming of the days to be spent within its airy rooms. Finally Laurie had broken the stillness to ask, "Tutu, just who was Samuel Kekela? I've heard Mummy mention him once or twice."

"He was a kahuna; he's dead now. At Mummy's wedding luau he sang a bridal song. In it he forecast that Mummy would have two children, a boy and a girl, and that the girl would marry a man of Kona. That's you, Laurie. Some of what Samuel said has come true. Maybe this will too."

"Perhaps so. But there aren't many people in Kona Father would approve of for me." Laurie had been bewildered by the wise glance of amusement and knowingness which Tutu had given her. The old lady often had an expression which made one believe she could see into the future, and Laurie wondered if Tutu thought she knew what was going to happen.

Laurie moved off from the hard boards of Win's bench and lay down in the grass; she cocked her feet on one end of the seat and continued to strum her ukulele casually, almost unconsciously. She thought of Mummy and wondered what slow altering in her nature had occurred to make Tutu change her mind. Mummy was like two people. With Father and with guests or friends, she was beautiful, fascinating, a woman whom one envied for her certain knowledge of how to live gracefully. Laurie was always reminded of a Gainsborough painting whenever Mummy was in that character; one could not escape admiring her beauty and yearning for her friendship, but at the same time one feared to disturb the gentleness about her, a gentleness which made her unapproachable in intimacy. The other side of her was simple, lovable, and she seemed to be a person thrilled with many of the same things that thrilled Laurie herself—the fragrance of sun-heated guavas, the wind crackling in the hala trees, going swimming on a day when the water was so crystal clear that your arms and legs looked like flashing bits of pale amber and the sand like moonlight sparkling on the sea bottom.

This second aspect of Mummy didn't come out very often, and then it was mostly when she and Laurie were alone or when they were with Grandpa and Nanna Bell. She even had a special voice for this part of her, a warm, emotional one, so different from the other polished tone. In that voice she had whispered to Laurie on a summer afternoon at the Hartwells', "Baby sweet, you are my very special child, because you are all I have left of Kona." Laurie had known that she must not ask what those words meant, that perhaps they couldn't be explained.

When Mummy was in this frame of mind, Laurie felt a core-deep kinship with her, something closely knit and precious and exciting. It was an awkward circumstance, she thought, that Mummy always made her feel important, special, while Father always made her feel as though she were inadequate, stupid. Yet, she knew that Daddy, after his stern fashion, wanted to see her established as Allie Lyons was who had married Keoki Tremaine and had a baby son and a new home built on the Lyons family tract up Nuuanu. Daddy always stressed the importance of Wendells in the making of Hawaii, and of their social responsibilities. Even Mummy echoed that at times.

Laurie turned her head so that half of her face was pressed close into the grass; the green blades were cool, fragrant, and sharp against her skin, and she felt a response through her body. "Oh," she murmured, kindled by the feel of the grass and by the tremor of well-being within her, "life is so wonderful!"

"Oh, it is, is it?" came Win's taunting voice.

"Win! I thought you were at a Boy Scout meeting."

He brushed aside her words. "Say, what have you got your dirty feet on my bench for? Gosh, Laurie, take 'em down!"

"I'm not hurting your bench."

"You know it's wobbly and has to be fixed."

"I know it never has been right," she said unkindly.

"Laurie Wendell! You're revolting! Why I had to have a sister like you—so undignified all the time, and lazy and dumb." He paused a moment and then stammered on in indignation, "You couldn't even get through the first year at the University! It's certainly lucky the war kept you home and Dad didn't spend all that money to send you to some expensive mainland school."

"Oh, shut up, Win, and go play with your friends. We know you are the family genius."

"What I can't understand is why you don't do something like the rest of the girls. You just sit around all day."

"I'm too dumb. You could have answered that for yourself."

"Gosh, I'd like to be proud of my sister!"

"You sound just like Father. Now, go away and leave me alone. I was perfectly happy till you came along."

"O.K., O.K., I was just trying to help you."

"Like so much! . . ." she said scornfully and turned away from him. She heard his clumsy boyish footsteps as he walked across the lawn toward the house. She and Win always wrangled when they were together. Yet she was fond of him in a careless sort of fashion; he was a child in many ways and had a queer sense of propriety. He was only fifteen and yet already he wanted her to be just like everyone else. Poor old Win!

The encounter with her brother had destroyed her mood, filled her with restlessness. She rose from the grass, went into the house and up to her room. She put her ukulele on top of the cabinet and picked up a flute, which was partially hidden beneath the untidy pile of sheet music. She dusted it off against her dress and then blew a few notes, softly, deftly; she liked the flute, but the family complained if she played it too much. She always had to wait until she was out at Sol's and Lissie's where they didn't mind noise and weren't worried about the neighbors. That was an amazing family! Lissie could be pounding at her typewriter, working on another book, Sol strumming his ukulele, Mele, their adopted daughter, practicing her singing, and she, Laurie, tooting on her flute, and no one seemed troubled by the commotion. In many ways she fitted more comfortably into the Hartwell way of doing things, of eating whenever they were hungry, deciding suddenly on a beach picnic, hurrying down to care for the Akiona children while Mrs. Akiona gave birth to her fifth baby.

Laurie blushed at the thought of the time she had threatened to run away to the Hartwells. She had had a quarrel with Father over some forgotten incident and had cried out that she would go and live with Sol and Lissie, "People who really love me!" That was the moment when she had discovered for certain that Father, in spite of his sternness and his seeming preference for Win, had a deep love for her. He had taken her in his arms and, much to her embarrassment, had smothered her with kisses, calling her his little daughter, his darling Hawaiian child. That incident, however, hadn't changed his ways toward her, and she still regarded the weeks spent each year with the Hartwells in Kona and at Waikane as the time when she could be the real Laurie Ululani Wendell. Mummy was the only person who truly understood how much the Hartwells meant to her, because Laurie had only to say, "Mummy, I simply *must* go to Waikane," and permission was granted.

Laurie blew a few more trills on the flute and then put it back on the cabinet. She sauntered to her closet to see if Lehua had pressed her green net gown. She took it out and examined it, shuddering at the prospect of tonight's engagement. Mummy had insisted that she go out again with Dick Waldron, who was somebody or other's cousin from Boston, and therefore she had to be nice to him; he was also a Navy lieutenant, and she had to be nice to him for that. She thought with a sigh of the young easterners the war years had brought to Honolulu. They seemed to consider themselves so superior, and they bored her. They had three essential topics of conversation, intellectual patter about music, art, or writing, cousinly talk of Boston, or a kind of flip repartee, which they thought was very smart but which she considered rather silly. The most amazing part was that they all said practically the same thing and held identical views on all subjects. Before the evening was over, they let her know, sometimes politely, sometimes bluntly, that they considered Hawaii a dirty, crowded, shabby, much overrated spot. They might as well have slapped her face, she thought, as to let her know they regarded Hawaii in that way.

There was another and more important reason why Laurie disliked these eastern officers who came bringing letters of introduction. She instinctively realized that Father hoped she might find from among them one suitable for a husband, someone who would efface the recollection of Jerry Wakinekona. Consequently she had made a secret resolution. She had determined not to marry a man who didn't feel with her a flow of warmth at the very word Hawaii, a man who didn't have an inner compulsion to live his years out in the Islands. She would not allow herself to look with favor on any of the young officers lest she fall in love. Once she was in love, she knew she would marry; Jerry had taught her that.

Laurie put her green net back into the closet. She went to the bed and stretched out, reaching for a cigarette from the cinnabar box on her bedside table. She lighted the cigarette and watched the smoke curl peacefully up toward the ceiling until it was caught in a draft which swiftly dispersed it. She sighed; and if not marriage, then what? What was she going to do with herself? Here she was almost twenty, a failure at the University, and a failure at everything else. Father did not like to have her sit around idly.

"The time is past," he preached, "when young women of well-to-do parents can be nothing but frivolous social butterflies. Laurie, my dear, plan something constructive for yourself. I was proud of your Red Cross work."

She had probed and questioned herself constantly on this difficulty, but no satisfying idea had come to her. Her friends studied to be nurse's aides, or took courses in occupational therapy, or helped at the Y.W.C.A., or did volunteer social work, but these activities seemed dreary to Laurie. If only there were something she could do with her dancing and her flute! But that was out of the question with Father feeling the way he did. He would allow her to teach, but he would never consent to her giving public performances. And she wanted to dance and play—not to teach.

She sometimes thought it might have been better if she had been brave enough to run off and marry Jerry three years ago. She would have a home now and perhaps a child or two, and her whole life would be mapped out. A home! Laurie smiled. A home with Jerry would be a small cottage in an alleyway, unless Father had softened his heart and forgiven her. She had to admit that on her few visits to Jerry's home she had been uneasy with his family and shocked at his poverty. She had even wondered in moments of cool thoughtfulness if it would be possible for her to live so simply and frugally; she loved good food, new clothes, running about the Island in a car. But when she was alone with Jerry, sharing his gaiety, singing and dancing with him, enjoying the poetic and sentimental way he treated her, she became certain that living simply and humbly with him would be heaven.

Laurie was not ashamed of admitting to herself that marriage was the future she yearned for; she wanted most a home and children. But she dared not mention it, even to Mother, lest she be accused of husband-hunting. That, among her friends, was the gravest of crimes. Also she wanted to be cautious; she had been sharply sensitive to the divorces among her parents' friends and to the unhappiness of the couples afterward. There were the Beaches, for instance; Aunty Juliette was still a bitter, melancholy woman, and she had been divorced from Uncle Sam for over ten years. Laurie had even wondered if her mother and father had been as happy as they should be; they were so studiedly devoted to one another that they seemed more like people in a play than people in life. Father was excessively polite and considerate of Mummy, and Mummy seemed, at times, to treat Father as though he were a guest in his own house. Laurie did not want a marriage like her mother's and father's. Hers must be simpler, warmer, and she thought she'd prefer to live in the country like the Hartwells and escape some of the dull, artificial social obligations of town.

She put out her cigarette and went to the cabinet for her ukulele; it fitted snugly, familiarly in her hands, and she enjoyed the rounded, vibrant quality of the strings against her finger tips. She lay back on the bed. Her ukulele was acquainted with all her moods and ready at any moment to comfort her. She whispered in Hawaiian the words of the songs she played and felt a cool peace blossom within her.

She was startled when she opened her eyes to find her mother looking down at her.

"Laurie, sweet! You look very happy."

"Oh, Mummy!" She felt guilty that her mother had caught her in this idle moment. "I guess I'm pretty lazy. . . ." Words rushed out of her. "Whatever am I going to do with myself?

Daddy asked me again this morning, and as usual I had no answer."

"Someday it will all simmer up from your subconscious. Don't worry about it." Mummy used her warm voice, and it was comforting.

"Is life always so difficult?" Laurie watched her mother's beautiful smile, which changed her whole face, made her eyes delicately slanted, her mouth curved as exquisitely as a shell, her cheeks round and tender. In her smile, Mummy was Hawaiian.

"What a question for a young girl to ask! . . . I have some news for you. Grandpa and Nanna Bell are coming to town next week."

"How nice, Mummy! But isn't this unexpected? Usually they plan so far ahead."

"Well . . ." Her mother hesitated, and Laurie looked sharply at her. "Nanna is going to visit the doctor."

"The doctor! I didn't know she was sick."

"Well, she's not exactly. But Dr. Corben thinks she ought to have certain tests."

"It sounds very mysterious."

"Oh, no! You know the way doctors are. . . . Now come on, darling. You haven't even washed your hair yet for tonight. And is the little tear near the hem of your skirt mended?"

"Lehua fixed it and pressed my dress, spoiling me as usual."

"Hurry, Laurie. It's three-thirty, and Richard is calling for you at five-thirty. Your hair will just barely have enough time to dry."

"I'll do it now, Mummy."

Laurie went into her bathroom and stripped off her clothes. She turned the hot and cold water on in the shower until they formed just the right tepid mixture which she liked. Then she stepped in and felt the little pellets of water sharp against her skin. She ducked her head under the spray; her hair was quickly drenched and lay heavily upon her shoulders.

She thought of her grandparents coming to town; there was always a subtle change in the household when they arrived. They seemed to bring with them an aromatic breath from the sun-bathed slopes, the hot sands, the glimmering moonstone sea of Kona. And then when they had gone—such an ache as of something precious lost irrevocably! Laurie thought of Nanna, of her leisurely ways, of the charm which made her irresistible to all types of people, a charm expressed simply in smiles, in gestures of the hand, in tender little words. Suddenly, inexplicably, the idea came to her mind, "What if Nanna were to die?" The water of the shower seemed to run icy across her body, and she shivered.

II

"Laurie!" It was Father's voice, and she hurried into the library. "Richard Waldron is on the phone."

She made a little grimace, and he warned, "Now, be courteous to him."

She picked up the receiver and said, "Hello, Dick."

The young lieutenant's polite, Boston-accented voice said, "Laurie, tomorrow is my last day in Honolulu. Then I'm off to the Philippines. I have a wonderful time planned—swimming at Kalama and a picnic. In the evening, dinner and a dance at the officers' club."

Laurie answered swiftly, "It's awfully nice of you to think of me, but I'm terribly sorry I can't. My grandmother and grandfather are coming to town tomorrow, and I have to be with them."

Laurie saw her father gesticulating, and she frowned slightly at him, listening at the same time to Richard's protests and disappointment. "Just a minute, Dick, please. Father wants me to tell you something." She held her hand over the receiver and asked, "What do you want?"

"Don't refuse the poor boy. It's his last chance to have a good time for many months. Grandma and Grandpa will be here for a couple of weeks, and you'll have plenty of opportunity to be with them."

"I know, but Mother said we'd have a Kona dinner, and I can't miss that. And all the family's coming. Besides, I don't want to go out with Richard."

"Laurie!" said her father in a way which seemed to her regretful but resigned. "Richard is going to do you the honor of asking you to be his wife tomorrow night. I was hoping you would consider it seriously."

She was surprised. "But I've only seen him five times!" Then with decision, "Father, I'd have to say no. My not going tomorrow will save him a disappointment." Laurie spoke into the receiver to Richard. "Father says to wish you lots of luck and to tell you we'll be thinking of you and looking for you when you come back to Hawaii. Now about tomorrow, Richard. I'm just terribly sorry, particularly as it's your last day here, that I can't make it. But I've promised Mummy I'd do so many things, and we're having a family reunion dinner."

She said good-by and hung up the receiver. When she turned to leave the room, she found her father gazing at her with both affection and anxiety in his eyes.

"Oh, Father, I know I'm a failure to you! But I can't marry Richard. I don't love him; I'm not even interested in him."

"Laurie, how you're going to spend your life worries me more than all the business troubles I had in the war years put together. I want to see you settled properly and happily as befits a Wendell and my daughter."

She looked into his eyes, then glanced hastily away; the words slipped from her, "And you're afraid of what I'll do, aren't you? You've been afraid ever since the Jerry episode.

That's too bad." She twisted a lock of hair which fell over her shoulder and then faced him. "Father, I may seem irresponsible to you, but I'm really cautious about myself. I've that much New England in me—to want to do what's right for me."

His voice was pompous in the way she dreaded. "Laurie, I feel as though I know you very well indeed, because you are your mother all over again. Consequently I know the pitfalls of your nature, where the danger lies. And I'm afraid that you don't recognize the danger."

She snatched at a thought which suddenly opened in her mind. "Father, what is danger for you may not be danger for me."

She saw his face settle into stern lines and the flesh pull like a mottled web across his cheekbones. "Laurie." He spoke with a slight gruffness in his voice. "I shall insist upon one thing—that you make a good, a suitable marriage. And you cannot have lived in this house for nearly twenty years without knowing what I mean by that." He paused and with a strange embarrassment, a flushing of his face and a lowering of his eyes, continued, "If you marry against my will, I shall be forced to forget that I once had a lovely little daughter."

Laurie looked at her father in disbelief. Those words! Did he mean them? Their syllables rang in her ears like an air-raid siren. She felt an impelling desire to laugh, to try to make the whole episode seem a joke. But there was the mottling of his flesh and the power in his voice. A curious feeling came upon her that she was already turned out of her home, and a huge loneliness engulfed her. She broke into sobs. "Father, you're—you're unkind!" she cried and ran from the library.

The feeling of aloneness grew until she ached. How could a father, in 1946, say such a thing! What if he did turn her out? What would she do? She stumbled blindly down the hall, felt for the doorknob of the side entrance, pushed the door open, and went out into the garden. She threw herself down upon the velvety Japanese grass under the mango tree and sobbed, her body trembling.

When she was spent, she began to think of Tutu and of Punaluu, of "her house." There in that old fragrant home would always be a refuge for her. She belonged there. She dug her finger tips deep into the turf and whispered against the earth, "Thank you, Tutu. With all my heart and soul, thank you."

At the airport while they waited for the plane to arrive, Win beckoned his father here and there, asking innumerable questions about the equipment and the different types of planes. But Laurie and Martha stood together silently, hand in hand. Laurie quivered with excitement at the coming and going of people, and she wondered about them. What island was that obviously mainland-looking man in his dark suit and felt hat bound for and why? Maybe he was a new schoolteacher or an accountant for a plantation. And that poor old Chinese lady dressed in her blue pajamas! She looked frightened and lonely as she sat stiffly on the bench with her little black purse clutched tightly in her fingers. It was certain that she was making her first trip by herself. Near the coke-vending machine a group of young girls of Oriental ancestry talked and giggled together and drank cokes. Laurie could hear enough of their conversation to know they were schoolgirls on summer vacation. They began to talk about an absent friend:

"And her brother when he came back from the war in Italy told her father that he was going into business for himself and that he was through with all this eldest son stuff. And the father burned up, and the family almost split. That's why Hazel didn't come back to school this semester. But everything's peaceful now, I guess. She's coming back this fall."

Laurie was roused from her observations by her mother's fingers closing more tightly around her hand. She glanced at Mummy's face and saw a worried frown on it. "What is it?"

she asked, and then continued, "You're worrying about Nanna. Is it really something serious?"

"We don't know. In a few days the doctors will tell us." Martha withdrew her hand and smoothed back a stray lock of hair from her forehead. "Oh, Laurie, it's a tragic thing to think of Nanna being sick. She's such a rare person! There are few like her left—with just that generous, sympathetic, joy-bestowing nature. The war, industry, are changing our Hawaiian people, filling them with an impatience, a discontent, and even in too many cases a cruel vulgarity they have not known before."

Laurie was startled at the tense emotion in her mother's voice and was about to reply when Martha grasped her arm and said, "Here they are—getting out of that plane. Nanna looks tired."

Later when they were in the car, Laurie sat next to Nanna, who took her hand. "Little Laurie Ululani!" she exclaimed in a low, rhythmic voice. "You grow more beautiful each time I see you. Luahine, this child of yours is the first real beauty of our family. I should think the young men would be groveling at her feet."

"They are, but she will have none of them. She has refused three proposals that I know of in the last year—and all of them from handsome, wealthy, eligible young men. What more she wants, I don't know!"

"Sometimes there's more wanted than that, as Laurie probably knows."

Nanna's words were spoken gaily, but they gave Laurie a baffling sensation of being entangled in something she couldn't quite understand. She knew it had to do with a recollection of Jerry. Nanna had not disapproved of Jerry; she had disapproved of the fact that Laurie was only seventeen when she wanted to marry him. At the time, she had said, "In spite of your parents, keiki, it's not the fact that Jerry will take you to a humble cottage or that his Hawaiian family will absorb you in its tender, quarrelsome embrace, but it's the fact that you're only seventeen. You have a whole lifetime to be married. Give yourself a few more years of girlhood."

Mummy had said very different things, and Laurie recalled the morning she had come in to awaken her, a task which was usually Lehua's, and had sat on the edge of the bed while Laurie stretched and forced the sleepiness from her mind. Mummy had said, "Darling, it may sound stuffy to you. But believe me that in the long run it's better to marry someone at your own level of society. You'll be happier! If you do otherwise, there are too many difficult adjustments." Laurie, remembering momentarily her uneasiness in Jerry's house, had wondered if there might not be some truth in Mummy's words. And then she had instantly denied it to herself; it was only love that counted.

Answering her mother's rhetorical question concerning eligible young men, Laurie said, "What I want is very simple. I'm just looking for someone with whom I can fall in love." Nanna and Mummy both laughed lightly at these words.

When they reached home, Mummy whispered to Laurie, "You'd better go out and jolly Yukie along a little. She's being obstinate about tonight's dinner." Laurie smiled at the thought of Yukie; she had grown old in their household and had developed the usual stubborn, tyrannical airs of trusted Japanese servants. When Mummy planned a dinner now, she could never be certain that she would find on the table the dishes for which she had asked.

"Hi, Yukie!" Laurie called saucily as she went into the kitchen.

"You no lady. You Kanaka kind girl!" Yukie said contemptuously.

"Sure, I'm Kanaka kind. But that make me more happy, yeah?"

"More silly!"

"Yukie, I hear we're having a Kona dinner tonight."

"That what your Ma says. But you no have anything old Mr. Wendell can digest. All this poi and pork and coconut stuff! By and by he sick. Then you sorry."

"I know what's your trouble, Yukie. You just don't like to grate coconut. You're lazy."

"You one bad girl! Go away. You tease."

"Yukie, you know I love you. I wouldn't tease you for the world."

"Go 'way. You bodda' me. You make Win come. He one good boy; he he'p me."

"Yukie, I'm jealous. I think you love Win more better me."

"That not so. But Win, he like a gentleman. You like a tomboy."

Laurie went over to the old lady, grasped her by the hands, and danced her around the room. "Here we go a-maying, tra la, tra la, tra la!" She whirled Yukie to a dizzy stop and then steadied her. "Now, Yook. Where's the coconut? I'll shred it for you."

Yukie sighed and looked at Laurie. "How you be so bad, so good all same time! Coconut scraper on back lanai."

Laurie sat on the back steps and grated the coconut into a large wooden bowl. She experimented, making different sorts of fancy curls of the meat, and once draped a curl in her hair as an ornament and ran in to show Yukie. The Japanese cook snatched it and threw it in the garbage, mumbling over and over, "You one bad girl!"

Laurie spent the rest of the afternoon making certain, partly by cajolery and partly by assistance, that Yukie would put a Hawaiian dinner on the table. It was to be a family affair in honor of the Bells, and the Wendells were coming over, and Laurie's twin aunts, Jane and Janet, and their husbands and children.

Just before the family was to sit down at dinner, Laurie went secretly to the dining room to tuck some Ixora about in the arrangement of breadfruit and pomelo on the table. She felt not only that the monotony of green should be relieved but that a touch of red would add to the festivity. She had finished and was about to return to the drawing room when the procession came in, headed by Nanna and Father. Laurie stepped unobtrusively to her place and looked at the members of her family seating themselves. Grandma and Grandpa Wendell were together at one end of the wide table. They were the same dignified, ageless, correct people. She acknowledged a connection with them because they were her father's parents, but she could not feel more than a frail and watered affection for them. She regarded Mrs. Wendell with tenuous pity; Laurie knew that the old lady lavished on her a love which was nearly abject, and she was embarrassed, almost appalled, by this emotion of her grandmother. She could not look at her without remembering the innumerable occasions during childhood when Mrs. Wendell had embraced her with impulsive, torturing affection and had stifled her with the fragrance of a musty perfume and the dusty scent of her powdered body. Nanna Wendell seemed artificial to Laurie in the sense that she was like a doll; her flesh did not feel warm and living, encrusted as it was with creams and powders. Her coiffure, though simple, was always exact and carefully netted like a wig. Although Laurie was ashamed of herself, she furtively tried to avoid Nanna Wendell on all occasions.

When the grace spoken by Mr. Wendell was finished, Laurie turned to look at Grandma and Grandpa Bell who were seated in relative positions to the Wendells at the opposite end of the table. Instinctively she smiled, and a flush of affection warmed her when she looked at them. Grandpa was such a dear little wizened Scotsman, filled with a love of teasing and a tender devotion for his grandchildren! And of course Nanna! She was very special in anyone's life. It wasn't that she went out of her way to do anything for you; it was simply that when you were with her, you felt happy and content.

Between these two old couples was seated the rest of the

family, now busily unfolding napkins and removing the lids from the lacquered soup bowls. Mummy was down near the Wendells and Daddy was up near the Bells. Daddy had Aunt Jane and Aunt Janet on either side of him, and Mummy had Uncle Willard and Uncle Joe on either side of her. The children were concentrated toward the center of the table. Win was next to his favorite cousin, Eloise, at thirteen already capturing masculine hearts with her long blonde hair, her fair, transparent skin, and her removed, angelic look. Eloise was Aunt Janet's oldest child. On the other side of Win was Anthony, Eloise's five-year-old brother who looked exactly like Grandpa Bell, so much so that the family laughed about it. Laurie had at her right David, Aunt Jane's son. David was six years old, and he and Laurie were the only two out of the seven cousins who showed distinctly their Hawaiian blood; that created a bond between them, a bond of which they knew the other cousins were jealous. Win and Eloise accused Laurie and David of having secrets and made them miserable by nagging, sometimes persisting so long that Laurie and David ran off to find a spot by themselves. At Laurie's left was Stephen, Eloise's ten-year-old brother, and beyond him was Elizabeth, David's sister, who was as fair as he was dark.

Laurie finished her soup and chattered with David and Stephen. The soup bowls were removed, and Kimi brought in the suckling pig, which she placed before Grandpa Wendell. He carved it with great solemnity and with the sureness of one performing a familiar ritual. Laurie was vaguely sorry for the Wendells this evening, because they could claim so little of this large, gay family. They had said but few words in the course of the dinner and sat in their places of honor as aloof and detached as Chinese ancestral portraits. Surely, Laurie thought, they must feel the distance between themselves and the group, and she wondered if they were lonely.

"Well!" said Aunt Jane. "This is quite a family gathering.

All we need is Tutu, our matriarch, and then everything would be complete."

Grandpa Bell offered, "Tutu is probably much happier at this moment eating her bowl of poi out under the breadfruit tree than she would be sitting here with all of us. And I don't know but what I agree with her. City life's all right for you young 'uns, but . . ."

"Daddy," teased Aunt Janet. "You sound as though you're going Hawaiian on us in your old age—and you without a drop of Kanaka blood for an excuse."

Laurie noticed that her mother put trembling fingers up to her face in a gesture of dismay when Aunt Janet said those words. It was a graceful movement but fearful.

Grandpa answered with a laugh, "It's just the renegade Scotsman in me, Janny." He looked at Mr. Wendell and continued with what Laurie realized must be an attempt to include the Wendells in the conversation. "Winslow, you and I are the oldest people here. Not that I'm sure it's something to boast of. But at least we can accept the prerogatives of age. We can insist that this bevy of strong young people wait on our every wish while we relax at leisure."

"You're right, Macpherson. And this very minute I'll ask one of the pretty girls here to go and fetch my pipe, that is, of course, if dear Martha will allow me to be a crotchety, impolite old man and smoke a pipe in place of the dessert course." He looked questioningly at Martha, who bowed her head and smiled in acquiescence. "Laurie," he continued, "will you go, please? I left it on the library table, I think."

"Of course, Grandpa." Laurie excused herself and went into the library. She quickly found the pipe, a pouch of tobacco, and some matches. She walked back to the dining room and paused on the threshold. The faces around the dinner table glowed palely in the candlelight. Or rather, she corrected herself, all but two were pale. Nanna Bell's was like a deep-colored Madeira wine and David's was a pale golden sherry. She realized that her own would shine with the same color as David's in the candlelight. The three of them were linked by this color, a bond mystical and warm. As she stood there regarding her family, the fair and the dark, she felt she knew suddenly what it was that Father meant when he told her she must make a suitable marriage, and why he was so stern about it. He wanted to be able to look around his family dinner table in years to come and see candlelight glimmering upon fair-skinned grandchildren. With this thought something started in her she had never known before, a painful gnawing sensation which set her heart beating wildly; she felt certain her father was ashamed of the darkness in her Hawaiian blood. That's why he had hated Jerry with such intensity, Jerry who would have brought more Hawaiian to the mixture. She wanted to turn and run from them all, but Grandpa Wendell's voice called out, "Come, child, what are you waiting for?"

III

Nanna Bell spent the greater part of the next three days at the doctor's office, and the family lived in a mood of increasing anxiety. A breathless, intent atmosphere settled over the house; Yukie and Kimi tiptoed about, and even Win tried to step lightly with his overgrown boy's feet. Laurie and Win heard the murmur of their parents' voices in the library each evening, a murmur suggestive in its tone of sorrow. Grandpa Bell paced up and down in the garden, his hands clasped behind him and his head bowed; his pipe was tightly clenched in his teeth, but it remained unfilled and unlit.

Laurie spent most of the three days hugging her ukulele in her room. Mummy urged her to go to the beach for a swim, to her friends' parties, to the Hartwells', but she stanchly refused. "How can I have a good time when my mind is on Nanna?" she asked indignantly. She remembered constantly the fearful thought she had had in the shower, but she did not want to worry her mother with it and bottled it up, tormenting herself.

On the fourth day Daddy asked her to come into the library in the late afternoon. When she arrived, she found Win already there, sitting in the big leather-covered chair. He looked small and pale in it.

"Sit down, dear," Daddy said, and Laurie perched tensely on the edge of the obi-covered sofa. Daddy continued, "I'm afraid I have something very tragic to tell you children, and I want you to be brave about it. Take it like Wendells."

Laurie felt moisture spring out on the palms of her hands and a dizziness in her head. She grasped the arm of the sofa and watched her father intently while he continued.

"The doctors have examined Nanna Bell very thoroughly, and their diagnosis is a most unhappy one. Your dear Nanna has cancer, and she has but a few months to live."

"Gosh, Dad!" Win exclaimed. "How awful!" Laurie saw the consternation and horror on his face and felt a moment of tenderness for him. Her own voice was locked in her throat, and she could not utter a word.

"Now, I want you children," Daddy went on hastily, "to be kind to Nanna and thoughtful of her. But you must be very careful not to give her the feeling that your kindness comes because you know she is going to die. Treat her as you always have; tease her a little and love her a little. She is being very brave about it. As a matter of fact it is your Grandfather Bell who is the person most upset. He is an old man who loves his wife very dearly. This is more difficult for him than for any of the rest of us. He has shut himself in his room, and you must under no circumstances disturb him. Your mother too is upset, but she is a courageous woman, and she has the consolation of knowing that the three of us are always ready to help her."

Laurie rose from the sofa and asked in a faint voice, "May I go now, Daddy?"

"Yes, dear. If you're all right."

"I'm all right, Daddy," she said and waved aside his offered assistance. She closed the library door very softly and overheard her father's words, "Win, old thing, we've got to be men together in this."

She went down the hallway and up the stairs with the vague idea of getting her flute and then walking over to the hillside and up the slope a way where she could play to herself. When she reached the top of the stairs, she passed the door to Grandpa Bell's room. In her mind flashed a vision of him, as she imagined him to be, standing at the window, his body motionless but tears streaming down his face. She wanted to rush in and throw her arms about him, but she remembered Daddy's warning. Next to Grandpa's was Nanna's door. Laurie tiptoed past it. What was it like, she wondered, to know you were going to die in just a few months? How would it feel? It must be a fearful thing! . . . Also, it might be a—an awesome thing; you could pray and feel closer to God. You could even visit the plot in the cemetery, sit on the cool grass, and think, "Someday I will be part of this grass forever and ever. And my bones will be in this earth, and over them in the sky such pure clouds as these will travel for centuries." And then would come the bitter realization that when your bones were lying in the soil, you could no longer look up at the clouds or feel the grass.

A sense of the horrible loneliness of death beset Laurie, and she ran to her room, slammed the door behind her, and threw herself on the bed. She was surprised that no tears came, only a hotness to her hands and her forehead. After a while she sat up and toyed with the tufts of her candlewick spread. She reached for her ukulele and strummed softly the song *"Mai Poina Oe I'au."*

The thought of her mother came to her, a strong, impelling thought. It was almost as though she felt Mummy calling for her. She rose from the bed, put her ukulele back on the shelf, and started toward her mother's room. When she reached the door, she tapped softly.

A faint voice asked, "Who is it?"

"It's me, Laurie."

"Come in, dear."

Laurie opened the door just wide enough to slip into the room. She saw her mother sitting on the chaise longue looking pale and self-contained. Her hair was perfectly groomed in the way she wore it now, brushed up into a roll around her face. She had on a tailored, lime-colored negligee, and her feet were bare. Laurie paused a moment appreciating the sad, graceful picture she made. "Mummy, I thought maybe . . ." she started, and when she saw her mother raise her arms, offering an embrace, she ran and threw herself into them. "Mummy, it's awful, awful!" she sobbed against Martha's neck.

When there were no more tears, Laurie sat up beside her mother and took her hand. "I'm sorry to be so, so . . ." she left off lamely.

"You'll feel better now, darling."

"Mummy, why can't they do anything about it? Isn't there a thing?"

"It's one of the diseases in which medical science fails." Laurie noticed a shrill tightness in her mother's voice.

"Mummy, dear, you're just terribly upset, aren't you!"

"There is nothing in all the world to protect one from the agony of this kind of thing. All the careful little controls and strivings of a lifetime are smashed." Laurie watched her with growing anxiety as she poured out her words. "Laurie, isn't it easier just to get down on your knees and wail against the cruelty of disease and death! Our ancestors did just that. Tutu's wise enough to do just that. But the most we dare is to shut ourselves in our rooms and when someone knocks, answer steadily so that they know our grief is carefully schooled. And they'll tell all the world how brave we are!" Martha's voice had reached a strident pitch at the end.

Laurie, only vaguely understanding her mother's words, looked at her tense face and blurted out, "Mummy, you don't have to be brave with me. I'm your daughter."

"One must be brave before one's children. It's expected."

"Maybe Win. But not me."

Laurie felt her mother's eyes upon her, and shyly she turned to look into them. They were even darker when they were filled with tears. For a moment Laurie felt that she gazed deep into a worn tide pool, where an ancient rhythm of the coming and going of the sea and of the living and dying of water creatures had established a frightening beauty. Her mother's eyes had an almost hypnotic effect upon her, but she continued to look bravely at them. trying to show that she was not afraid of whatever emotion her mother might show.

In a husky voice Martha said, "You're right, Laurie. With Win, but not with you."

Laurie put out her arms, and her mother yielded, leaning against her breast. Laurie felt the coming of the storm, the sharp fingers pressing into the flesh of her arms and finally the stertorous rhythm of fierce dry sobs. She clasped her mother tightly and rocked her back and forth. She didn't know why she rocked, but the motion was soothing, and for the first time in her life she felt stronger than her mother. It was almost as though Mummy were a child. She hummed in her mother's ears little words which came to her, "Mummy, dear! Sweet Mummy! Cry all you want. Darling Mummy!"

The violence of Martha's sobbing abated, but Laurie continued to rock her back and forth. The room was quiet, peaceful once again. They both heard the gentle opening of the door and saw Win standing in the doorway. He looked at his mother, and slowly an expression of shock came upon his face. "Gosh, Mom!" he gasped.

Martha pushed Laurie away, and hiding her countenance

from Win hurried into the dressing room. She saw in the wall mirror her swollen blotched skin and started daubing powder on her face. "Win, come in," she called.

"Mummy," said Laurie quietly. "He's gone already."

"Then he must come back! . . . Darling, will you bring me my white linen with the aqua border." Martha worked at her face, bathing it in cologne, massaging it with cream, and Laurie stood at her side waiting, holding the dress in her arms.

"Run now, Laurie, and bring Win back. It's important."

"Mummy?" Laurie ventured. "Are you . . . are you . . . you know!"

Martha took the dress and slipped it over her head. She zipped up the side with a deft movement and fastened the belt. Then she took Laurie's arm and walked her toward the door. "I'm fine now, Laurie. Please find Win for me and bring him here."

Laurie opened the door and went on her mother's bidding. She found Win in his room, looking out the window.

"Mother wants you," she said.

Win remained with his back to her, but he said, "Gosh, I've never seen her like that before."

"Well, forget about it. She's all right now."

Win turned away from the window, and Laurie saw that his face was pale and his eyes big and shocked. His hands almost seemed to tremble. "She must be just—just tortured."

"Buck up, Win. Mother's the same as ever. After all, a woman can cry at a time like this, if she wants."

"Of course. But I just . . ."

"Skip it. Come on. She's waiting."

He moved to go but let Laurie pass through the doorway first. She smiled a little to herself. Daddy's insistence on courtesy to women was already beginning to be instinctive with Win.

"Now just be normal," she warned as they went down the hall.

"I'm normal. I'm always normal."

When they reached their mother's room, Laurie opened the door and pushed Win in ahead of her.

"Hello, children," Martha greeted them. She was sitting in the middle of the chaise longue. In the white dress and with her hair more loosely brushed than usual, she looked young and almost happy. The unsightliness had gone from her skin, and it was now the usual smooth gold. Martha patted the chaise longue on each side of her. "Come, a seat for both of you."

Laurie and Win sat down as they were bidden. Martha put an arm about each of them. "I know that Daddy has told you children of the fearful tragedy which has come to Nanna . . ."

Laurie noticed that her mother's voice had assumed its polished tone. She glanced at Win. The relief on his face was so obvious that he seemed almost to smile. The ruddiness had returned to his skin, and he was an untroubled boy again. Laurie turned her attention to her mother's words.

". . . brave. Yes, we must be brave at all times—when we are alone and with each other as well as when we are with Nanna. Our whole thought must be to help her bear this frightful thing and to fill her with our love so that when she thinks of the darkness, she may be wrapped in warmth."

The next morning was cool and noisy with trade winds. When Laurie rose from bed, she moved, still in her nightgown, to the cushioned window seat and curled up on it, clasping her knees. The palm trees, a deep midnight green marked with stripes of silver, were sharp against the sallow morning sky; she sat absorbing this beauty, trying to push remembrance of Nanna from her. But the word cancer—evil, cruelly curved as a savage fist—was not to be routed from her mind. Now the two syllables were like a chant, beating in the rhythm of her blood against the hollow of her throat. Perhaps, she thought, if she could pray, it would help. Prayer—the idea reminded her of old Mrs. Wellington who spoke her devotions aloud in church; she had been deeply attached to her husband and was distraught at his death, but she had found comfort in talking to God. Laurie knew this because often she was in the pew ahead of Mrs. Wellington and heard her repeating the service to herself in the husky whisper of the aged; when the time had come to pray for those "afflicted or distressed in mind, body, or estate," Mrs. Wellington had boldly prayed for herself, adding, "especially Thy servant, Elizabeth."

Laurie and Win and their friends had laughed at Mrs. Wellington and behind her back called her "thy servant, Lizzie." Laurie felt a warmth of shame mantling her throat and cheeks. How unkind they had been toward the poor old lady. . . .

She looked again at the coconut and mango trees swaying and trembling in the trades, and she heard their music. Such wind and blowing of trees often filled her with a spasm of joy at her own being, but that mood seemed gross this morning. She slipped from the cushioned window seat to her knees on the floor. "Dear God," she said aloud. And then as words were hard in coming, inadequate, she allowed herself to feel intensely for a minute. Before rising, she muttered, ". . . and help Nanna."

While she was dressing, she thought of how inarticulate she was before God and of why it should be. All through her childhood she had been sent to Sunday school, and now that she was grown, Mummy and Daddy took her to St. Andrew's almost every Sunday. The service of Morning Prayer was so familiar in her ears that with Canon Stokely reading, she never needed to refer to the prayer book. But strangely, without his guiding voice she could not remember more than the Lord's Prayer and the Creed.

Downstairs she found Win sitting alone at the table. She smiled when she saw him twirling his spoon in a bowl of cream of wheat; he would have to eat all of the cereal before he could have the coveted sausages. Yukie was a tyrant and saw to it that he finished the cereal—every spoonful.

"Cheez, I wish I were sixteen!" he lamented.

"Come on, baby, eat it up," Laurie teased him. She remembered the pleasure of her sixteenth birthday when the cereal bowl had disappeared from her place at table. "It won't be long now."

She sat in her chair and squeezed lemon juice over her papaya. "Where's everybody?"

"Mom's eating upstairs with Nanna. Dad had to go to Kahuku early this morning."

"What're you going to do today?"

"Some kids and I are going up Tantalus to hunt land shells."

"Does Mum know?"

"Sure! Yukie's fixing a lunch for us."

"I almost wish I could go with you."

"You've got to go to Grandma Wendell's this morning."

"Yeah, I know. Too bad it's so close to yesterday. . . ."

"Maybe Grandma won't want to go."

"Oh, she'd get off her deathbed to go. . . . I don't mind too much ordinarily. And from her pictures Aunty Laurie looks as though she might have been a pretty little girl."

"Too old-fashioned."

"Don't be so stupid. Thirty or forty years from now your pictures will look old-fashioned too."

"Thirty or forty years!" he grunted and helped himself to a generous portion of sausages and fried pineapple. He took a large mouthful. "Umm!" he said.

"You certainly look greedy."

"Glad I don't have to worry about my figure like you."

"Well, you'd better. You're a chubby enough little rascal."

"You're just jealous because all you eat is papaya and coffee."

She finished her cup of coffee and rising from the table said, "Good-by! Don't fall down the mountain."

She went through the kitchen into the garden to pick a spray of flowers for Aunty Laurie's grave. This was the day each year she and Nanna Wendell went to the cemetery with flowers. When she was a small girl, Laurie had hated the obligation and had often lamented to Mummy about her name. But after she had begun to read poems and romantic tales, the cemetery had become a beautiful and interesting place, and she enjoyed strolling under its plumeria and shower trees and hunting for curious tombstones. Also, Nanna Wendell by the stories she told on these excursions had made Aunty Laurie live as a real person, and Laurie began to imagine her as a cherished companion whose face and form were like the Madonna in the Fra Angelico reproduction which Mummy had in her dressing room. And the fact that they bore the same name became a mysterious, significant bond. For several years Laurie had confided to this lovely phantom her innermost secrets—until Jerry Wakinekona came along.

Laurie picked a full, rich bouquet of begonias and framed it in fern fronds. She sprayed the bouquet with water. Then she went to the dressing room off the back lanai and combed her hair and put on her shoes. She glanced hurriedly at herself in the mirror and decided she looked neat enough to go to Nanna Wendell's house.

Nanna Wendell was sitting in a pool of sunlight on the side lanai. She had a pale blue chiffon scarf tied about her throat and a challis shawl over her legs and feet.

"Hello, dear child," she greeted Laurie. "My, what lovely flowers you have today."

"Have you got a cold?" Laurie asked abruptly as she noticed the scarves.

"No. Just a little achiness. And my throat seems sore."

"I hope it's not flu."

"Oh, no! I'll be all right in a day or two."

While Mrs. Wendell said those words, Laurie had the sudden feeling that she was inventing the illness. But what could be her reason? The old lady held out her arm toward her granddaughter and as she did so, Laurie was aware of the strong, musky scent of her perfume. Nanna Wendell needed only to rustle her clothes a bit, and this aroma escaped clumsily into the air. She said, "We are terribly sorry, dear Laurie, about sweet Nanna Bell. It's—one just hasn't words to express it."

Laurie listened to her grandmother's soft, high voice with its slight southern accent and wondered what thoughts were really in her mind. She had always felt that Mrs. Wendell instinctively stiffened whenever she was with Nanna Bell and only reluctantly offered her a hand or cheek in friendship. Yet Nanna Wendell was drawn to Nanna Bell, just as everyone else was. Perhaps if Nanna Wendell could be assured that she never actually had to touch Nanna Bell. . . .

"Shall we go now?" Laurie asked suddenly and saw that she had startled her grandmother.

"Well, I think—that is, the day is rather windy, and I'm not feeling quite well—and—well, I think today we'll not go. Our Laurie will forgive us and perhaps in a week or two we can go."

"Shall I go alone? I have these nice begonias."

"That's very sweet of you, darling," Mrs. Wendell said, and tears filled her eyes. "But you, sweet child, have enough to—er—think of today."

And then Laurie realized: Grandmother Wendell in her gentle, circuitous way was trying to spare her further remembrance of death so close upon yesterday's sorrow. She was even pretending illness. Laurie thought indignantly, "What utter nonsense to be so excessively delicate about it! Why not say, 'There's enough unhappiness in your family today! We'll not visit Laurie's grave.' "

"All right, Nanna," she said. "Why don't you keep the flowers? After all, you're sick. Good-by!" she called and ran down the steps.

IV

The first time Laurie saw her Grandfather Bell after the doctor's diagnosis of Nanna's illness, she was shocked. He had changed from a weather-toughened, wiry, energetic man to a slight, frail-looking person from whom all sturdiness seemed to have been drained. He was coming out of his room for the first time in four days just as Laurie went by to go downstairs. She smiled at him with affection and said, "Hello, Grandpa." She was pleased with the casualness she had achieved in her manner.

He looked at her, and as he did so, a little fire of enthusiasm sparked into his eyes. "Laurie!" he exclaimed. "You dear child for coming by at this very moment!" His tone implied that a refreshing idea had just come to him. "Where's your mother?" he went on. "We must find her."

"She's in the lath house, I think. Choosing orchids for the show." Laurie looked carefully at her grandfather's face, trying to imagine what thought had struck him.

"Come on then, let's go," he said and taking her arm in a firm, urgent grip marched her down the stairs and out to the lath house. "Martie!" he called as they drew near.

"Yes, Daddy," Martha replied. Laurie noticed she used her polished voice; she was probably thinking so much of the orchid show that she had not realized fully it was Grandpa to whom she was speaking. "Here I am," she continued.

He opened the door and ushered Laurie in ahead of him. "Martha, it has come to me! What we need—Ululani and I."

"Daddy, how nice to see you!" Martha exclaimed, seeming to ignore his words and now using her intimate voice.

"Never mind me right now. I've come to ask a favor of you. And it concerns Laurie here. Martie, your mother—and I too—need Laurie in Kona. Let her come and be with us until . . . the end. Her presence will be a constant reminder to Ululani that life continues as beautifully as ever."

"Daddy!" Martha gulped. She sat down involuntarily on a low stool. "Let me catch my breath! . . . I had hoped and planned that you and Mummy would stay here."

"Martha," he said sadly, "how far from us you have grown! You know that your mother would want to die in Kona. She wants to return right now. Only yesterday she said, 'I can't bear it. So little time left and to be away from Kona. Let's hurry home, Macpherson.' "

"Of course, I should have known," Martha murmured. "She would feel that way. . . . But you must give me a chance to explain it to Winslow."

Mr. Bell turned abruptly to Laurie. "Poor wee thing! I haven't even asked you if you cared to come with us. Forgive me!" His look was tender and eager.

Laurie's words came out of her mouth almost before she realized it. "I would like to come, Grandpa." After they were said, she began to think of what they meant. She was timid about living in a house where death was imminent. Could she behave naturally toward Nanna? Yet she must go, because they wanted her.

Grandpa Bell's next words came huskily. "It won't be easy. Especially toward the last."

"I'll be there then, Father," said Martha.

"But even with you. . . . She's young, sensitive—"

"Don't worry about me, Grandpa," said Laurie. "I can do this for Nanna." She picked a white Phalaenopsis and pinned it in her hair. "How soon do you think we must go?"

"As soon as possible. In a couple of days, probably."

"Mummy, may I go out to see Mele now?" Laurie asked. "I want to say good-by to her today. If I'm not back for dinner, don't worry."

"Go ahead, Laurie. But be careful driving over the Pali. The traffic is so frightful now."

"I will. G'by, both of you," she said and started toward the house.

Laurie hurried up to her room and changed from her dress into an old pair of white gabardine slacks, which she rolled up to just below her knees. She pulled on over the slacks a green-and-white-striped T shirt. After brushing her hair vigorously with a few strokes, she tied it with a ribbon at the nape of her neck and tucked the Phalaenopsis in the ribbon. She felt the slacks cool along her legs and the T shirt easy against her back; it was a fine sensation, almost as though she were relieved already from the atmosphere of a house of grief. She took her flute and lauhala purse and ran downstairs and out to the garage for the car which she and Martha shared. In the car was the familiar odor of grease and sun-warmed upholstery. She started the engine and raced it. Although Daddy had always warned her against racing it to warm it up, she continued to do so because it gave her a thrilling sense of power. The smell of the fumes whirled about her, and she backed the car out of the garage in a rush of speed.

On the Pali road she was delayed behind a slow truck, and the stream of traffic up the mountain was so continual that she dared not pass. She could lean back against the seat and, keeping her hands firmly on the wheel, glance from time to time at the steepy landscape. This view of the Kaneohe mountains and the sea never failed to fill her with a quiver of excitement. The first glimpse of it always recalled poignantly her happiness at the Hartwells'—swimming, charcoal-broiled steaks, fragrances of ginger and salty seaweed. Today the mountains had shreds of clouds wreathing their peaks and hiding the mysteries of their deeply etched crevices; what could be seen of their precipitous flanks was a rich dark green, thickly foliaged. The sea was its usual mingling of blues, greens, and violets. When her first brief ecstasy at seeing this beauty again was gone, she began to notice the war scars of the countryside, the abandoned tent and shack cities of the Army and the Marines lying drab against the red, gouged-out earth. The feeling she knew so well began to boil within her, an anger piercing as wind-whipped rain pellets. She realized that these camps had been necessary, but she hated them. The war had stirred a bitterness in Laurie which even now, many months after the fighting was over, she could not control. She hated the destruction and the ugliness caused by large encampments of men. She hated the insults heaped upon Hawaii and the assumption by many of the men that the islands were nothing but a military fort and that the residents could be shifted, ordered, forced about at military whim. She had resented the imposition of regulations long after the need for them was past and had trembled at the stories told at her father's dinner table of injustice and oppression suffered by luckless souls in the provost courts and even in their own homes. Above all, she was concerned over the racial hatreds brought to Hawaii by the influx of multitudes of strangers. She waged her own private battle against these prejudiced visitors, and whenever she came upon one, poured out a lecture of hot, impetuous words.

Laurie knew that she did not think altogether justly or coolly about the problems the war had thrust upon Hawaii. But she could not prevent herself from growing rigid with a defiant sorrow. Sometimes she yearned to escape to a spot ignorant of, and untouched by, the injustice, cruelty, and hatreds she had seen in the past few years. The men of the armed services were fine and gallant on the battlefield, in the hospitals, and as she met them in her own and her friends' homes. But there had been those she met every day on the streets and in the restaurants of Honolulu, drunken, insulting, blaspheming men from whom she recoiled in horror. Once she had asked her mother, "Mummy, can these be American men?"

When she finally reached the bottom of the Pali road, she swung around the truck and turned toward Waikane. Driving through Kaneohe and Heeia, she stared hard at the road whenever passing an abandoned tent city or a training center, and bitterness remained like alum on her tongue. She was thankful that the stretch of countryside between Waiahole Valley and

Waikane had been untouched. How lucky the Hartwells had been! In their broad view of the sea and mountains, there was not a single military installation visible.

She turned into the driveway at the Parken place and stopped the engine. "Mele," she called, jumping out, "Mele!"

Mele appeared at the back door. "Laurie! How swell to see you! We've missed you!"

"I've been pretty busy lately; Grandma and Grandpa Bell have been visiting us."

"How perfectly elegant! They're such old dears. . . . Come on in. I've got a surprise."

"What is it?"

"You'll see."

Laurie ran up the back steps, and Mele grasped her hand, leading her through the kitchen and toward the living room. In the kitchen Laurie sniffed at the chicken Asano was frying and determined to accept the invitation to dinner which the Hartwells would certainly extend. She looked through the door to the living room and saw a stranger, a young man, sitting there. A moment of disappointment crossed her; if they were having guests, they might not ask her to dinner.

"Who's that?" she whispered to Mele.

"Wait, you'll see! . . . Mom, Dad! Look who's here."

Felicity came to the doorway and exclaimed, "Laurie, dear! How nice! Come in and meet our visitor."

Felicity moved toward Laurie, put her arm around her waist, and led her into the living room, straight up to the stranger. "Laurie, I want you to meet Mele's brother, Hal Phillipson. This is Laurie Wendell, our dearest friend."

Laurie searched Hal for any resemblance to Mele. The curved lines about the mouth and the breadth of the forehead were the same. But Hal was darker than Mele, more like a full-blooded Hawaiian. She said, "Hello, Hal," and looked into his eyes to show that she felt warmly toward him because of Mele. The expression in his eyes was penetrating, and it rebuffed her.

She was suddenly engulfed in shyness. This made her angry with herself as well as somewhat angry with Hal that he should arouse such a feeling in her. She mumbled, "I'm happy to meet you," and in an agony to escape him, turned to Solomon and said, "Hello, Uncle Sol!"

In her confusion, she stumbled against a footstool and sat down abruptly on it. "Oh! How clumsy I am!"

"What's the matter with you, Laurie?" Mele asked. "You're acting too, too dopey."

"Oh, it's nothing," she answered. She ventured to look at Hal again, and although his glance was more friendly, she felt the same uneasy shyness; her pulse throbbed loudly in her ears. She was disgusted with herself, and to cover up her perplexity, plunged into the story of Nanna Bell.

"The most horrible thing has happened to our family. Nanna went to the doctor, and he told her she has cancer and that she has only a few months left to live. It's just like the end of everything, and we're all so confused!" The words tumbled from her.

Mele sat down on the footstool with Laurie and hugged her. "Laurie, darling, no wonder you're acting dopey. It's too awful!"

Felecity sat on the floor in front of Laurie and took her hand. "Is there anything we can do?"

"Nothing," Laurie replied. "There's really nothing to be done."

"And how's your mummy?"

"Mummy!" Laurie said and looked with tear-filled eyes straight into Felicity's. "Oh, you know Mummy. She's a brick."

"She's really quite . . . all right?"

"Yes. She got over the shock—she let it out of her."

"I'm glad. She needs to do that."

Laurie glanced over Lissie's shoulder in time to see Sol and Hal tiptoeing from the room, and she felt more comfortable.

The oppressive excitement left her, and she sighed involuntarily. Mele must have felt her relax, because she released her from the embrace.

"I'm going over to Kona to stay till the end. That's what I came to tell you. We're flying probably day after tomorrow—Grandpa, Nanna, and I. Mummy will come for the last month. And probably at the very last, Win and Daddy."

"You're a brave girl, Laurie," murmured Felicity.

"Not too brave. Besides, I'll enjoy it in Kona. . . . Let's talk about something else."

"Of course, Laurie. . . . Tell us. What do you think of Hal? He's Mele's oldest brother." Her eyes fogged with memory as she continued, "I recall him very distinctly the day I went to get Mele. He was sitting in the middle of a mud puddle and was holding a puppy tightly to his breast. Both he and the puppy were filthy. I laughed at the two of them, and he looked up at me with great wistful, chiding eyes. He succeeded in making me feel rather ashamed of myself—almost shy."

"He's quite good-looking," Laurie said in a noncommittal tone.

"Laurie Wendell, he's handsome!" broke in Mele. "Gosh, it sure is a funny feeling though, to have a brother and yet not to have one."

"He's your brother all right," said Felicity. "Now, Laurie, what about it? Can you stay for dinner?"

"Thank you. I'd love to." She looked mischievously at Lissie. "How could I refuse when I saw the chicken frying!"

"You're a rascal," Lissie said. "Now go and hunt for the men, you two. We're eating in about forty-five minutes."

Laurie and Mele went out the front door and down onto the lawn. "Mele, have we time to go up to the gulch?"

"Sure. We can hurry."

"I'd like to go up there just once before I go to Kona."

The girls made their way through the grove of mango trees, across two hilly meadows bordered by old, lichen-encrusted rock walls, and started over a third. Halfway across, they came to a stream which had cut for itself fifteen-foot banks, almost perpendicular. At the bottom of the banks was a little valley floor about twenty feet wide which was thickly overgrown with guavas and occasional monkeypods. The stream twisted and tumbled round the boulders and the trees and over little falls. Laurie and Mele climbed down the steep sides and went to a spot where lush grass grew under a large, spreading guava. The light in the ravine was crepuscular, tinctured with a lingering hint of the unknown. Not a sound was heard, not even the wind through the trees, and there was a dank, woodsy scent to the air.

They sat down close to one another. Laurie thought of all the times since they were seven years old that they had come to this place and sat in this way. It was their secret spot, and they had told no one of it. Here they had plotted all of their childhood schemes and once a year held a mystical candlelight ceremony to cement their friendship. Under that hoary old rock was buried the metal strongbox in which they kept the candles and the crude wooden image which had been part of the ceremony. It had been four years since they had dug the box up, and Laurie imagined that it must be rusted away by now and the wooden figure full of termites. In this spot she had first told Mele that she was in love with Jerry, and they had whispered together in excitement. Once, in an ecstasy of adolescent religious fervor, they had made a little altar on the flat-topped rock; Laurie had brought from town the large black onyx cross which belonged to Grandma Wendell, and they had propped it up against a little screen of greenery. On each side they had placed candles and vases of meadow flowers. But they had soon grown tired of it, because once they had the altar set up, they didn't know quite what to do next.

Now they were here again in "their spot." Laurie wondered if perhaps it would be the last time. In the past year, she had wondered that every time they came to the gulch. The darkling atmosphere and the farawayness renewed the spirit of mystery about it, but their necessity for that kind of place was disappearing.

Mele broke the silence. "Whatcha thinking about?"

"I was remembering all of the things we used to do here."

"We did some silly things, didn't we!"

"They seem silly to us now. But then we were very serious."

"Yes. Remember the time we thought we saw a ghost?"

"I was certaintly scared. The place still kind of scares me in a way. It's so unnaturally still and dark. Have you ever thought how strange it is that the stream makes almost no noise?"

"Laurie, for heaven's sake! You're giving me the creeps."

"But it is strange."

"Uh-huh . . . Laurie—" Mele carefully pulled up a blade of grass and nibbled the tender, whitish end. She seemed embarrassed. "Laurie, I—uh . . ."

Laurie waited a minute and then asked, "Is something bothering you?"

"Yes. I s'pose it's silly." She paused for a long moment. Then with a sigh she said, "I wish Hal weren't my brother!"

"You wish Hal weren't your brother!"

"Yes. Because, because, well—I'm afraid I'm falling in love with him!"

"Oh, Mele, darling! How awful! How did he ever happen to come to your house anyway?"

"Mother ran across him in town the other day, and in her uncanny way recognized him. She brought him out to stay with us for a week. I've had to avoid him somewhat."

"It's a shame!"

"Laurie, I wish you'd fallen in love with him. Then I wouldn't be tempted."

"Oh, Mele, he's not my type."

"No. I suppose he isn't. All I can say is thank heaven he's going back to town day after tomorrow. And I hope I never see him again!"

"You probably never will, Mele."

"The thing I'm worried about is that Mother will try to keep track of him."

"Tell her you'd rather not. Pretend you don't like him—something like that."

"I guess I'll have to. You know Mother; she's so friendly." Mele looked at her watch and exclaimed, "We've got to go! Half an hour has passed, and we haven't found the men. Let's hurry!"

At the dinner table, Laurie's uneasiness in the presence of Hal came back upon her; it was made more poignant by the knowledge of Mele's trouble. Every time Laurie looked at him, he seemed to be looking at her. Finally she dared not glance in his direction, but kept her eyes on her own plate or on Mele. It was embarrassing, she thought, this curious thing which was always drawing her eyes and Hal's to each other.

Soon after dinner she excused herself and said that she must be on her way or her mother would be worried.

"Will you be all right alone?" Felicity asked anxiously.

"Of course. After all, I did night canteen work."

Hal shook her hand in farewell, and her palm tingled when she drew it away. It was like the stirring of blood after her hand had "gone to sleep."

On the way home her thought turned persistently to Hal. To remember him was much pleasanter than to be with him. From a distance he seemed a quiet, sympathetic person; she could not recall a single clumsy remark or action. And yet, when he looked at her there was that embarrassment. She remembered his eyes distinctly with an almost scientific detail. They were large and dark brown, and around the iris the white was bluish and brilliant; she suspected that the eyes bulged a little to make the whites appear so prominent. In the darkness of the iris were occasional yellowish flecks. His eyelashes were long and reminded her of delicate stamens. She smiled to herself as the thought came that he had beautiful eyes, more like a girl's.

She wondered where Hal lived; no one had mentioned it. Several years ago she had overheard Aunt Lissie telling someone in detail about getting Mele, how difficult it had been to find the place, and what a poor, tumbled-down little shack it was when she reached there. Aunt Lissie had told of entering the house and being dismayed by the scantiness of furniture and the untidyness. However, after five minutes' talk with Mele's mother, the shack had taken on a romantic aura, and the fact that the children slept in a row on the floor with only two thicknesses of lauhala matting for a bed became in Lissie's mind a healthy, Spartan way of living. A fresh sea wind blew through the house constantly, and during the day the sun beat upon the mats and baked them with its clean heat. Hal had then been the little boy clutching the puppy. What would growing up in that environment have done to him? Laurie wondered. Could he be as nice as Mele?

She swung into the garage with a startling suddenness. Her whole drive had been absorbed in thinking of Hal. When she was out of the car, she walked slowly up the path and across the awai bridge. A little shudder of unhappiness made her stumble when she thought of her father's reaction if he knew that she had spent so much time thinking of the Hawaiian boy.

Later, when she was undressing for bed, a tap sounded on her door and Mummy came in. "Laurie, darling," she said, "everything is arranged now, and you're going on the late afternoon plane tomorrow."

"So soon? But how can I be ready!" Laurie felt a blade cutting across her mind; the change was coming too quickly.

"We'll just pack a suitcase with your slacks and shorts and a dress or two. You won't need much. And later I can send you some boxes of things."

"Oh, Mother, do you think I can do it?" An emotion she couldn't define was growing within her.

"You are the only one who can really help Nanna, Laurie."

"I wonder if that's true. . . . You know," she said despairingly, "I'm such a failure about everything except the Red Cross. Daddy can't understand why I'm so stupid and idle since the war ended. And I know you're always afraid I'll do something horrible—something dramatic, maybe, and disgrace everybody. Even Win says I'm not like other people."

"Laurie, what is this you're saying? How did your little mind get so full of these ridiculous ideas?" Martha went to her daughter and took her hands. "Dear child, what's the matter with you? If you don't want to go to Kona, say so now."

"Oh, I want to go! I want more than anything to help Nanna Bell," Laurie cried and felt words moving within her. She poured them out. "But, Mother, year after year things pile up, and I get to know that you and all the Wendells are scared to death of everything I do for fear I'll be a disgrace. Especially since Jerry." When she mentioned Jerry, she remembered how much she had thought of Hal Phillipson on the way home. If Mummy knew that!

"Laurie, the Wendells are your family and they love you. That is why they are concerned about what you do. Perhaps it has been too smothering a concern for you. But remember it grows out of a deep love for you."

"I don't like that kind of love!" Laurie rebelled. "I want something warm that accepts me the way I am. It's like Nanna Wendell the other day—being so considerate and not taking me to Aunty Laurie's grave. But how did she do it? She made me think first that she was ill, then that she was holding back something, and finally that I was a child who could not face the truth. Mother, why can't they come right out? They're always trying to appear to overlook the sad or unpleasant things."

"That is their way, dear. They live by quiet manners and a careful propriety."

"But I don't like it! Sometimes I just want to go outdoors

and scream and scream and scream! There's something inside of me that's too closed up."

Laurie felt her mother's arms warmly about her and heard the muttered words, "My little Kona child; you feel too much!" Laurie resented these words, for they separated her from her mother. She released herself from the embrace and calmed by the feeling of separation, said, "I guess we'd better get my things together." She knew Martha's eyes were upon her, questioning, unhappy. But she went stolidly to her dressing room and began pulling clean blouses out of a drawer.

Her mother's next words came clearly, separately as the first few large drops of a shower. "In Kona, Laurie, you will find your way. Consider it, enjoy it, find out if it's what you really want. Nanna and Tutu will show you, although they'll not be conscious of it. But, Laurie, don't forget us. We really love you."

"Oh, Mum, I know it! I'm terrible!" Laurie cried and flung herself into her mother's arms. "I'll miss you—awfully."

V

The first morning in Kona, Laurie unpacked her suitcases and put her things away. She smiled at the thought that there was no Lehua to spoil her at the Bells'. But she enjoyed the work and imagined that she was settling in her own home while she made her bed, laid her linen in neat piles in the chest of drawers, and hung up her dresses in the closet. She even rearranged the furniture to suit her own taste. Nanna had reminded her that the room was Mummy's, and she felt a comfortable sense of the presence of her mother. What could Mummy have been like when she was a girl? Laurie stood quietly for a moment, trying to picture her mother as a little girl with long black hair and childish rounded cheeks. Mummy was so beautifully grown-up, so polished and graceful that surely she could never have been a clumsy, uncertain child.

The room was small with only two windows which looked out to the sea. The line of the steep-sloping roof imposed itself upon the walls, shaping the room curiously and giving it strange little corner nooks. Laurie rather liked the smallness; somehow one could fill it with oneself. In Honolulu, her bedroom was large, with bath and dressing room adjoining, and it never seemed completely a part of her; even now, four years after the decorator had redone it, there were portions which Laurie had left untouched by her own personality.

When she had finished unpacking and had found a place on the bookshelf for her ukulele and flute, she sat on the bed a moment to look at the room, to establish herself in it. The spread and curtains were a pallid, splotchy blue. She must ask Nanna if she couldn't dye them a nice rich green or even a warm gray, and then she could put a yellowish border around them. She lay back upon the bed and examined the sloping walls of the room. Up in one dark corner was a large spider teetering on his long legs. She stared at it with vaguely focused eyes, consciously creating for herself the illusion that it was a huge creature inhabiting all of the ceiling. As her imagination played upon the spider, she felt lonely, almost afraid in the little room. What lay ahead of her in Kona was obscure, difficult. Mummy was not here to restore a wounded integrity with that deep sense of kinship which warmed Laurie's heart more than anything else. Father with his queer, stern love was not here to frown and put out a restraining hand when she was nearing the danger zone. Even Mele, who could comfort her, was not planning to be in Kona for the summer.

In the places of these loved people were dear Nanna and Grandpa Bell. But Nanna was dying, her whole body dedicated to death, her whole spirit dedicated to something one could not know. And Grandpa—poor sweet! He was watching Nanna with his tears shut in, his hands trembling. They had brought her, Laurie, here as a buffer between them and death, as a constant reminder that living and dying go on in a bittersweet rhythm until eternity. Mummy had said on that day she had sobbed in Laurie's arms that it was better to get down on your knees and wail against the cruelty of death. But Laurie was not certain of that. Right now Daddy's way seemed safer—quiet, controlled dignity, a way approved by society. When one began to wail, so many things might happen, horrible unknown things which accompany abandon. And what of afterward? Exhaustion and despair, probably.

Laurie shook these thoughts from her mind and rose to go to the window. She looked at the shore line which had been molded into jagged, almost fantastic shapes by lava flows. Upon the hillside where the Bell house stood, the vegetation was lush, because the weather was cool and the rain fell. But down along the coast it was desolate and hot. She had a vision of herself walking along the harsh shore in some deserted spot, stumbling over the lava, scratching her legs against its shards, pausing to rest in the thin shadow of a starved *kiawe* tree. She sensed poignantly her solitariness. Impatiently she wondered why, on occasions, she felt this gripping loneliness. In the heart of her family, in the midst of her friends, her mind would suddenly detach itself, and she felt estranged; curiously it was they who seemed to shut her out. She was not at ease with them nor with herself, and she never mentioned it for fear of incredulity or ridicule. Sometimes she wondered if it were not better to recognize that she would always be alone in certain ways and to learn to rely on herself. But then fumbling and nuzzling its way into her heart was the desire and hope that someday there would be someone who would know and understand. She loved people, to be with them, to feel the warm fingers of friendship, the embrace of love. She didn't want to be locked within herself; she hoped to find friends who could repudiate the interior, lonely Laurie by showing her that just talking to them or fishing with them or swimming with them was enough.

A sudden trembling of wind in the banana plants filled her little room with rainlike sound, and she noticed a quick massing of pinky cloud shadow on the sea. These small movements of beauty filled her with a darting, inexplicable joy. The happiness astonished her, as it always had when in the past she had felt this reversal from loneliness to joy within a second's time. She took down her ukulele. She would go and sit under the kukui tree and play to herself.

As she went down the stairs, she slid the palm of her hand along the balustrade of koa wood. So many fingers had slipped along the handrail and Pua had polished it with oil so many times that the wood appeared to be filled with a liquid, translucent gold and felt like cool wax to the touch. Laurie never went down these stairs without enjoying this beauty. At the bottom she hesitated between going out the back or the front door. She knew that Pua was in the kitchen cleaning vegetables. Right now she did not want to speak with anyone; her mind was not yet resolved in complete peace.

She turned toward the front door and stepped into the living room. Nanna was sitting in a rocker near the window, apparently watching for Laurie, whose footsteps she must have heard on the stairs. She greeted her granddaughter, "Hello, keiki, dear."

Laurie went over to her and said, "Hello, Nanna. I'm all through with my unpacking. Just as cozy as a bird in a nest."

"I hope you like that room. Of course you could have the twins' room if you prefer."

"No, I'd rather have Mummy's." Laurie noticed that Nanna had a lava stone, black and elongated, lying in her hands. "What's that?" she asked and pointed to the stone. She bent over and saw that caught in one of the larger holes of the stone was a mauve-colored piece of shell.

"It's just on old stone I picked up. . . . Sit down, Laurie, and play for me."

Laurie sat on the floor under the window and leaned against the wall. She tuned her ukulele carefully and then tried a few chords. "What would you like?" she asked.

"Whatever you want."

"You're easy to please. Now, Win would have a carefully prepared list." She began with a song which described the various regions of the Island of Hawaii, and when she came to the verse about Kona, she sang it slowly and tenderly, repeating it twice. When she had finished, Nanna whispered, "Play 'Sweet Leileihula,' " and Laurie started that song, a gayer and more lilting one. Nanna joined in the singing. Laurie played on, melody after melody; she played until her fingers tingled, and she felt herself a part of the pure rhythmic sweep of the songs.

After a while Nanna leaned over and took the ukulele from her hands. She played a hula tune, singing its words with vigor. Laurie rose from the floor and started to dance, her body attuned to the simple rhythms. She swayed her arms and hips, felt her bare toes gripping the floor in the surety of slow, carefully devised movement. She laughed lightly and tossed her head, flipping her hair about her shoulders. Nanna turned the ukulele over and beat gently on the back as though it were a gourd. She chanted to the throbbing rhythm she made, and Laurie knelt to dance an old hula. At the end of the chant, Laurie lay down on her back and stretched her arms above her head, waving them in traditional hula gestures, describing with her fingers a house, the stars, the moon, the falling rain, a mountain. "Oh, Nanna," she murmured in her happiness.

Softly the old woman said, "I guess, then, we weren't selfish."

"Selfish?"

"Yes. I've been afraid of that. Taking you away from home, from your friends. I thought you might be lonely."

"Oh, don't worry about that. Besides, one is always lonely sometimes—wherever one may be. It's funny—change makes you lonely; it's like leaving part of you behind. When I used to go and stay with Mele, I'd be lonesome at first, and then again when I went home, I'd feel the same thing."

"You strange child! But I guess it's true for lots of people. . . . Laurie, while you're here I'd like to teach you some of the songs and hulas I knew as a girl. Many of them are disappearing, and it's too bad."

"Oh, Nanna, I'd love to. Let's have a lesson every day!"

"All right. Tomorrow about ten. In this room."

"Nanna, you old darling!" Laurie rose from the floor and took her ukulele from her grandmother's hands. As she did so, the black stone slipped to the floor with a clatter.

"Oh, here's your stone," Laurie said, and bending over, she picked it up. "It looks kind of like a fish, and this piece of shell is his eye." She turned the stone over in her hand, rubbing her fingers against it. "It feels good. So light and smooth." She thought it felt almost as fine as a polished gem, and she was interested by the little click, click, click of the shell when the stone was turned.

"The smoothness came from my hands," said Nanna.

"From your hands?"

"Yes. It was once rather rough—years ago. I like to hold it in my hand, rub it with my finger tips. The piece of shell clicks."

"Yes, a nice little noise."

"I've never talked much to anyone about this stone. But I'd rather like to to you. . . . You know, Laurie, we country-women often have much time alone when our husbands and children are out for the day, and we think in those hours a great deal about our families. Some women do this thinking while they are knitting or mending. But I never could sew or knit. And this stone came to my hand. It was a good substitute for the needle."

"Nanna, how interesting!"

Nanna fondled the stone. "It's been a handy thing to have around."

"Wherever did you find such a nice stone?"

"It's quite a story. Do you really want to hear?"

"Yes, yes! I love stories."

"One day when I was eight, I was a very naughty little girl. I ran away."

"You ran away!"

"Uh-huh. Papa had hurt my feelings. Poor Papa! He had such a capacity to hurt my feelings. But this time it was worse than ever before. I can remember to this day . . . but that's by the bye." She sighed and reached for the stone from Laurie's hands. "I tied up a nightgown, a toothbrush, and my favorite doll in a scarf, and at dawn of the morning after the quarrel I set out for some friends at the beach; they were fishermen. It took me two hours to get there, even with the ride I had part of the way with old Mr. Kawika in his wagon. When I reached my friends, I went straight to Mrs. Kanahele and said, 'I'm to be your daughter now. My mother sent me.' Mrs. Kanahele embraced me, fed me a bowl of poi and some dried fish, and sent me out to play with her children. Aggie, her daughter, was just my age, and we were close friends. I told Aggie I was going to be her sister now, and she was delighted. She kissed and hugged me. The affection of the Kanaheles was a soothing balm for my hurt."

"Tutu must have nearly died with worry while you were gone."

"Tutu was wise in such things, and she knew me through and through. It was Papa who suffered. He never scolded me again to his dying day. Papa loved me, but I could not understand his way of showing it."

Laurie interrupted, murmuring, "Yes, to understand . . ."

"Well, Aggie called her numerous brothers and sisters together and told them that I was now one of them and suggested that they let me in on a secret. I swore by a solemn childhood oath never to reveal what I learned. They took me down a little trail through the *kiawe* thickets till we came to a place where the lava had heaped itself up like a miniature mountain. On top of this was a small cairn made of chunks of coral, looking very white and gleaming against the black lava. On top of the cairn was this black stone. 'Look!' they cried.

" 'What is it?' I asked.

" 'A big lizard was in that stone,' Aggie said.

"I replied with disgust, 'A lizard couldn't get in that stone.'

" 'But it's not a real lizard. It's a god!' Aggie answered with awe. 'It's like the stone down at the next beach which people say is a shark, and the fishermen leave offerings,' she continued.

" 'Where'd you get it?' I asked.

" 'We found it and put it there, and we piled up the coral.'

"I had been taught to regard such superstitions as nonsense, and so I boldly climbed the miniature mountain and picked up the stone. The Kanahele children were horrified, and loudly protesting that something awful would happen to me, they ran off. I looked at the stone, and the little bit of shell caught my eye. I turned the stone in my hand and heard the click of the shell. It was exciting, and I wanted the stone very much. So I hid it in my dress and took it back to the house where I tied it in my nightgown. When my parents came for me in the afternoon, I took it home and have had it ever since."

"What an interesting story!" Laurie said and felt a vague, disturbing wish for the stone herself.

Nanna looked intuitively at her. "If you want the stone, Baby sweet, you may have it when I'm. . ."

"Nanna darling! Don't say that! You'll want to keep it a long time!" Laurie reached gently for the stone and held it pressed between her palms. "It's nice; it just fits your hands."

This stone had helped Nanna through her hours of loneliness. Perhaps one day it would help her, Laurie. She imagined herself sitting by an unknown window of the future, looking out at rain falling and streaking silver light among the trees, and she would be holding this stone, thinking of the story Nanna had told her, remembering Nanna, and being relieved of her own burden of loneliness.

Laurie put the stone back in her grandmother's hands and said, "Nanna, if you'll excuse me, I think I'll go out and explore a bit. Mummy wanted me to visit certain places for her."

"Of course. But remember, Grandpa wants lunch at twelve sharp."

"I'll be back on time."

Laurie left the house and walked down to the opening of the lava tube. The place had always fascinated her, especially after Mummy had told her the story of meeting the old lady there. She liked to imagine that the tube led to the very heart of the mountain, perhaps to Pele's own place. A clump of ferns grew just outside, and she sat down among them and gazed into the gaping darkness of the tunnel.

Why had Nanna run away? Maybe her father was . . . well, like Daddy in some ways. It was possible.

The sun beat warmly on her and stirred the fragrance of the verdure. She stretched and lay back in the ferns, arranging herself so that one frond shaded her face. She pushed her fingers deep into the green, feeling the coolness of plant life and the earth; a voluptuous sense of relaxation came over her, and sleepily she imagined that she turned Nanna's stone in her hand.

VI

One morning when Laurie had been in Kona a fortnight, Grandpa knocked on her door soon after breakfast. She was writing a letter to Mummy, telling her of the hula lessons and of the sweet laziness of living in Kona.

"Come in," she called. "Oh, hello, Grandpa," she said when he opened the door.

"Hello, keiki. Writing letters, I see."

"Yes, to Mummy."

"I wondered if you could drive Nanna down to Kailua this morning. Her old friend Mrs. Awai has a gift, something she says will spoil."

"I'd love to. Right now?"

"As soon as you're ready. Why don't you poke around in Kailua while you're there? Maybe have lunch at the inn. You might find some of your Honolulu friends vacationing there."

"A good idea! Tell Nanna I'll be down in a minute."

Mr. Bell closed the door, and Laurie made herself ready. She tied her hair at the nape of her neck in the way she liked to wear it while driving. She took off her bright yellow shorts and put on aqua slacks in their place. Then she went downstairs.

Nanna met her at the car, and together they set off for Kailua. Rain in the night had washed the roadside foliage and disturbed the fragrances so that the air was heavy with the scent of ginger and moist greenery: The sea was that lustrous blue, the shimmering of which always stirred in Laurie's mind faint imaginings of a simple life at the beach.

Along the way, Nanna talked of the changes in Kona since her childhood. She pointed to a crumbling rock foundation overgrown with morning-glory. "Here's where Mr. Mason had his coffee mill. But he fell over a cliff and was killed while hunting wild pig. After that his widow gave up the enterprise; it wasn't doing very well, anyhow. . . . And oh!" She held out her brown thinning hand. "At this very junction there used to be a church, a Catholic church. And everyone said it was haunted. If you'd go there at night, a strange white figure would precede you into the church. It was like a bit of mist which rose from the ground. Finally the wraith didn't confine itself to the church but began to roam round the neighborhood and visit homes of people living near by. And then one night the church burned. They never discovered who did it."

"Nanna," Laurie said after a few moments of silence. "Whose is that old house? It's so rambling and so curious."

"It belonged to the Thrinly sisters, six old maids who lived there nearly fifty years; whenever they thought they needed a room for something, they just added it on. One of them was an ardent gardener, and she kept the grounds looking like the jungle they are. Another one did quilts; almost every respectable bed in Kona at one time or the other was decked by her efforts."

"Six sisters and none of them married!"

"The oldest was, but her experience was tragic, and within a year she was back in the family home and managed to embitter all of her sisters about matrimony. She took back her maiden name, and most people in Kona today don't know that Theodosia was once married."

"You know so many wonderful stories, Nanna! I hope I can remember all of them." Laurie glanced at her grandmother's face and saw that she was enjoying herself; she seemed to have forgotten for the moment that she was going to die.

They drove into Kailua from the Kainaliu side, and Nanna directed Laurie to turn left and to stop at the third house from Mr. Naehu's church. Laurie parked the car on the grassy shoulder at the side of the pavement. She opened the door to help Nanna out. Then she looked at Mrs. Awai's place. The tiny house was right in the middle of a large square of green lawn. In one corner near the fence were some nets spread out to dry. Three coconut palms grew in the front yard, a lone *kiawe* in the back, and clustered near the house a few scraggy crown-flower shrubs, but otherwise no plant interrupted the fine expanse of closely clipped lawn. The house was a weathered gray, but there were signs that at one time the lanai had been painted blue. Laurie realized as she and Nanna drew near that the house contained only one room. The front and back doors were open, and she caught a glimpse through them of a brick oven covered by a palm-leaf shelter on the back lawn.

A large Hawaiian woman seated on the lanai shouted at them, "Ululani! Aloha! Come in. Who's that? Your granddaughter?"

"It's Laurie," Nanna answered in a hearty voice.

"Good. I'm glad you brought her."

Laurie and Nanna walked up the lanai steps, and Nanna said, "Mattie, this is Luahine's daughter. You saw her when she was a baby—and then again when she was five or six. She used to come and stay with the Hartwells."

"Sure. I remember. Sit down, you two. Have something to eat."

Mrs. Awai was dressed in a large shapeless gown of a faded blue material. Her wedding ring had been removed to the little finger of her left hand, where it fitted snugly. Her thick hair was caught up in a large loose bun at the nape of her neck, and her brown skin was smooth and shining.

"The kids are all fishing, and Jasper went up to Holualoa to get some string to mend his nets," Mrs. Awai said. "Come on in the house. I've got a piece of cake." She heaved her large body out of the chair and moved into the house as gracefully as a wave across sandy shallows.

The space in the one room was occupied chiefly by four iron beds. Against the back wall taking up most of the remaining space was a large wooden table around which were seven or eight chairs. On the table were dirty cracked dishes of every shape and description. Above, against the wall, hung a cupboard. Mrs. Awai opened the cupboard and took from it a half-eaten cake, which she set on the table. Then she walked over to one of the beds and pulled from under it a case of orange soda. She took out three bottles, opened them, and offered one each to Nanna and Laurie. She cut three pieces from the cake and said, "Come and eat."

Nanna and Mrs. Awai sat down at the table, but Laurie

leaned against a chair and sucked at her bottle of soda. She looked carefully around her at the room, letting the older women chatter to their hearts' content. She was amused by the clothes draped in every possible spot, pajamas over the bedsteads, dresses across the chairs, and even trousers hanging from the lamp. This was the same kind of poverty she had seen in Jerry's house. And yet—there was a difference. Through this house blew the fresh, salty fragrance of the sea, and from its windows one could see clean, green grass, the sand and water, a sweep of pure sky. Through Jerry's house blew the fetid odor of a courtyard into which careless people dumped their slops, and from his window one could see the blank, dirty wall of the brewery. Mrs. Awai's children played by the sea every day, but Jerry's little brothers and sisters had played in the courtyard filth. Laurie had been uneasy with Jerry's mother, because she seemed nervous, strident, quick-tempered. She was a large woman, much the same type physically as Mrs. Awai, yet she was dirty and often vulgar in her speech, especially when she had had too much "*oke.*" But Mrs. Awai one instantly liked; she was warmhearted, gay, and though her dress had smudges on it, her skin and hair gleamed in their cleanliness. What made the difference? Laurie wondered. Was it living in the country?

When Laurie had finished her orange soda and nibbled enough at the dry cake to be polite, she said, "Nanna, do you mind if I wander down to the beach for a while?"

"Go along, child. But don't get lost."

"If she do that, the kids can find her," said Mrs. Awai with a grin.

Laurie left the house, went across the lawn and the hot pavement of the street down to the shore. A small beach of coral sand nestled in the black lava rock, and she idled along it, picking up shells, pausing to watch the waves, and feeling the sand warm and comfortable between her toes. She came to the end of the beach and started across the lava in which little tide pools had been worn. She stopped every now and again to watch the small fish and black crabs that darted about the pools. Walking over the lava was slow and sometimes hazardous; she stepped carefully to avoid the fissures or sudden jutting up of jagged pieces. Landward, the rock was edged with dense kiawe thickets, whose leaves looked a piercing yellow-green against the stone blackness. Laurie thought that the sea as well as the kiawe was more intense in color when bordered by lava. There was a quality of dark shadow in the water, a hint of the vast, dimmed world beneath it.

She continued south along the shore, lured by a desire to know what lay beyond the next curve of the coast. Sometimes she paused to sit in the shade of a kiawe; the hum of bees contended loudly with the noise of the tea, and she had the curious sensation of being in a hot summer garden while at the same time feeling in her hair the wild, salt wind of the coast. These two sensations clashed within her, and she thought with amusement of eating spiced green olives while at the same time drinking syrupy hot chocolate. Once, as she rested in the shade, a fisherman with a throw-net passed by. He did not even glance at her; his eyes constantly scanned the sea.

She realized that some time had elapsed since she had noticed a house tucked in among the trees. She must now be in an isolated spot, visited only by fishermen. As she walked on, the impression of her solitude enlarged, and a heretofore unsavored, intense mood grew upon her; she felt the vastness of the sea and the vastness of the great mountain mass which rose from the sea. In this largeness she was withdrawn, remote from her fellow men, but she was not lonely. A kinship was established with her surroundings; something in them was also in her, and it was that which made her intense, alert. She felt herself to be a creature whose home and living were on the lava shore, and a spirit untrammeled by logic or consideration, deep stirring so that it seemed to tug at the core, possessed her. When a black crab skittered from a shallow pool up onto a rock to stare at her, she halted instinctively, remained motionless, watching him, straining her ears, feeling the sense of touch highly intensified. The crab slipped down into a fissure, and the spell was broken.

She went on, noticing that her bare feet found by themselves secure, smooth footholds. Her newly quickened eye caught sight of a young squid stranded in a tide pool. He thrashed his many arms about as though in fury over his imprisonment, and she squatted on her haunches to watch him. In her own body she understood the yearning, angry movements of the small sea creature. A cloud passed over the sun, creating a brief moment of shadow; the squid slunk under a ledge of rock, and Laurie, herself momentarily frightened, looked up to find the reason for the dimming of the light. She rose and sped along the lava, which seemed more than ever her proper abode. Her eyes swam with a vision of the sea wavering in the heat and the green-yellow of kiawe foliage burning like a flame against the black pahoehoe lava.

Abruptly her way was blocked by an ancient stone wall which ran almost to the water's edge. She paused as if undecided, then scrambled over it and dropped down on the other side. She noticed she was panting, that her heart beat too rapidly, and the remembrance of her humanity returned. She was exhausted and lay in the shadow of the wall to find coolness and refreshment. The exhilaration of her mood of kinship with land and sea was gone, and loneliness besieged her. This wall; it was the work of men of long ago. They had lived solitary lives here by the sea, fishing, fearing the coming of Pele whenever the mountain erupted. . . . How far had she come from Kailua? It must be miles. She looked at her watch; two hours had passed. In this remote spot, she could slip down and injure herself and might not be found for days. Why had she come so far alone? She was a fool! People were easily injured or drowned along this coast—a sudden wave, a turn of the tide. Panic stirred in her, and she rose and started back over the wall.

She must return, start now, walk carefully so as not to fall, watch the waves; the tide was coming in and she mustn't be caught.

When she reached the other side of the wall, she saw at the sea's edge a fisherman casting a throw-net. A man, a fellow creature! She must speak to him, smile at him, laugh with him, reassure herself that the old familiar world of human beings was not lost. He was a tall, solidly built Hawaiian. A violet sheen glistened over the strong brown muscles of his back, and his legs were sturdy like carved rock. He watched his net, unaware of her presence, and she walked hesitantly, quietly, toward him. He drew in his net, slowly, carefully; there were no fish in it. He picked it up by the center, shook it slightly, and then twisted it into his grip, making ready for another throw. He turned toward her, paused a moment, startled.

"Oh! Hello, Laurie! What in the name of heaven are you doing way out here?"

She stared at him, searching for recognition. Those large eyes, the whites gleaming around the dark iris. It could be no other! . . . There was no shyness this time when she looked into his eyes. Instead there was happiness, relief.

"Hal!" she said. "How wonderful to see you! But however did you get out here yourself?"

"I live at Keauhou."

"I thought you lived in Honolulu."

"No. When Grandma died seven years ago, Pa brought us back here to live in her house. He didn't much like Honolulu, anyhow. He was a country boy."

"Keauhou's a nice place."

"You'd be bored after Honolulu, but we don't mind."

"I don't think I'd be bored. . . . Say, how far have I strayed from Kailua? I'm afraid Nanna will be worried. I just got started and went on and on and on."

"You're not too far. Would you like a ride back?"

"A ride?"

"My car's near here. On the highway about an eighth of a mile inland. Can you make it that far through kiawes and lava?"

"I've come all this way over lava!"

He smiled. "Come on then. You're just like a Kanaka, bare feet and all."

He took her hand, and it was a casual, friendly gesture. There was no tingling in her palm this time. They trudged along a crude trail to the highway. They did not speak, for the heat was oppressive, cloaking them in a moist, heavy veil. Half a block from the water the cool sea breeze was dissipated among the kiawes.

Laurie almost laughed when she saw the car. It was a model T built in the high, old-fashioned way. He must have felt her inclination, because he apologized, "It's not much of a car to look at. But it runs pretty well. I tinker with it all the time and keep it in good order."

When they were in the car and riding, the coolness of the sea came back. "You're staying with the Bells at Kealakekua?" he asked.

"Uh-huh. You know about Nanna? She has cancer."

He didn't speak for a moment. Then with a low sigh he said, "It's terrible! Gosh, you poor kid, to have to suffer this. And poor Mrs. Bell!" He put his hand on her knee for a moment.

"I can't exactly say that we in the family are getting used to the idea. But we've built up a little wall of defense—we had to. Of course, when she actually dies. . ."

"Gosh!" he said and then remained silent.

Laurie felt a return of the loneliness she had felt by the sea. She tried to think of something to say. He was solemn now, withdrawn, probably thinking about Nanna's tragedy. Finally she asked, "Didn't you know before this summer that Mele Hartwell was your sister?"

"No. I think my parents promised when they gave her up

for adoption not to see her any more. But Mrs. Hartwell recognized me and said I looked like Mele, and she invited me down. I didn't much want to go at first. But I had a good time with Mr. Hartwell. Mele was queer toward me, though. I guess she felt kind of mixed up suddenly having a brother."

"I guess so. . . . Mele's my best friend."

"Yeah, I know. Funny you should pick her. You a Wendell."

She bristled. "And why not?"

"Oh, nothing. 'Scuse it." He looked down at her and smiled. "Honolulu made me feel my place—a fisherman."

"That's too bad. You shouldn't take it all seriously, though."

"I don't. But after the country, well—"

"I know. Before the war, Honolulu was spoiled enough. But now!"

"We'll just have to take it. Even Kona is different."

"The old saying—change is inevitable. I guess that's right. We just have to get used to the rawness of it."

"What a couple of old fogies with long beards we sound like!"

She grinned. "How's this? It's the new atomic age, and we're young, and what more can we want?"

"Swell! But honestly, I do feel that way a lot too. I feel both ways."

"Me too."

When they reached Kailua, Hal asked, "Where do you want to go?"

"Mrs. Awai's."

He parked in front of the house and reached across her to open the door. "Thank you," she said. "I was really tired and wondering how I'd ever get back."

"May I come and see you at the Bells'?"

"Of course. Any time. Thanks again," she said and slipped out of the car.

VII

When a week had passed and Hal had not as yet appeared, Laurie found questions growing within her and impatience disturbing her tranquillity. Perversely, the longer he stayed away, the more she wanted to see him. She was eager to talk with him under what she considered normal circumstances. At the Hartwells', shyness and embarrassment had plagued her, and on the shore she would have welcomed anyone, even the ugliest, oldest fisherman of the whole Kona coast. What was the real, everyday Hal like? And what was delaying him?

At the end of another seven days, Pua invited Laurie to go to a church supper at Kailua. She said that as Grandpa and Nanna couldn't go this year, it would be nice for some member of the family to take their place. Laurie replied quietly, "At Kailua!" Then more brightly, "I'd love to go!"

On the day of the supper Pua baked three large white cakes, and Laurie grated coconut for the frosting. They packed the cakes carefully in tin boxes, rolled up their bathing suits and towels and fitted them in a lauhala basket. In the late afternoon they set out for Mr. Naehu's church. Nanna and Grandpa waved good-by from the back door, rather wistfully, Laurie thought.

Pua said as she watched them, "In the old days Ululani Bell was always at the supper. People will miss her. She danced the hula like no one else."

"Poor dear Nanna! . . . Do many people go to these affairs?"

"Oh, yes! There's not too much to do around here. And they're fun. Mr. Naehu has caused quite a revival in the church. He combines his religion with social affairs. You know us Hawaiians—we like our religion, but we like fun too. And when it's combined!" Pua left her sentence unfinished and grinned at Laurie.

"How come Mummy goes to the Episcopal Church in Honolulu?"

"Your grandpa started her in that. That's what he was as a kid. . . . It's funny. Some say that in Kona the important people are Episcopalians. But that's not true with Ululani Bell. Why, she could go to the Buddhist Temple and she'd still be the most important woman in Kona!"

When they reached Kailua and drove along the sea, Laurie rejoiced in the topaz light of early evening, which had settled in the sky above the water and over the embracing foliage of the kiawe and monkeypod trees. She felt a pleasant trembling at the turn of the day toward the night. Now one could look forward to the happiness peculiar to the dusk and the dark, the softening of light and the slowing of pace, the cozy feeling of being inside and safe from the unseen movements in the black. She parked near the church, and with Pua carried the cakes and swimming things to the churchyard. The long tables were already laid with ti leaves for covers and with soda bottles and paper napkins. Women were busy at the back tables preparing the food, and most of the men were lounging about in a clear grassy space. A few were working over the imu.

"Hello!" "Hi!" "Aloha!" came the varied greetings. "The keeds is all swimming now. You go?"

Laurie and Pua answered that they wanted a dip and after leaving the cakes, went across the road to the ancient bathhouse. Lurie put on her suit and hurried down to the beach. She plunged into the midst of the swimmers and rolled over and over, porpoise-fashion, relishing the pleasant vertigo which filled her body. A ten-year-old girl who was bathing in her dress pointed a finger at Laurie and shrieked, "Look at her! Like one fish!" And she began to laugh with exaggerated vehemence. Soon many of the youngsters were rolling about, imitating Laurie, and complaining, "I get dizzy," or saying, "Plenty fun, yeh!" Pua dove into a wave and came up alongside Laurie. "What kind of stuff you teach these kids! By and by they all get dizzy and drown."

"Don't be silly, grouch," replied Laurie, and ducking under a wave, she swam out beyond the surf line. Then turning, she came back into the breakers and tried to catch a wave. She missed, and the others, body-surfing, laughed and taunted, "You no flying fish, you swimming pig!"

Laurie laughed and as if to mock them, caught the next wave, which carried her right up onto the beach. She swam out again and caught another wave. The water was cool and stinging with salt against her face, and her body felt light as a shred of coconut husk bobbing on the surface. She grasped a bit of crisp, smooth seaweed, chartreuse-colored, in her hand and held it tight against her cheek. "Oh!" she murmured to herself. "My body is singing, singing!"

Swift as an unexpected wind gust came the remembrance that she, as an adult, should be doing her part in preparing the supper. She clambered out of the water and dressed inside the old bathhouse. Across the street again, she opened the gate of the churchyard and started down the graveled path. There ahead of her was Hal walking with a girl. Laurie darted off the path and went over to the table where the women were slicing hot roast pork and putting it in individual paper dishes. "Let me help," she said, and her face burned with the vision of Hal.

"Whassa matta you?" Mrs. Awai asked. She appeared to be in charge of apportioning the pig.

"Nothing. I just want to help."

"Your face is plenty red. . . . How's your dear Nanna?"

"She's—failing."

"*Auwe!* Such a terrible thing!"

Other women working at the table muttered, "*Auwe, auwe! Ma'i 'a'ai, auwe!*" Their voices sounded to Laurie like a lament, and she sensed their acceptance of the inevitability of death from *m'ai 'a'ai,* cancer.

She heaped the dishes before her generously with pork and

hoping to hear trifles of gossip about Hal or his family, listened to the chatter of the women. When some time had passed, and the Phillipson name had not been mentioned, she timidly asked the woman standing next to her, "Mrs. Kapena, are the Phillipsons here today?"

"Only Hal, I think. He brought his girl, Flora."

"Oh! He has a girl!"

"Of course! But since he came back from Honolulu, they not so steady. Everybody gossip and say he met one girl there."

"I wonder!"

"I'm not so sure. He only there two weeks, and one week he spend with the Hartwells in the country. He met his sister."

"I heard."

"I never did think Flora his kind. She too much like go *holoholo,* he like stay home. Also she Catholic; her pa is one Portuguee. Hal's family Congregational long time. From beginning. His great grandfather is talked about in old missionary writings. He was one good man."

"His family always live in Kona then?"

"Yeah. Long time. Long as anybody round here. . . . There he is." She pointed, and Laurie turned to see Hal walking toward them. He was alone. Mrs. Kapena called to him, "You come here! We give you some pork."

Hal hurried toward them and greeted Laurie, "Hello! How are you?"

She muttered an ineffective "Fine" while Mrs. Kapena gave Hal a fistful of pork. He ate it in two mouthfuls and said, "*Ono! Ono!*" When he had finished chewing, he asked, "Mrs. Kapena, may I take Laurie away from you? I want to show her my grandmother's famous quilt."

"Sure. Go ahead. We're almost pau now, anyhow."

Hal took Laurie's arm and led her among the tables toward the other side of the churchyard. "How have you been?" he asked.

"All right."

"I've wanted to come up and see you, but things prevented me. I hope you'll still let me come."

"If you want," she said and felt the blood beating against her forehead. Did he really want to come? Or was this just his way of being agreeable.

"What's the matter? You don't seem so friendly!" he complained.

"I'm just the same. This is a different place."

"Yeah. I guess you were really scared that day you were lost."

"Oh, I knew I could follow the shore back. I was just tired, and the tide was coming in. I don't know the tides on this coast."

"No. And it's dangerous in places, if you don't know."

"I thought it might be."

At that moment the girl Flora came up and said in a low, husky voice, "I've been looking for you, Hal." She possessively took his arm.

"This is Laurie Wendell, Flora. Laurie, this is Flora Mendonça."

Laurie smiled at Flora and nodded. She examined the girl as best she could without seeming to stare. Flora's eyes, lustrous and dark, gazed innocently from her pale even-featured face. Her lips were full and tender and pink, and her hair, a brown veil about her shoulders, was high-lighted with amber streaks. She looked like a guardian angel pictured in a Sunday school paper, as beautiful, sentimental, and without character. But her figure belied this otherworldly quality of her face. She was mature and plump, her breasts firm and obvious under the tight-fitting lines of her flimsy rayon dress. Around her neck she wore a tiny gold cross, and her arms and fingers were decked with silver bracelets and pale-stoned rings. Laurie felt a moment's repulsion from Hal that Flora should be "his girl."

But she was ashamed of this and tried to make up for her snobbishness by being friendly to Flora. "Hal is very kindly taking me over to see his grandmother's quilt." Then as if further explanation seemed necessary, "You know, Hal's sister, Mele Hartwell, is my best friend. Mele wanted me to be sure and say hello to him for her."

Laurie's efforts were embarrassingly obvious to herself, but Flora was apparently content with them. Her little manner of belligerent possessiveness disappeared, and she chattered to Hal and Laurie about some exciting incidents at the church supper —how Mrs. Hanahana's baby had almost fallen into a tub of poi, how Mrs. Apo wasn't speaking to Mr. Wong because she had overheard him saying her quilt was the worst one on exhibition, how Mrs. Nakamura's seventh son was so lucky, being discharged from the Army in time to get home for the supper. "You know," Flora said, and her eyes glowed, "this is the first time I've been to such a party. I don't belong to Mr. Naehu's church, but this is fun!"

After they had admired Hal's grandmother's quilt, Laurie excused herself and said that she must find Pua. She sat with Pua at the supper table and spent the rest of the evening with her. Just before they were leaving, Hal came over and whispered, "I'm really coming to see you. Don't forget."

Laurie waited expectantly each day for Hal to come. She put fresh flowers around the house and straightened things up, although she knew he probably wouldn't notice such niceties. Ten days slipped by, and he did not come. Laurie wondered angrily why he had asked to call on her if he didn't intend to do it! She began to cram her days full of activities to make herself forget him. She played for Nanna on the ukulele and the flute and learned more of the ancient hulas, typed letters and records for Grandpa, helped Pua can the guavas and mangoes, took charge of a rummage sale for the guild of the Episcopal Church. But in spite of her busyness, she was acutely aware of waiting, and the remembrance of Hal forced itself upon her mind. As time went on, she could do nothing but lie in the grass or stare vacantly at the sea, her thought brooding upon Hal's behavior.

Expectancy had sharpened her nerves so that each time she heard a car in the driveway, her body began to tremble and her stomach to churn. She hurried to the window, hoping to see the old Model T. At every unexpected knock she rushed to the door. Her disappointment was so acute when he wasn't there that frequently she could not greet a visitor with the proper cordiality. One day after a caller had gone, Grandpa spoke to her gently and tenderly. "Laurie Ululani, you should try to welcome our guests a little more warmly. I'm afraid Mrs. Stone was hurt by your manner. Dear, you mustn't let Nanna's illness bother you in this way. If it does, we must send you home."

"Oh, Grandpa, it isn't that! Honestly it isn't. I'm sorry; I'm an awful person!" She felt overwhelmingly and uncomfortably guilty that she had thought so little about Nanna in recent weeks.

"Don't blame yourself, lass. We only want to help you."

"Believe me, Grandpa, it isn't Nanna's illness. It's my own selfishness."

"Can you tell me what's bothering you?"

"It's nothing," she said, recoiling. "Guess I'll go upstairs now and write a letter."

She started toward her room and heard her grandfather's tender voice calling, "Any time, keiki, I can help you. . ."

It would be a relief if somehow she could share her anxiety. The old loneliness was gnawing at her. If she could just talk to someone! . . . And why not Grandpa? Surely he would not ridicule her. Her decision flashed warmly upon her, and she ran back to him and blurted out, "Oh, Grandpa! Hal Phillipson asked if he could call on me, and he's never come. Every time the bell rings, well, I . . ." she ended lamely.

"Lassie, lassie!" Mr. Bell said, keeping a solemn aspect on his face. "I'll watch for him too, and the minute he arrives, I'll let you know. I couldn't mistake his car. And don't you worry. He'll be coming along one of these days." He took her hand and after stroking it gently said, "Go now and play some songs for your Nanna. She never tires of hearing you."

"I'm glad I told you," she said. "It helps."

Laurie ran upstairs and took her ukulele from the shelf. She tuned it and went down the hall to Nanna's room. "What about a concert?" she asked as she went through the door.

Nanna was beginning to look pale and thinner, and sometimes her lips were pinched firmly together as they had never been in the past. Laurie wondered if she suffered pain and was not mentioning it. Right now there was a yellowish, strained look on her face, but Nanna said merrily, "Good! It's just what I need."

Laurie sat on the couch near Nanna's feet. She fingered through some chords, savoring the wonderful relaxation which came from the knowledge that Grandpa shared her burden. It was like the refreshment of a shower, she thought, after several days of heavy, glaring heat. She began to play Hawaiian cowboy songs and comic hulas. Nanna joined her in the singing, and together they swayed back and forth to the rhythm. Finally Laurie could stand the restraint of her motions no longer, and she thrust the ukulele into Nanna's hands and said, "Play for me. Please! I've got to dance." She rose from the couch and started her arms and hands curving in the traditional movements which marked the intervals between the verses of a song. When she recognized the hula Nanna was playing, she started her dance, moving her hips and arms in contrapuntal rhythms, feeling the music humming in her head, sensing exhilaration through all her body. In the middle of the dance she suddenly knew that Hal would come tomorrow. His coming was there in her mind, bright as a sea-washed pebble, and she danced on in wilder vigor.

At the end of her fifth hula, she muttered, "Oh, Nanna," and slipped limply to the floor, leaned back against her grandmother's knees. She looked up and saw on Nanna's face a great happiness. "You're happy too, aren't you. Isn't it fun?"

Nanna laid her hand gently on top of Laurie's head.

The next morning Laurie stood before the closet fingering her clothes; she had been standing there for half an hour pondering whether she should wear the chartreuse sheer, the blue with the white eyelet edging, the dark green linen, or be more casual and just wear slacks as she did every day. She took the green linen out again; it looked a little partyish. Pua's voice loud and impatient startled her, "Laurie Wendell, come down and get your oatmeal before it's cold. I won't heat it up for you!" Laurie was spurred to action by these words, and she put on gray slacks and a pale yellow blouse. She twisted a few leaves of *maile* in her hair and ran down the stairs.

She sat at her place in the kitchen to have her fruit, coffee, and oatmeal. Nanna and Grandpa breakfasted at six-thirty, but Laurie couldn't manage to get down until eight-thirty. So she ate in the kitchen near the broad window looking out on a clump of mango trees and the vegetable garden. The sun came in the window this morning and blinded her with its brilliance; she had the feeling of being isolated in a little pool of light, and her mind remained unruffled, almost detached, while she ate. She toyed with the oatmeal, because today eating seemed inexplicably vulgar. In the aura of the sun's brilliance, she was filled with an awareness of Hal's coming, and she couldn't be sure whether it was the sun or her thought which made her body so pleasantly warm and comfortable.

After breakfast Laurie spent the morning in self-invoked reverie while she lay on the hikie in a shadowed corner of the living room. She drew together all the threads of her relationship with Hal, the moments at the Hartwells' when she was breathless in the awkward allurement of their mutual glances. She wondered if he had felt something of that too. The very fact that he was Melle's brother forced her and the Hartwells to presuppose that the two of them would share a relation of friendship. But on that day a wall of embarrassment had risen between them which had made friendship impossible. She thought of her journey home in the evening, how she had remembered his eyes and wondered in what way his life might have been similar to Jerry's. She recalled vividly her moment of intense unhappiness as she swung into the garage and thought of Daddy. The bitterness of the fear of Daddy's censure lurked at the core of everything she enjoyed. But her mood, as she lay on the hikie, was too well cushioned by a vague, irresponsible bliss for her to be long troubled by worry of her father.

From the day at the Hartwells', her mind traveled to the meeting on the shore. There was a quality about this meeting which made her wonder if it might not have been predetermined by something she couldn't understand. In Kona it was easy to believe in such things. Only an encounter such as that could have effaced so speedily the awkward intricacy of emotion stirred by their first acquaintance. And then there was the church supper when he had sought her out; that must mean something.

At noon, eating with Nanna, she talked and joked. Her tongue traveled on lightly, airily, and she scarcely knew what she said because her mind was concentrated on the flow of consciousness that Hal was coming. After luncheon she took Nanna upstairs and helped her to undress for her nap. She was shocked by the gaunt thinness which seemed to be coming over Nanna's body, and very gently she lay an afghan over her and tucked a challis scarf around the old lady's shoulders. "Sleep tight," Laurie said and stooped to kiss her.

"Keiki, sweet!" Nanna answered and looked into Laurie's eyes with a faintly smiling but inscrutable glance.

Laurie, puzzled, questioned, "What?"

"Nothing in particular. I was just saying that for the comfort of the words."

"Oh!" Laurie tiptoed out of the room and closed the door.

The afternoon passed in a drift of pleasant idleness until three-thirty, and then Laurie began to worry. Her certainty that Hal was coming began to be shaken, and she wondered why it was that she had trusted an intuition so vague. At four-thirty the house seemed too small and confined her, and she went out into the garden and down to the entrance of the lava tube. She sat on the fern bank and tried to invent plausible excuses why nearly four weeks from the day on the shore had passed and still Hall had not called on her. Maybe since the church supper his car had broken down and he was unable to get parts; perhaps his mother was sick or he himself was sick. This last idea spurred her worry. What if he were sick and she sat complacently all the time waiting for him to call? Of course he might have written her a note, but no, that wouldn't be like Hal. "Oh, Hal, Hal, Hal!" she moaned aloud and pounded her hands in despair against the turf.

She forced herself to think of Nanna and was ashamed of her neglect of that dear person. She remembered the frailness of Nanna's body and how her once rounded cheeks were now almost hollow. And her hands! The bones were sharp and obvious through the flesh, and each time Laurie held them, she thought of death. She must remember that her duty in Kona was to Nanna, and she told herself firmly that she must make every moment of Nanna's living count.

Laurie looked at her watch; it was five-forty. Reluctantly she rose from the ferns and started toward the house. She must face the inevitable—that he wasn't coming today.

When she reached the main expanse of the front lawn, she saw him walking down the drive. His trousers were dusty, and his forehead was bright with perspiration. His shoulders sagged from heat and weariness. She moved slowly toward him; he seemed more phantom than real. Finally she said, "Hello, Hal. Would you like a drink?"

"I sure would. Just walked two miles in this heat."

"Two miles!"

"Yeah. From my cousins' down the road. I'm staying with them for a while."

"Oh! That's nice."

"I just came up from Keauhou today."

"Oh? Come in, won't you? I'll get some beer."

"Let's stay outdoors. What say? It's cooler."

"O.K. I'll call Pua to bring some beer."

She ran to the kitchen window and delivered her order. Then she returned to him, glad that she was wearing her slacks and that they were slightly mussed from the day's wearing.

"How's Mrs. Bell?" he asked and stretched out on his back in the grass.

Laurie seated herself near him and answered, "She's as to be expected."

"God, it's awful!" he said and rolled over to hide his face in the grass.

She felt tears start into her eyes and appreciated the depth of his sympathy for Nanna. They remained silent for a while; she did not feel the uneasiness, the lack of communion which she had felt with other young men when silence came upon them. There was rather a restfulness, a feeling of herself flowing out to meet the peace of the grass and the trees, something as gentle and imperceptible as the first turn of the tide from low to high. She was aware of his presence and relaxed by it.

He suddenly moved and sat up. Smiling at her, he said, "Hello, Laurie! It's swell to see you. Tell me, what do you think of living in the country? Do you miss Honolulu?"

"Not too much. I'm not too fond of living in Honolulu. I always escaped to the Hartwells' whenever I could."

"I missed Honolulu terribly at first. I was cross with my family for weeks when we first moved to Keauhou—and with myself. No movies, no pool halls, no place to go; I was bored. But my pa taught me lots of new ways of fishing. And we built a canoe and fitted sails to it. Now Honolulu makes me nervous."

Pua brought a tray on which were two large glasses of beer and a plate of crackers spread with cheese and oyster paste. She set the tray on the grass near them and looking at Hal said in a warning voice, "Hal Phillipson! Don't you go getting any ideas."

"Pua, I haven't a thought in my head."

"I bet!" Pua said indignantly, and turning her back on them, she strode quickly and rhythmically toward the house.

They both snickered at Pua, but she had left a slight sense of embarrassment between them. To cover it up, Laurie handed Hal a glass of beer and then offered him a cracker. She took a glass for herself and holding it high said, "Skoal!"

They drank and ate in an uneasy silence. Pua's insinuation brought to Laurie's mind a remembrance of her father's words, "I shall be forced to forget that I once had a lovely little daughter." And she counted her friends who had done the correct, the safe thing. Sylvia Chantery had married Albert Fyfe, and only a few knew of the Russian-Jewish musician she had loved so devotedly. But Honolulu had been excited over her marriage to Albert. "The union of two great *kamaaina* families," the newspapers had simpered, and described in a double column the solemn, beautiful ceremony in Kawaiahao Church. And there were the others, Marianne Smythe, Phyllis Haldane, Emma Laurence, all of whom had had not simply the usual approval but also glowing felicitations over their marriages from family and friends. If she, Laurie Wendell, dared to marry anyone like Hal Phillipson, Honolulu would be startled. Wendells always did the proper thing and were noted as being among the most conservative of island people. How Father had drilled into her the significance and responsibility of being a Wendell. One other thing was certain; if she married someone like Hal, she could no longer maintain the same relationship with her friends. They would kiss her and say how brave she was to marry for love in spite of everything, but they would begin to forget her, slowly but inevitably.

She gulped down the last of her beer and scolded herself. What was all this thought of marriage! Why, she didn't even love Hal. To break the silence, she said, "Are you taking a vacation at your cousins'?"

"I guess you could call it that."

"I feel as though I need a real vacation myself. As soon as I can, I'm going to the mainland and stay away for years." She knew as the words slipped out of her mouth that they sounded brittle, shallow.

"You don't seem like that type."

She smiled at him. "I'm really not. After two weeks on the mainland, I want to turn around and come right home again."

"I thought so. . . . Laurie, I didn't really tell you the truth about my staying at my cousins'. I really came up to be near you. I'd like to call on you every now and again, if I may."

She was confused and startled and murmured, "Yes, if you want to." She had the sensation of plunging toward something which, even if she wanted to, she couldn't avoid. It made her pleasantly dizzy.

He rose from the grass. "Well, I've got to get along now. It's a long walk home, and it's almost suppertime."

She went down the driveway with him and out to the road. He paused beside the mock-orange hedge and took her hand. "Laurie, may I come back tomorrow?"

"Yes, of course."

"G'by!" he called and started off down the highway. She watched until he reached a curve and she could no longer see him. Would he really come back tomorrow? Surely this time. . . . She sauntered toward the house. Pua met her at the back door and said briefly, "Nanna wants you."

Laurie found her grandmother sitting on the lanai holding a stalk of white ginger in her lap. A smile softened her thin face; she was smelling the ginger in long, deep breaths and touching the petals gently, lingeringly. When she saw Laurie, she said, "Keiki, I want you to do two things for me."

"Anything, Nanna."

"The first is really for you. Baby sweet, I want you not to be afraid of yourself—of what you really want to do. There is nothing safer than doing what is in accordance with your nature."

Laurie looked into her grandmother's brown eyes. Light drifted across them in such a way that she seemed to see a little golden flower blossom within them; it was stirring and beautiful. Her own eyes filled with tears as she understood, and she said urgently, "Do you really think so?"

"Real courage comes from the heart for people like us. Our hearts won't listen much to our minds. It's probably just as well, because we do not like to be lonely people."

"Not lonely," Laurie repeated and thought of all the loneliness she had suffered and against which she had rebelled.

"Second, darling, is for me. I haven't the courage to do it myself," Nanna continued. "I want you to write your mummy and ask her to come."

"Right now?" Laurie queried, and fear constricted her throat.

"Right now, keiki," Nanna said. "Tell her to come within ten days or so." Her words sang out as richly as the start of a song. The very tone and music which she put in those words comforted Laurie.

"I'll go write," Laurie said and walked to the desk in the living room. With trembling fingers she reached for pen and paper.

VIII

The memory of this ride to Hilo would remain like a cold blade in her mind, Laurie thought. Mummy's coming was, fearfully enough, a herald of Nanna's going. And when Nanna was gone, something of the Hawaiian would leave the family. Then there'd be only Tutu who was so old, Mummy, David, and herself left of that fellowship. A rush of warmth flooded Laurie's throat and face. I'll never let them forget that warm bond, never, she thought.

When this morning she had asked Grandpa to go with her on the trip to fetch Mummy, he had said emphatically, "No! There is too little time left to be away." And she had not asked Hal; Mummy would have enough to make her unhappy without the troubling question of Hal's presence. Laurie felt a dramatic quality about the journey, which, she could not escape remembering, would bring Mummy to visit her mother for the very last time.

Early morning light was opaline as it lay on the clustered foliage of the trees and along Mauna Loa's flank. On the sea it was more brilliant and crystalline. What was Nanna thinking as she looked out at this morning, at all the shining mornings of the past few weeks? Did she regard them as jewels set in fast-flowing time, things always yet never there? Did she yearn to capture them forever?

Tears distorted Laurie's vision at this last thought, and she took out her handkerchief to brush them away. She must think of Hal, of happy things. She concentrated her mind on their past week together. They had twice hiked up the mountain. He knew all the trails, and when she was certain they must be lost, he would tell her that five miles down that trail was Kealakekua or eight miles down this other trail was Captain Cook. She had never known so intimately the mysterious beauty of the lehua forest; its color was not the green, blue, and brown of other forests but rather a mingling of grays and red, the gray of bark, foliage, and mist, and the red of the blossom. The air in the forest was cold and trembled in her blood, exhilarating her in a way to which she was not accustomed. She knew the flow of spirits caused by a swim in the sea, by a sudden shower on a sharp, hot day, by a gust of trade wind disturbing tranquil warmth. But this exhilaration of a real coldness so that the breath was crisp going into her nostrils and her cheeks felt icy to the touch was something she had known only on trips to the mainland in the winter.

"This kind of feeling doesn't belong to Hawaii," she said to Hal.

He had laughed and retorted that she didn't know her islands. "Let me take you up Mauna Kea this winter. Then you'll feel island snow."

During their second hike the mist and rain had suddenly sifted down about them while they were still on the trail toward a small crater where they planned to rest and have lunch. Hal had stopped abruptly and said, "We'll go no farther today." He picked a lehua blossom and held it a moment in his hand. Then he laid it tenderly on a clinker of lava. Immediately after this, he set about building a flimsy shelter of fern fronds. That simple gesture of his, picking the flower and offering it to Pele, stirred in Laurie an awe beyond any she had known; she felt that in another moment she could almost believe there was a Pele, but Hal disturbed the mood by saying, "Come. Let's eat under here."

They crouched under the woven mat of fern fronds and unwrapped their sandwiches and hard-boiled eggs. Hal poured coffee into the lid of the thermos for Laurie. The fragrance of the beverage made her forget that her clothes were drenched and that her shoulders ached with coldness. She took the cup in three fingers, and he said, "No! Wrap your hands around it. The heat'll warm you." He gently placed her hands around the cup and held them there a moment. She smiled and lifted the cup for him to have a sip. He drank and then said, "The rest is for you."

She replied, "There'll be a second cup—and maybe a third. We'll share."

He answered, "O.K.," and started to munch his sandwich.

She thought, "Someday when we're married, I'll remember this moment and tell you that that was when I first knew I loved you."

Laurie slowed the car down to go over a bumpy, torn-up portion of the road in Kau. She smiled at the assumption in her musings. After all, Hal had never once said that he loved her or hinted that he might want to marry her. He had been tenderly attentive, and obviously he enjoyed her company; sometimes he had held her hand, and once in the dusk she thought she had felt the touch of his lips upon her cheek, but beyond that, there had been nothing.

He had been wonderful to Nanna. The three of them often sat together through the evening on the lanai, sometimes singing, sometimes talking. He and Nanna exchanged tales of Kona and neighborhood gossip. Though Laurie knew only casually the people and places, Hal and Nanna gave her the feeling that their experiences were also hers. She belonged with them to the tranquillity of Kona.

When she reached Hilo, she parked near the Inter-Island Office. She had come early because she wanted to shop for Nanna and to find some especially nice leis for Mummy. She walked to the front of the Inter-Island Office and looked at the displays of several lei women; from among the profusion, she finally chose a wreath of *akulikuli* and one of hala twined with sweet-smelling maile. She paid for the leis, joked a moment with the Hawaiian women, and then went on her shopping tour. In a small dry-goods store, she found the soft flannel jacket for which Nanna had asked. As she opened her purse to take out the money, the sudden thought of what a short time Nanna would have to wear the jacket overwhelmed her. Tears filled her eyes, and she noticed that the clerk was gazing curiously at her. When she had found one or two small presents to take back as surprises, she went to the Hilo Drug to order a large, rich sundae, dripping with chocolate and strawberry sauce and garnished with nuts and bananas. She ate leisurely and watched a booth full of soldiers devouring with the gusto of ranch hands great chunks of sirloin steak. A radio was blaring forth a morning ad and record program, and although the drugstore was comparatively empty of people, the noise of the radio gave the impression that it was teeming with buyers, lookers, and gossipers. It was the atmosphere, Laurie thought, that soldiers would like. They were rapidly teaching island people to prefer the noise and the confusion.

When she had finished her sundae, she drove to the airport. She amused herself by watching a Hawaiian family gathering its numerous parcels of luggage and children in readiness for the plane to Honolulu. The mother had a huge lauhala basket from the top of which one could see a baby's bottle, a pink blanket, a box of paper diapers, and a battered black imitation leather purse. Baby was reclining in the father's arms while the mother tied the sash of a three-year-old. Two boys of about seven and ten years kept a solemn guard over the worn suitcases and cardboard boxes which were the family luggage. Laurie wondered if they lived in Honolulu and were returning from a visit to relatives. Somehow they had the melancholy look of people at the end of an outing.

When the plane finally arrived, the waiting people clustered about the gate. A boy wheeled the ladder out to the side of the plane, and the stewardess opened the door. Mummy was the fifth person out, and she was carrying an Oriental baby. Following her was the mother of the child, helping a small boy to step down the ladder. Mummy handed the baby to the mother and hurried toward Laurie. She kissed her warmly and then grasping one of her hands, asked, "Darling! How is Nanna?"

"You'll see a change."

"Poor, poor dear! Oh, Laurie, why did this have to happen to her of all people!"

Laurie had that feeling once again of being older and wiser than her mother. She said, "Mummy, in a way Nanna is happy. She knows she's had a wonderful life and that she's been lucky to have so little sorrow. One day she told me that she was glad to have the misfortune of her life happen to her alone. . . . Really, we've been very gay, dancing and singing and eating out on the lawn. Only now, she is in bed much of the time."

"Laurie, Nanna is braver than all of us."

"Certainly, Mummy. . . . I never used to like to think of death. It always seemed frightening to me, even a little embarrassing. I was afraid of the emotions about it. But now . . . Nanna has made death not such a fearsome thing."

Laurie felt her mother's eyes searching her face. Martha's voice was low and vibrant when she said, "So-o-o. . . . I'm glad. Tell me, Laurie, what it is about you. You've changed somehow. You seem more—well, I don't know exactly. You haven't—it can't be that you know what you want to do now?"

"Oh, no! I haven't changed," Laurie said and flushed faintly. She knew that she had changed; she couldn't remain the same Laurie after all this Kona experience. She felt strongly the new self growing within her. "Mummy," she continued, "we're to call for Tutu on our way. I guess we'd better start. . . . Oh, I almost forgot! Here are some leis for you." She put the leis around her mother's neck and kissed her.

"Thank you, darling. Now we must get my bags," Mummy reminded her.

They inquired at the desk for the bags and stowed them away in the car. Laurie helped her mother into the front seat and closed the door for her, then went round to her place as driver. In the closeness of the automobile, she smelled the gardenia fragrance of Mummy's perfume, and it recalled the unfathomable quality of her mother, the something which always faintly excited her. One could know Mummy only so far; it was as though she were an artist, the essence of whose genius makes one wonder what compounding went into the creation of this special person. Mummy vibrated to everything, the rain or wind in the weather, the sorrow or joy of her children, rooms full of people, landscape of sea or mountains. When Laurie was with her, she could often feel in herself a reflection of the trembling of this response.

Laurie drove swiftly up the volcano road; it was wide and straight through the fern and lehua forests. When they passed the Volcano House, Martha said, "Oh, I nearly forgot! I have a letter for you from Daddy."

"Oh? What have I done now?" Laurie felt her face bathed in warmth and her hands grow wet.

"The only thing you've done is something nice. Darling, why is it you always think Daddy is going to scold you?"

"I always seem to do things wrong for him."

"That's not true. He's very proud of you now."

"I'm glad. . . . When are he and Win coming over?"

"Well, it depends. . . ."

"I know."

When they had passed the forest region and the landscape became more desolate, a melancholy settled over them, and they did not speak. Laurie drove at high speed, and from the corner of her eye she could see Martha gazing as though mesmerized at the drab countryside. She turned abruptly down the road to Punaluu and up to Tutu's front gate.

When the car was stopped, Martha reached in her purse. "Here's the letter from Daddy. Why don't you read it and then come in. He wanted me to give it to you the very first thing. I'm sorry I forgot."

Laurie took the letter and went over to the black sand beach to sit down. Although the day was cloudy at Punaluu and inclined toward rain, the sand felt warm. She took off her shoes and pushed her toes deep into its tepid softness. Then she put the letter on the sand and buried it until only one white tip showed. What if she left it there for the waves or the wind to carry away; no one ever need know what it said. But perhaps that would be dishonest to Daddy; she realized that he would never speak of it unless she herself mentioned it. The truth was she didn't want to read his rationalizations, his twisting of her efforts in Kona. And once she had read and acknowledged the letter, it would take its place in the family strongbox, a lasting record of what there was between her father and herself.

She muttered, "Coward," in a low voice and with swift decision snatched the letter from the sand, ripped it open with a bit of coral, and read:

My dearest Laurie,

I am writing to express my pride and delight in you, my daughter. You have entered willingly into a household filled with sorrow and anguish, and you have turned it into a place still capable of happy, everyday living. Your grandfather has written at length of your accomplishments, of your sweetness and naturalness and understanding. There is no way I can adequately express my pleasure except to say that my heart glows when I think of you, my child.

Laurie, this is a talent which lies deep within you and one which is needed in this world. Isn't this, the utilization of this precious ability, the work you are looking for? Can't this be the mold around which your life is formed? Think about it, my dear.

Your ever loving Father.

When she had finished the letter, she stuffed it impatiently back into the envelope. Why couldn't Father have complimented her and left it at that! It was his usual way—spoiling for her everything that might have been pleasant.

She brushed the sand off her feet, put on her shoes, and

hurried back to Tutu's house. Tutu and Mummy were on the lanai directing Jiro to put the bags in the back seat of the car. "Hello, Tutu!" Laurie called.

"Hurry up, keiki, we're all ready," Mummy said.

Laurie ran to Tutu, kissed her vigorously, and encircling her waist with an arm, marched her down the path to the auto. "First Tutu," she said and opened the door to help the old lady climb in. "Now Mummy," she counted off.

"We're off to London to visit the Queen!" she said gaily as she started the engine. This must be a difficult moment for Tutu, knowing that she was leaving her home to watch over the deathbed of her only child. Laurie wished she could somehow relieve the old lady of part of her burden of suffering. She drove toward Kona, regulating her speed with a consideration of Tutu's eighty-year old frailty, and talked of the months she had spent with Nanna, how happy they had been and how she would always remember them with delight.

When after supper the excitement and activity of arrival had settled down to a quiet hum of voices from Nanna's room, Laurie walked out on the lawn to look at the evening sea. It always comforted her to look at the sea and realize that its coming and going continued in endless, unmeasured rhythm. The water usually appeared placid from this height, even in case of storm, and this placidity was a mood of which she was quickly envious. She realized that already her role was changed. With Tutu and Mummy in Kona, she had become the child again—for them. But for herself, she was the new Laurie Wendell who had tasted of love and of death. She must remember that Tutu was Nanna's mother and Mummy was her daughter; they were the central three, the three most involved in the sorrow and the love. That is, all except Grandpa; but he was the one who stood apart. How full of despair he must be, alone, far from his own land and from the comfort of familiar childhood things. When he looked out at this sea did he yearn for the sight of gray, misty Scotch city streets? Would their bleakness comfort him more than this gentle, scented landscape? It was hard to believe so, but when death was near, one yearned for the things of childhood. How many times Laurie had thought of Lehua's brown arms and of the little cushioned window seat in her own bedroom; in those two places she had been safe from all the world. Did Grandpa remember such spots?

She walked farther down the hill until she was free of the shadow cast by arching trees and the house. She sat in the grass and looked at the sky which curved dark and starless above her. Strange that there were no stars; she had not been aware of clouds hiding them. And strange this feeling of being shut in and almost haunted by nothingness. There was no stir in the dusk, just the faint murmur of voices from Nanna's room, and she was now far enough away for that to take its place as part of the humming of night silence. The universe was a dark luminous gray, everything in it, the land, the sea, the house, the trees, the sky. This melancholy color did not make her lonely; she felt rather a kinship with it, and she recaptured the mood of the day on the shore, without the exhilaration. She felt a quiet belonging to this gray, gently breathing universe.

The crush of footsteps in the grass was quite close to her before she was aware of another presence. She turned and saw Hal coming toward her.

"I'm sorry if I'm butting in at the wrong time," he said.

"You're not butting in."

"The first night your mother and Tutu are here, I ought to stay away."

"Well, I'm down here and they're up there. I had a feeling I ought to let them alone."

"You're probably right." He didn't say anything more nor did he move to sit down near her.

She wondered if he were thinking of going, being sensitive to a mood which wasn't in her. So she said, "Let's go up on the lanai and have a coke."

He took her arm and together they walked back across the grass and up the steps. They sat near each other on the hikie, and he kept her hand in his. Laurie enjoyed the profound quietness of the mood, and in her happiness at the rough, strong feel of his hand, she forgot her offer of a coke. She thought, this is a kind of peace one might hunt for and never find except in an act as simple as two people sitting together quietly in the growing night. With Hal, such a peace might become a thread through all the texture of life. Curious that since she had been with Nanna, she had thought much more of what made up living and of what one would want to remember when the time of one's own death was near. Nanna had tried to explain to her one day that living was not the achievement of a desire, but rather the winning or the losing of that desire. Life was not only a rising to a point but also a coming down again. Laurie knew that every moment of being with Hal was living sharply, happily. The difficult thing was remembering to realize it so that the moments did not slip unnoticed through her fingers.

Breaking the silence and her thought, his voice came, "Laurie, darling, the next few weeks are going to be hard for you. If there's anything, I want to help."

"I'll tell you if there is."

He continued stumblingly, "I know that now is not the time to speak of such things. And probably I am not the person to say this to you. After all, I'm just Hal Phillipson, Kona fisherman. But I must say it before things have changed too much. Laurie, I love you. I want to marry you."

Now that he had spoken the words, it seemed inevitable that he should have said them. She felt a warm kindling of happiness in her and leaned over to kiss his cheek lightly. She smiled at him and said, "Nanna and I both approve."

After his long kiss, he asked, "Your father? Your mother?"

"My mother? Don't worry about her. My father?" She shrugged her shoulders. "He never yet has approved of anything I wanted to do!"

IX

The next morning Laurie was aware in her slumber of the light of dawn upon her eyelids, and as she moved toward consciousness, she felt a thrust of excitement in her body. She could not remember, at first, why it was that excitement should come, and why at this solitary hour there was no longer loneliness. When remembrance came, her body warmed and claimed a joy of its own. She moved her legs and arms along the cool expanse of sheet, delighting in a voluptuous comfort. She thought of marriage with Hal, of living in a little house near the sea, of the cotton dresses smelling of sea wind she would wear, of the dampness of salt spray constantly in her hair and on her skin, of worry about Hal when he was out fishing, of Hawaiian friends, of children, of baking and sweeping and washing and picnicking on the shore. It would be a full life, devoid of loneliness and of the restless wondering what to do. Moreover it would be different from anything she had experienced for any length of time. A quiver of fear stirred in her; could she change from luxury and servants and bridge-playing, from mainland-tripping friends to these other laughing, swimming, quarreling, dancing people? She thought of Lehua, how secretly she had once loved Lehua even more than Mummy, and of Lehua's friends. With them she had known a comfortable happiness. They had accepted her casually, warmly as another little part-Hawaiian girl. How differently her school friends had accepted her! She was a Wendell, and she was pretty; that was the criterion for them. She had always enjoyed sharing the activities of her school friends and being one of them successfully. But sometimes in the midst of her playing, she felt apart from them, alien to their efforts. Then she would pray silently that they would never know; she must not let them guess her double experience, her strangeness. On some occasions she felt that she was wiser than they and through her duality had an advantage over them. They must have felt it too, because they frequently accepted her suggestions without the questioning and bantering which might occur if someone else had offered a plan. She knew they sometimes considered her the most resourceful, the most imaginative of them. Yet in spite of their tribute to her, she needed the association of Lehua's friends to assure her happiness.

Laurie flung the sheet and light cotton blanket from her and slipped out of bed. Before the mirror, she examined the silhouette of her body through the thin nightgown. Her figure was slender and finely molded. The pale honey color of the skin was pleasing, particularly in contrast to her black hair. She twirled and danced in front of the mirror, watching the flowing drapery of her nightgown and the fluid movements of her body. She looked and felt like a sprite from a Botticelli painting. This thought pleased her—a sprite from Botticelli. She danced more strenuously, whirling and leaping, imagining flowers twined in her hair and wreathed about her gown.

Martha opened the door, and Laurie stopped abruptly. "Oh, Mummy!" she exclaimed and went over to kiss her on the cheek.

"My goodness, Laurie, what are you doing?"

"Nothing really. Just dancing."

"You are the dancingest child!"

"It's the Hawaiian in me."

Martha looked startled, and Laurie grinned at her. It wasn't often they mentioned this fact out loud. Polynesian blood was something they felt and cherished within themselves. But now the situation was different, and on this morning, Laurie wanted to cry to the world that she was Hawaiian.

She took her mother's hand and relapsing to a little-girl mood, she said, "Mummy, what'll I wear today?"

"Why not your yellow slacks and white shirt?" Laurie heard the tone of happiness in her mother's voice. Mummy always liked it when she pretended to be a little girl again.

"Mummy, sit down. I'll take a quick shower and then I

want to tell you something. ' Laurie pushed her mother into the big overstuffed chair, thrust a magazine into her hands, and went to her bathroom and stepped under the shower. She didn't soap herself but simply stood under the spray of pipe-cool water for a few seconds. Then she briskly rubbed herself dry, patted a generous amount of bath powder over her body, and dressed in the slacks. She stood before her mother with her hair as yet uncombed and blurted, "Mummy, I'm engaged!"

"Engaged!" Laurie felt the mingled surprise and consternation in her mother's voice. "But to whom?"

"Daddy won't approve, and I'll probably be disinherited—or something."

"Don't be ridiculous! You won't be disinherited. . . . But who is it?"

"It's Hal Phillipson, Mele Hartwell's brother. I met him first at the Hartwells' just before we came to Kona. He lives in Keauhou."

Martha's voice was low, almost a whisper. ". . . So old Samuel Kekela was right!" She rose from the chair and walked to the window and stood before it, twisting her fingers together languidly and gracefully.

Laurie watched and wondered what she was thinking. It must be something deep-laid, peaceful, like a bed of dried leaves in the woods; her shoulders were relaxed, her head thrown slightly back. Laurie said, "Daddy will disapprove, I know. I hope you don't. I couldn't bear it if you did."

Martha turned to her daughter. "Laurie, I don't disapprove. Far from it. It's the unfolding of the inevitable. . . . I don't know Hal, but I'm sure that if you chose him, he's a fine person. The only thing I wonder is if you realize the kind of life you will lead."

"I do know, Mother. I've thought of it."

"Eight or ten years ago you would have fitted nicely into Hal's sort of life. But now—in growing up, you seem to have changed."

"Not really. . . . Mummy, you must have known this would happen. I'm not too much like Win and the rest." She saw tears start into her mother's eyes and said impulsively, "Mummy, don't cry."

"I'm not crying. It's just an old thought, an old dream. Laurie, you are fulfilling a part of me I could never have fulfilled, except in snatches, for myself."

"What—what do you mean?"

"Let's say it this way, keiki. You love music. You play a flute nicely and have your ukulele. But you know you never will become a musician in the world's eye. Let's pretend that you wanted more than anything else to become a great musician, but you knew you never would. You bear a child who inherits your ability. You watch that child grow and develop into what you yourself had wished to be. And it is as though you yourself are fulfilled."

Laurie knew that she would have to think quietly and alone about her mother's words to understand their full purport. But something of what they meant gave her the comfortable feeling that in marrying Hal she was doing the right thing, and not only for herself. She put her arms around Martha and murmured, "Oh, Mummy, Mummy!"

Martha returned the embrace and then pushed Laurie gently away. She looked at her, examining her hair, her skin, her slender body, and then she seemed to try to nuzzle her way into Laurie's mind. Laurie felt the scrutiny as a warm cloak of love. Finally Martha said in a voice of tenderness, "My Kona child!"

Laurie smiled in response and then asked the question which troubled her. "But what of Daddy? He'll not like Hal—you know why."

"I feel certain of one thing. Once you are married to Hal, Daddy will accept it. Although he might not realize it now, that's the way of Wendells. . . ." Martha paused and gazed toward the window absorbedly. Then she turned away from it and in a quick voice said, "But for the time being we must think only of Nanna. Her passing may change certain things. We can't tell."

"Yes, of course we must think only of Nanna . . ." Laurie persisted, "But, Mummy—once Daddy said he would have to forget he had a daughter if I married someone of whom he did not approve."

"Those are words, Laurie. Actions are different. Wendells on occasions say harsh words. But their actions are usually just."

"You talk about the Wendells so queerly sometimes—almost as though you were thousands of miles apart from them."

"But actually I'm one of them, through choice and understanding. . . . Now we must tell Nanna of your wonderful news. She and Grandpa are all who need to know for a while."

Laurie ran a comb hastily through her hair and said, "Let's go."

She and Martha went to Nanna's room, knocked gently, and without waiting for an answer, pushed the door open.

"Nanna, good morning!" Laurie said and went to kiss the old lady.

"You two look up to no good, considering the grins on your faces," commented Mrs. Bell. "I can probably guess, however."

Laurie looked at her with mock despair. "You probably can. You are always so omniscient."

"What a word for my granddaughter!"

"It's a good word! But come on, now. Guess if you can."

"All I need to say is Hal!"

"Nanna, you're a rascal. I'll bet you've been eavesdropping."

"That wasn't necessary. Sometimes one can foresee the inevitable without too much trouble. And, Laurie, I'm glad. Now I can die happily."

"Why, Nanna, dear!"

"Yes, Laurie. After all, you know I'm going to haunt Kona; I'd like to have someone of my own blood to whisper to from time to time, someone to whom I can tell the old secrets. Only Hawaiians will listen to such whisperings." Nanna grinned as she spoke.

"I'll teach my children to listen to you." Laurie was amazed to discover she felt quite serious about the promise, although she laughed in an echo of Nanna's mood as she said the words.

"Luahine," Mrs. Bell said, "you must help Laurie. Get them married as quickly as possible after I'm gone. What's the sense of their waiting?"

"We'll do our best, Mummy. . . . And now, Laurie, go down and get your breakfast. Nanna and I have some planning to do."

Nanna became rapidly worse in the following fortnight, but Mummy spared a little time from caring for her to meet and talk with Hal. Laurie watched them anxiously in their first few minutes together.

After the introduction, Mummy said in her warm voice, "Hello, Hal! I understand you are taking my daughter away from me."

Hal had blushed and said, "Not exactly."

And Mummy had continued, "But you are giving her to Kona which, after all, is a part of me. So shall we say you are also giving her back to me."

Hal, brightening, had answered, "Mrs. Wendell, you speak in riddles, but nice ones."

"Thank you, Hal," Mummy had said. "I like you, and I'm glad that Laurie found you."

Later Hal had confessed to Laurie that he in his turn liked Mummy. "She's swell," he said. "But I was sure scared to meet her!"

Grandpa called Honolulu and asked the twins and their families to come, and when they arrived, he established them at the inn in Kailua. Each day they drove up to the house; the older people sat quietly on the lanai or waited on Nanna in the stillness of her bedroom, and the impatient children played in the garden or on rainy days teased Pua in the kitchen. It seemed to Laurie that now with the family gathered in this fashion, Nanna had determined to die quickly to spare them the anguish of lingering illness. She felt she could almost see her grandmother fade each day.

Nanna had asked that she be buried with some of the old Hawaiian ways, and Tutu and Mummy were already busy planning the food and the watches for the bier. Laurie was at first shocked at the way in which Tutu talked of the events to take place just after Nanna's death, and she confided this to her mother. Mummy had comforted her, saying, "Darling, I felt the same way until I realized that Nanna herself is happy to have this activity around her and to have a glimpse of what will take place at her passing. It's the one time she can be certain of the future."

A few mornings later, Laurie heard her mother leave Nanna's room and hurry downstairs. Something in the urgency of her movements led Laurie to follow. She reached Grandpa's study door in time to hear Mummy putting a call through to Honolulu for Daddy to come and bring Win. She waited at the door for her mother to come out. "Is it really the time?" she asked.

Mummy replied, "Yes, dear. The doctor says so. Tomorrow you must go to Hilo to pick up Daddy and Win. The nine-forty-five plane."

The next day Laurie waited at the airport. She had not bought leis; it seemed somehow improper at this time. When she finally saw the two walking down the gangplank toward her, the tall handsome man, the boy an image of his father, she felt herself no closer to them than a casual acquaintance might be; her world touched theirs only at intervals. The last time her father had seen her she had been a girl, anxious and undecided about her future, baffled in her attempts to fulfill herself. Now she felt herself to be a woman, with a future already planned, and most wonderful of all, she knew herself to be a fulfillment of her mother's other self. She was richly established in life and had already forgotten the uncertainty of a child's status. She reached out to shake her father's hand and was startled when he pulled her toward him and kissed her. He regarded her questioningly. "Laurie," he said, "you've changed. I hope . . ." He broke off his statement, and she knew that it was just in time.

"I hope I've not changed for the worse," she said to be conversational. "Hello, Win. Are you afraid to kiss me?" She kissed her brother's cheek and laughed at the flush which covered it.

Laurie went instinctively to the driver's seat of the car. As she pulled away from the airport, she remembered that this was the first time since he had taught her to drive that she had taken the wheel from her father. On the way to Kona, she answered Win's questions about Nanna and how she looked. She tried to prepare the boy for the emaciated look of his grandmother and at the same time to reassure him that her spirit and mind were the same.

Martha was waiting at the kitchen door when they turned into the driveway. She ran out to greet them, and Laurie watched while she kissed Winslow and while she hugged Win and then stood him away from her to regard him with pride. Laurie felt a stab of jealousy, of which she was immediately ashamed. But nevertheless it was there—ineradicable. It had been a fine thing to be Mummy's only child for a while and to feel that she, Laurie, had become what Mummy had wanted of her. But in this moment Laurie realized that Win too fulfilled a part of Mummy. She was proud of his resemblance to his father, of his manner, of his caution. For a moment Laurie felt the old loneliness and uncertainty. Was there always to be that difference between them, she on the dark, the ambiguous side and Win on the light, the established side? Then she thought of Hal, and her heart warmed. The right thing for her was not the right thing for Wendells. If she remembered that, she need never be troubled again.

Martha said, "Laurie, Nanna wants to have a little talk with you before Daddy and Win come in to see her. Go now, will you, dear? And when the men have had a chance to clean up a bit, they'll follow you."

Laurie hurried into the house and ran up the back stairs two at a time. When she reached Nanna's room, she was breathless.

"Hello, keiki," Nanna said in her rich voice, her only physical aspect still untouched by the disease. "I suppose it was raining as usual in Hilo."

"It was. A gentle shower."

"Old Hilo! Always fresh and damp and green. I love it that way."

"It was raining in Kau too."

"And the lava was shining black and smelling like wet charred stone. And at Punaluu you could hear the rain falling on the sand with a little swoosh. I always loved that sound, and rain was so precious in Punaluu."

Laurie saw that her grandmother's eyes were large and brilliant and remembering. There was a mournful loveliness about the old woman's countenance as she framed it with her hands, whose bones and veins now proclaimed the frail, perishable stuff of life. "Nanna," Laurie murmured, "you are beautiful today."

"Thank you. It's been long since anyone's said that to me. . . . Laurie, I have something for you."

"For me?" Laurie repeated, not thinking of what she said.

"Yes, the stone."

"Not yet!"

"It's not too soon. In a few days. . . . Besides, the stone is too rough for my hand now. It's funny how the nerves begin to feel too near the surface."

"Nanna!" Laurie cried and grasped her grandmother's hand.

"Don't, don't!" She realized in that moment how irrevocable Nanna's death would be.

"Keiki, keiki, remember I'll be whispering to you, to your children. Tell them of me. Keep my stone well for me. The time is coming when you will want to use it, to find comfort in it, as I have for so long. It's our secret. As long as you have the stone, I'll be in Kona."

X

It was not until she heard the choking, muffled sobs of Grandpa Bell that Laurie knew the moment had come. Wondering what should be done now, she glanced at her family; Tutu had flung herself across Nanna's body, and the nurse had bent over to soothe her. Mummy was tight in Daddy's arms, and Win looked frightened. Laurie turned her gaze back to Nanna to search for some proof beyond the utter stillness of her figure that she was gone. It was hard to believe that the inscrutable transformation had actually taken place, and Laurie was ashamed of her numbed heart.

The doctor and the nurse created a slight stir as they hurried out on their death obligations. After they were gone, Laurie went to the window to look at the landscape and search for a little relief from the stifling feeling of the moment. She saw an owl soaring just above the tips of the guava thickets; it moved back and forth on its great powerful wings, apparently hunting. Abruptly it turned and flew toward the window from which she was watching. She had a sensation that it would fly straight through the window, tearing the screen, shattering the glass, and instinctively, she dodged away. When she looked out again, the owl had alighted in the kukui tree, one of whose branches reached across the window. It sat there staring with round, glowing eyes into the room, and Laurie peered concentratedly at it, her vision absorbed in the magnetism of the great, yellow-green eyes. For one fleeting second she felt again that going out of herself, out of her humanity, that she had known the day on the shore. She tore her gaze away from the owl; now when she was concerned with a very human grief over Nanna, this mood was unnatural, uncomfortable.

If she could only talk to Hal or even just be near him; she was so alone by the window. No one had followed her or even noticed her movements. She glanced around and saw her mother and father standing together with Win between them. Father's hand was on Win's shoulder, and Win like a small child clung with his fingers to Mummy's belt. Tutu and Grandpa were seated at the bedside, still holding together Nanna's hand. Aunts Jane and Janet stood huddled, each with their families as though they were protecting themselves from too great a sorrow. Laurie thought, "I'll not be missed from this group. And I must see Hal."

She glided quietly from the room, hurried down the stairs and out to the garage. She climbed into Grandpa's car and drove the two miles down the road to Hal's cousins' house. Hal was at the side of the car almost before she was parked. She said breathlessly, "It's come," and he reached through the window and put his arms tightly around her. She waited for the tears she had expected, but they did not come. Somehow they were not necessary now; this is what Nanna would have wished—for Laurie to find refuge in Hal's arms.

The days passed for Laurie in a haze of bewilderment at events and ceremonials which she had never before experienced and which she realized she would go through many times in her Kona life. She watched Tutu emerge as the directress of these days of sorrow; Tutu, who had always seemed gentle and easy-going, was now energetic and demanding. She organized the watches at the bier and ordered fresh flowers and leis whenever the blossoms began to droop. She hired three Hawaiian women to help Pua in the kitchen; rich, bounteous refreshment must always be ready to offer those who came to mourn the dead and to visit with their friends. "Laurie, you are to keep the record of flowers and messages," she said, and Laurie felt relieved to have a part in the activity.

When Nanna was brought home to lie in state, Tutu took Laurie's hand while they listened tearfully to the welcome song chanted by Mrs. Awai. The guttering flames of the fat wax candles that burned at the bier pierced Laurie's eyes, and she wondered how the women who took turns watching could bear these tiny darts of light. In the afternoons she sat near the bier with Mummy or Grandpa and watched the people who passed by to pay their respects; some of the old friends glanced embarrassedly at Nanna, others stood a moment quietly, and a few even spoke soft words in Hawaiian.

When Nanna was at last laid in the cemetery under a white-blossoming plumeria tree and the Rev. Mr. Naehu had sung out with his deep voice the final words of the Christian burial ceremony in Hawaiian, Laurie turned away with the movement of gathered family and friends and felt a strange relief. Now she could settle down to remember Nanna in a normal and loving way. She need no longer be repulsed by the presence and alien quality of a creature whose body death had taken; Nanna could become a sweet image within her heart.

As she neared the cemetery gate, Laurie was aware that Hal had stepped to her side, and boldly, under her father's glance, she held his hand. She watched their feet as they moved along together; Hal's shoes were new and brown and shining, but her own white suede pumps were slightly smudged by the rocks and earth of the cemetery. After the island custom, she was dressed in white, but Hal was in his brown suit, the only one he owned. She thought of the picture they must make together, brown and white figures against the lava rock and sparse green of the landscape.

She was conscious suddenly of soft fingers breaking her clasp on Hal's hand, and she glanced up to see Mummy stepping between her and Hal. Mummy took Hal's arm in her left one and Laurie's in her right, and the three walked along intimately together. Laurie felt a swift surge of mingled emotions in her until she could barely prevent herself from sobbing. Grief for Nanna who would have done just this, love for Mummy who was showing public approval, love for Hal—all mingled within her until she thought her small body could no longer contain such giant forces. She saw Mummy smiling delicately, sadly at her and heard her soft words, "For Nanna."

When they were home again, Laurie sat quietly with Grandpa for the rest of the day and held the stone in her hands. He roused from his grief enough to notice it and placed his bony, browned fingers briefly over hers. She felt he had been a little comforted. In the dusk she brought him a bowl of soup which he refused.

"It would be better," she said.

He answered docilely, "All right, keiki. For you and for her." Later she took him to his bedroom door and kissed him good night.

She was awakened early the next morning by a knock and called, "Come in." When the door opened, she saw her father.

"Good morning, Daddy," she said and felt a quivering of unpleasant expectation.

"Good morning, dear. Do you mind if I come in?"

"No. Of course not. Excuse me a moment and I'll put on my slacks."

"Don't bother. Besides, you probably won't want to wear slacks today."

"Oh?" she remarked and wondered what was coming.

"I don't think so. . . . I'd like to make a suggestion—well, more than a suggestion. I want to urge you to go back to Honolulu with me today. You've been away for so long now;

you've spent enough time for a young girl in a house of death."

"I promised to help Mummy and Tutu with going over Nanna's things."

"I know. But Mummy and Tutu can handle it very well alone. I think for Win's sake either you or Mummy should go back with me. And it's obvious that Mummy should be the one to stay."

"What does Mummy think? She's never suggested it to me."

"Laurie, my dear, I've missed you these summer months. Please don't make me think you prefer to stay away from home."

"Oh, Daddy, you know it's not that. It's just that—well, I wanted to help Mummy." She paused and then continued hopefully, "I've been here with Nanna for all this time, and I know what she wanted done with some of the things."

"Laurie, you have many reasons for staying. But the fact is that I want very much for you to come back with Win and me."

Laurie flared, "I don't want to right now!" She reviled herself inwardly, because her voice had been shrill and because, as usual, she was unable to cope with her father deftly.

He replied crisply, "It's true that you're no longer a child. You have a will of your own which should at your age be respected. But in this instance I must insist that you obey me."

"Are you always going to force me to do what you want?" she cried out. "Is my judgment always so miserable? Oh, Daddy, let's face it. You know and I know the reason why you want me to go back right now. But my going back won't help one bit. This time I know."

As she was speaking, the door opened and Martha came in. She paused on the threshold, looking first at daughter and then at husband, but her eyes held no discernible expression. "I thought I heard voices," she said. "This is rather early for you to be up, Laurie."

Winslow interrupted, "We're discussing Laurie's going back to Honolulu with me today."

"And, Mummy, I don't want to go," Laurie said excitedly. "I want to stay here and help you."

"Of course you must stay here and help me. I didn't know there was any plan to the contrary."

"Daddy has different ideas."

"Oh! Winslow, what is this?"

"It's just that I think it's time for Laurie to come home."

"I see. This time, Winslow, I differ with you."

Laurie watched her father's face as Mummy spoke her sentence. He set his teeth firmly, and she could see the strain of the flesh along his jaw. He drew himself to his full height, towering above the two women, and she felt that it was inevitable that he have his way. When he spoke, his words rang with a cold hardness. "Before everything, we must consider the family."

Mummy's words sounded as resolute and unfaltering as his. "The family will not be dishonored. Perhaps such an alliance will not be to its financial or social advantage, but Hal Phillipson is a fine young man and from a fine Hawaiian family."

Laurie gasped audibly when her mother mentioned Hal's name. Somehow she wished she hadn't; she didn't want to hear his dear name dragged through the argument which would follow.

Winslow turned to Laurie and said, "Do you remember what I said to you on the day you refused to go out with Richard Waldron? Well, I meant it. Every word of it. Furthermore, I shall not relent. The choice is yours."

Laurie struggled against anger and hurt to form an answer in her mind, but before she could speak, she heard her mother saying, in a voice controlled by inward calm and firm determination, "Winslow, in the twenty-one years we have been married, I have given up my life to yours. I did it happily—don't think otherwise—because that was my temperament. But you have never shown more than the faintest indication that you understood what my problems were. The question now is not of me, but of Laurie, our child. Together we are responsible for her happiness, and you *must* understand her. You can't guide or mold her as you did me. And I know that it is not in her to form her life happily according to ours."

Winslow started to speak, but Martha moved quickly toward him. When she was close enough to touch him, she said, "Winslow, Laurie has in her all of the Kona qualities you were attracted by in me—all of the things that made you call me your Kona sweetheart. The difference between us is that in her they are real, living. In me they were, fortunately, because I married you, a passing mood of girlhood."

She took his hand and held it firmly. "Think of this, Winslow. Think of all it means. . . . Do you remember that day a few months before Win was born, when we decided I should go to Kona for a rest? You said you realized that I needed to refresh myself, that you were afraid you had afflicted me with some of your sense of responsibility and worry about doing the right thing. Do you remember?"

"Yes, Martha," he said, with a strange gentleness.

She smiled up at him and went on. "You said you wanted me to be your Kona sweetheart again. In that moment I knew why we had married. We were attracted by certain qualities for which we each yearned and which we each saw in the other. For you, it was not possible to attain the qualities, nor would they have fitted you; but in my case it was possible. This child has those qualities we both loved and rejected."

Winslow brushed his free hand across his eyes as though he had just awakened from a long and wounding dream. When he seemed to have recollected himself, Martha continued, "Winslow, darling, it is important for Laurie to stay. I promise you that I shall allow nothing to happen to her which is not right for her."

Laurie watched with astonishment while her father suddenly

clasped her mother in his arms and kissed her ardently. She had not thought such passion existed between them.

After the kiss in a voice husky with emotion, he whispered, "Martie, darling, you know best—for our Hawaiian child."

In the week after the funeral the Bell household settled down into quietude. Laurie wondered when she had ever been so aware of the country delights of Kona. Bees were busy among the plumerias and hydrangeas clustered near the house, and their throaty hum filled the lanai with warm and pleasant sound. Ginger and lime blossoms mingled their fragrances to spice the air with sweet pungency, and light afternoon rains kept the atmosphere fresh, newly distilled.

Grandpa Bell spent the mornings digging heartily in his garden, praying for an exhaustion to carry him through an hour's forgetfulness in sleep after luncheon. At two-thirty he retired to his study to write.

"I'm simmering down my journals," he told Laurie. "I want to do a book on Nanna's era in Kona." And Laurie thought, "You have filled your daylight hours to the very brim, dear Grandpa, but at night you suffer unutterable loneliness." She had heard him pacing his bedroom floor long after he was supposed to be in bed, and she had heard the scratch of innumerable matches as he lighted his pipe. Sometimes she yearned to go in and talk with him, but Mummy had warned her not to. She said briefly, "He's Scotch, Laurie. He's got to fight it out for himself."

Laurie, Tutu, and Mummy passed their days in the bittersweet task of going over Nanna's things, dividing them among the children and grandchildren, laying away unwanted clothes for poor families in Kona. One morning Laurie sat at Nanna's desk. She had four sheets of paper before her, each with its heading: jewelry, books and papers, clothing, miscellany. Tutu was seated in an armchair with a jewel case in her lap. Mummy sat on a cushion on the floor with rolls of tissue paper and boxes of varying sizes at her side.

Tutu took from the case a strand of jade which she warmed a moment in her hand. Then she said, "She wanted Janet to have this. I've heard her say it many times."

"Yes," Martha commented. "Janny always loved jade more than any of us. Put down dark green jade beads, Laurie, and write Aunt Janet's name after it."

Laurie did as she was asked. Her left hand lay in her lap, and in it was Nanna's stone. She turned it about and rubbed her thumb against it. She thought of Nanna's telling her that the stone was too rough for her fingers; she must have been very ill to feel any roughness. The stone seemed smooth as a fine pumice in Laurie's hand.

After Mummy had wrapped the jade in tissue paper and labeled it Janet, Tutu held up the next object, a polished strand of kukui nuts. "Well, well!" she said. "I'd forgotten all about these. They were given to me by Princess Likelike when I was a small girl. See, they're hung on a golden chain and each one has a tiny gold leaf across the top." She paused a moment and fingered the shining nuts. Then she continued, "Laurie, how would you like these? I think they suit your coloring more than anyone else in the family."

"Thank you, Tutu, I'd love them. That is, if no one else really wants them. I love polished kukui nuts."

"And somehow they're more fitting for you, keiki."

The next item which Tutu drew from the jewel box was a heavy golden band, much worn and scratched. "And this," she said dramatically, holding the ring above her head, "is for Hal."

"For Hal!" Laurie and Martha exclaimed together.

"Yes, Hal. This was my mother's wedding band. Laurie, Nanna wanted it to be yours, too. In her letter to me she lists it for Hal, and the day before she died, she mentioned it."

"How darling of her!" Laurie said, feeling tears rising in her eyes. "She was always too good to me."

"She loved you very dearly, Laurie, especially in the last months when you were so wonderful to her. Another promise she exacted from me the day before she died was that I make certain that you and Hal do not delay your marriage. She said she could not rest if her death put off the ceremony, and I swore that I would see to it that you were wed within a month—or at most six weeks."

"Tutu, darling!" interrupted Martha. "You know that's impossible! People would be horrified. And Winslow, who is already enough against it, would never permit such a slight to Nanna, and such a break with propriety."

"Pfui on Winslow and anyone else! The important thing is Ululani's last wish. You don't think I'm going to let anything as thin as that interfere with my child's dying wish! Besides, people won't be horrified. The marriage can take place right here on this island and can be quiet—as it should be. . . . Laurie, you can convince Hal, can't you?"

"He would understand."

"That's fine. We'll have the ceremony in Punaluu in about three weeks. That ought to be time enough. Anyhow, you won't need a fancy trousseau for life here. I've already sent word to Jiro to groom the garden to its very best."

"Tutu," Martha protested. "You must give us a little time. We can hardly catch our breaths in three weeks."

"Nonsense! We'll just have the families to the wedding, and I'll circulate around Kona and Kau that it was Ululani's request to have the ceremony as soon as possible. After the wedding, Laurie, you and Hal can stay on at Punaluu as long as you want. Or if you prefer, you can go to my Milolii beach place. You can have Lei to do the cooking and what not."

Laurie went over to sit on the floor by her mother. "Tutu's right, Mummy. We can be ready in three weeks. I won't need much."

Martha was startled by Winslow's softly modulated but firm words, "I give this woman." She did not recall having heard such a response in a wedding ceremony and wondered why he had made it. Only the Rev. Mr. Naehu, Laurie, Hal, and she could possibly have heard it, but—oh, Winslow still had his inexplicable moments!

Until his words, the sound of the ceremony had been for her but a part of all the gentle noises of a halcyon day—the waves sinking into Punaluu sands, the wind through the mangoes, the gentle swishing against the grass of the holoku trains of Laurie and Mele, her bridesmaid. With that sentence Winslow had made the occasion into something essentially Wendell. For Martha his voice had transported the whole ceremony from the Punaluu garden to the dim spaces of St. Andrew's Cathedral where he had so much wanted it to be. And now his part was over; he had given his daughter away and he stepped back to stand stiffly and properly at his wife's side. Martha wondered unhappily if he realized how completely beyond his reach Laurie would still be.

The soft muttering of first Hal's and then Laurie's voices while they made their vows to one another restored the ceremony to its tone of Hawaiian warmth and informality. But Martha could not recapture her mood of belonging and sharing in it. She thought briefly of Felicity Hartwell's wedding; her remembrance of it now boded well for Laurie's happiness. But she was intensely aware of Winslow at her side, of his having given up his daughter. In that gesture he had also unwittingly gathered his wife wholly to him.

Martha felt within her a bitter taste of the loneliness of change. The doves that called from the mango trees, the sound of the surf on black sand, the leaf-veiled glimpse of the old church on the hill, had been her company in the past and had remained for her always constant, comforting. But people were different; they changed, sometimes slowly, sometimes with mercurial action. Tutu was a frail, aged woman; Laurie had matured and chosen the Kona way of living; Winslow was growing more like his father every year, and Win in turn like Winslow. Even Kimo, who had been invited to the wedding, was now a loud-voiced, rough-mannered fisherman, his gentle ways and sharp insight sloughed off in the rugged life he led. . . . And in this moment she herself, Martha Wendell, was changing. She was relinquishing the last trace of Luahine Bell to her daughter. No one could know it but herself, and for this she was lonely. Lonely for the moment, but content.

TALES OF THE PACIFIC

Stories of Hawaii by Jack London
Thirteen yarns drawn from the famous author's love affair with Hawaii Nei.
$3.95 ISBN 0-935180-08-7

A Hawaiian Reader
Thirty-seven selections from the literature of the past hundred years including such writers as Mark Twain, Robert Louis Stevenson and James Jones.
$3.95 ISBN 0-935180-07-9

Best South Seas Stories
Fifteen writers capture all the romance and exotic adventure of the legendary South Pacific including James A. Michener, James Norman Hall, W. Somerset Maugham, and Herman Melville.
$3.95 ISBN 0-935180-12-5

The Spell of Hawaii
A companion volume to *A Hawaiian Reader*. Twenty-four selections from the exotic literary heritage of the islands.
$3.95 ISBN 0-935180-13-3

South Sea Tales by Jack London
Fiction from the violent days of the early century, set among the atolls of French Oceania and the high islands of Samoa, Fiji, Pitcairn, and "the terrible Solomons."
$3.95 ISBN 0-935180-14-1

The Trembling of a Leaf by W. Somerset Maugham
Stories of Hawaii and the South Seas, including "Red," the author's most successful short story, and "Rain," his most notorious one.
$3.95 ISBN 0-935180-21-4

Kona by Marjorie Sinclair
The best woman novelist of post-war Hawaii dramatizes the conflict between a daughter of Old Hawaii and her straitlaced Yankee husband. Nor is the drama resolved in their children.
$3.95 ISBN 0-935180-20-6

Love in the South Seas by Bengt Danielsson
The noted Swedish anthropologist who served as a member of the famed ***Kon-Tiki*** expedition here reveals the sex and family life of the Polynesians, based on early accounts as well as his own observations during many years in the South Seas.
$3.95 ISBN 0-935180-25-7

The Golden Cloak by Antoinette Withington
The romantic story of Hawaii's monarchs and their friends, from Kamehameha the Great, founder of the dynasty, to Liliuokalani, last queen to rule in America's only royal palace.
$3.95 ISBN 0-935180-26-5

Rogues of the South Seas by A. Grove Day
Eight true episodes featuring violent figures from Pacific history, such as the German filibuster who attempted to conquer the Hawaiian Islands for the Russian Czar; "Emma, Queen of a Coconut Empire"; and "The Brothers Rorique: Pirates De Luxe." Foreword by James A. Michener.
$3.95 ISBN 0-935180-24-9

Horror in Paradise: Grim and Uncanny Tales from Hawaii and the South Seas, edited by A. Grove Day and Bacil F. Kirtley.
Thirty-four writers narrate "true" episodes of sorcery and the supernatural, as well as gory events on sea and atoll.
$3.95 ISBN 0-935180-23-0

Russian Flag Over Hawaii: The Mission of Jeffery Tolamy, a novel by Darwin Teilhet
A vigorous adventure novel in which a young American struggles to unshackle the grip held by Russian filibusters on the Kingdom of Kauai. Kamehameha the Great and many other historical figures play their roles in a colorful love story
$3.95 ISBN 0-935180-28-1

Other Mutual Titles

Celebration: A Portrait of Hawaii Through The Songs Of The Brothers Cazimero
Songs, photographs, illustrations and an informative narrative present a fascinating image of Hawaii including its music, culture, dance, history, and legends.
224 pps., color, $31.95 10¼ x 13¾" ISBN 0-935180-11-7

Panorama Hawaii: Scenic Views of the Hawaiian Islands
As the eye sees it. Panoramic landscape scenes and historical photographs. Unusual photography about an exciting and beautiful place.
96 pps., color, casebound
$19.95 7 x 14" ISBN 0-935180-10-9

Hawaiian Journey
A pictorial history of Hawaii from the early Polynesians to the present day. Over 200 duotone photographs. Now into its seventh printing.
128 pps., $9.95 9¼ x 10 ISBN 0-935180-04-4

Hawaiian Yesterdays: Historical photographs by Ray Jerome Baker
Now into its fifth printing. Old Hawaii as it really was. People, places, and events.
256 pps., 600 color-tinted and duotone nostalgic photographs.
$28.95 Oversized 10⅜x13¼″ ISBN 0-935180-03-6

History Makers of Hawaii: A Biographical Dictionary
by A. Grove Day
Over 500 movers and shakers of Hawaii's exotic history, 100 legendary figures and thousands of other facts for easy reference.
192 pps., $16.95 casebound 8½x10¼″
ISBN 0-935180-09-5

Maui on my Mind
Over 400 color photographs from 50 of Hawaii's best photographers present a breathtaking portrait of the Valley Isle.
256 pps. Oversized, casebound $40.00
ISBN 0-935180-16-8

Kauai: A Many Splendored Island
The photography of Doug Peebles and text by Ronn Ronck combine to portray the Garden Island. Includes a 16-page guide.
160 pps., 11x8″, casebound $25.00
ISBN 0-935180-18-4

How to Order

Send check or money order with an additional 10 percent to cover mailing and handling to:

Mutual Publishing
2055 North King Street, Suite 202
Honolulu, Hawaii 96819

For airmail delivery add an additional 20 percent
For further information and trade inquiries telephone (808) 924-7732